THE
STRANDED

THE STRANDED

ANNO INITIUM 1

DINKO SKOPLJAK

Podium

For my parents

Podium

THE
STRANDED

PROLOGUE

Whether it was a blessing or a curse to be able to lose himself in his work for hours on end and notice nothing whatsoever that was going on around him, George Morel himself was least qualified to say. Looking up from his computer screen that sunny Tuesday in late winter, the first thing he wondered was what time it was.

Was it possible that he had failed to notice it was five o'clock and time to go home?

A glance at the digital display at the top right of his screen confirmed it was only early afternoon. He strained his ears to hear what was going on out in the hallway. Where normally there was a constant hustle and bustle, today it was refreshingly quiet.

Was there a meeting he didn't know about?

George opened his email. He quickly ran his eyes down his unread messages but couldn't see any subject line that was even remotely relevant. His attention was briefly caught by a teaser email that had probably been sent by a careless intern who had used his superior's login details to scan documents; it had been sent to all the accounts stored in the copier.

Who picked these interns anyway? It was the third time that month that sensitive content had ended up somewhere it was not supposed to be. Yet again, it would take in-house investigator Julienne days to track down all the messages that had been sent to the wrong computers and destroy them. It wasn't legal, but who was going to complain and run the risk of being charged with the unauthorized possession of sensitive government documents?

George had grown accustomed to dutifully ignoring such misdirected communications—even deleting some of them immediately—and going about his business. As one of the external consultants on the French Ministry of the Interior contract, he was by no means underworked. Shaking his head, he closed the program without deleting the message for now. His attention was still focused on the strange state of affairs around him. He rose from his chair, reached automatically for his cell, and stepped out into the hallway. As he neared the elevator, he could hear his pants legs rubbing against each other with every step. The soles of his shoes rustled almost inaudibly on the carpet. He passed empty offices, peering into them, involuntarily recalling that old *Twilight Zone* episode where the hero woke up one morning in a world devoid of people. He had walked the deserted streets of the city all day, calling desperately for his fellow humans but never receiving an answer.

While George waited for the elevator, he dialed his wife's cell. Her voice mail picked up, and he disconnected. He didn't like leaving messages. Miriam would soon see that he had called and get back to him. After twenty-three years together, these things had become automatic.

In the silence, he could hear the mechanism hoisting the elevator up the steel shaft. Unease flitted across his mind. He hoped Miriam would call soon. The next moment, he wondered why he was so worried. Of course she would call! His analytical mind swung into action, laughing at him.

There was no indication of any kind of threat, and the current situation would soon be resolved. It was probably just the paranoia that came with the job.

George jumped as a shrill ringing sound shattered the silence in the corridor, announcing the arrival of the elevator. Nervously, he rubbed his face and found that his hands were damp with sweat. He stepped inside. Using his index finger, he jabbed at the button. It took only seconds for the ride down to begin, but George felt his impatience rising.

It was his job to get to the bottom of unusual things. He put the current situation at the top of his list of priorities.

As he stepped out into the ground-floor hallway, he was relieved to see some of the junior consultants. His mood brightened abruptly. But then he realized they were hurrying toward the door and out the building, singly or in small groups, as if they thought they might miss the last train home. Someone dropped a folder and some files. No one picked them up.

George frowned. He noticed that far fewer people than usual were standing around the foyer and sitting in the open-plan office. He saw one of the new consultants quickly hang up the phone and leave his workstation, pulling on a thick winter jacket.

"Where is everyone?" George asked as the younger man approached, his voice taking on the habitual authority of management. But the man strode past him without a word and disappeared from the building.

George looked around in disbelief, raising his right hand questioningly. He was alone in the hallway once again, and that now made him very uncomfortable.

In the near silence, he heard a soft, monotonous beeping. It had been going on since he exited the elevator, but it was only now that it entered his consciousness. Following the sound, he entered the copy room. Whenever classified documents were scanned or duplicated, the machine checked that they had been removed after thirty seconds. If they were still there, the warning signal would sound, increasing in intensity each time. This was purely precautionary, to prevent information from falling into the wrong hands.

George looked at the documents that had been left in the catch tray and saw that they were classified as top secret. A glance at the digital display told him the scans had been emailed to everyone. He frowned again and remembered having received a message with an attachment during the day. The empty beige folder lay next to the machine. He tucked the documents inside. The name of the special committee on the cover meant nothing to him at first—but then it suddenly hit him. Fighting his natural inclination, he opened the file and looked at the reports.

The special unit it mentioned had been set up a number of days ago and was tasked with dealing with the incidents that had occurred recently in a wide band around the French capital.

The documents had not been sent accidentally by some intern.

George skimmed the less relevant parts, automatically scanning for key terms. When he reached the conclusion, he read every line in detail. His heart skipped a beat in fear. He called his wife's cell phone again, breathless. She did not pick up.

Engrossed in the report, he made his way back to the elevator and pushed the *up* button. That's why the whole place was empty, he thought.

The report had sent them all into a panic. Now they were desperately trying to save their own skins. As he reread the final lines, he genuinely wondered if anyone would succeed.

Once again, Miriam's voice mail picked up. "Putain," he cursed, immediately reproaching himself for using the term. Then he thought about how he could get his family to safety. As soon as the doors slid aside, he sprinted for his office. He pulled on his winter jacket, grabbed his wallet and keys, and ran right back to the elevator. On the way down, he looked through the report again, impatient to finally get outside. He squeezed through the doors when they were scarcely halfway open, racing toward the main entrance and pushing open the large frosted-glass door before it could open automatically. George rushed through it and came to an abrupt stop after only one step.

Michelle Gerin, dressed in a thick winter coat, was coming toward him up the last few stone steps. George saw that his superior had registered his indecision and was raising a questioning eyebrow. At that moment, the door closed behind him, catching on the folder.

Reacting quickly, he pulled on it. The force of the movement sent the papers flying. George and Michelle looked at the sheets as they fluttered to the ground.

Crap. He'd taken classified documents out of the building. No one needed to tell him it was a serious disciplinary offense. George should know that better than anyone.

As if to mock him, the title page—the name of the special committee clearly legible—came to rest next to them on the step. He saw the unspoken question in her almond-shaped eyes as she scrutinized him. As her anger rose, her skin seemed to darken even further.

"What the hell are you doing, George?"

"Michelle," he began irritably. But then he remembered everything that had happened in the last ten minutes—and what he had learned. He quickly regained his composure. "Did you know about this?" George gestured toward the documents without taking his eyes off her.

"What do you think? I'm the senior advisor to the Department of Homeland Security! These reports come across my desk before anyone else even sees them. But as far as I know, this one wasn't addressed to you or your department. So how do you come to be in possession of it?"

George, who was in no mood for any back-and-forth about hierarchy, bent down and picked up the scattered papers. Without looking at

Michelle, he said, "They were lying in the copier on the ground floor for anyone to read. Jérôme had scanned them and sent them to everyone. So regrettably, they're not quite as top secret as they were. And the team has decided to take off early for the day."

Michelle looked around in amazement. It seemed to George that she had only just noticed that the parking lot in front of the office building was empty save for one or two vehicles.

"What's going on, George?"

"You're asking me? You're the top advisor on domestic security; I'd have thought you'd be the first to know."

She lost her temper. "Other people had access to the documents?" she hissed at him. The empty parking lot spoke volumes. Everyone must have read the communiqué and fled, literally. George was at the point of making a break for it as well. She tugged at the report in his hands. But he did not let go.

"George!" Michelle rebuked him. "It is not permitted to remove classified data or documents from the building without authorization. You will hand them over to me immediately, and I will refrain from mentioning this incident in my reports." As if to emphasize her words, she yanked at the folder several times. George kept ahold on it. He thought releasing the report would lead to widespread chaos. But if people saw it in time, it could also save many lives. That was why it was a good idea. Even if it would bring a whole world of trouble down on his head, he had spontaneously—and irrevocably—decided to make it public himself if necessary. Unless his superiors beat him to the punch.

George thought they were unlikely to. He knew their political tactics all too well. They would not want to make such explosive information public, and if they did, they would only release it after it was too late. As always, they would sit on their hands and afterward carry out only essential repairs.

Human casualties?

Merely collateral damage. He felt more obligated than ever to share with the public the information that had fallen into his hands so unexpectedly and illicitly. But he quickly pushed the thought aside. His priority had to be the protection of his own family. He did not question the report's veracity for a second. These kinds of investigations were entrusted only to the top experts. It had all been realistically appraised and drawn up with painstaking precision.

It was one hundred percent accurate.

"George, let go of the folder!" Michelle yelled, pulling harder. He couldn't let her take the documents. Small rips were appearing in the cover. But suddenly, he remembered he had been sent the files by email. He could print them out at home—the message was still there, after all. The papers in his hand could be replaced and were not worth arguing with his boss over. When she tugged on it again, George let go without warning.

She clearly hadn't remotely expected him to relinquish the folder and was using all the anger and determination she could muster to snatch it from him. The documents slid from his fingers almost without resistance. The huge force Michelle was applying caused her to stumble backward. George reacted a split second too late, reaching for her hand, but only catching the edge of the file. At the same time, Michelle let go. One of her feet found the top step, but the other found thin air. The physics of her momentum sent her flying, falling almost two and a half meters unchecked. She landed on her lower back, almost on her butt.

The tension generated in her body during the flight meant her upper body whipped onward on impact in the direction of the fall, like a taut bow. As her shoulders hit the broad stone landing, her neck muscles released. Like the mechanics of a medieval catapult with a built-in slingshot, the back of Michelle's head slammed hard into the ground.

The sound was to haunt George for the rest of his life. At first, he couldn't move his legs or take his eyes from the ever-growing pool of blood spreading beneath her. He took several deep breaths, regained his composure, and briefly considered calling an ambulance.

But what was the point? There was nothing to be done for Michelle. A grayish mass was already mixing with the blood. And according to the report, there was little chance of averting the impending catastrophe. He remembered his original plan to find his family and print out the documents. He had to do this, to save as many people as possible—but first he had to get to Miriam and the children.

George stepped around the body, fumbling in his jacket pocket for his car keys while trying to remember where he had parked. He couldn't see his vehicle in the company's valet parking a lot. Then it came back to him. When he arrived that morning, he had unexpectedly spotted a space right on the street and had left the car there. He had not felt like making the short detour to the inner courtyard. Running at full tilt, he looked to his left and saw the Renault. He forced himself not to think about Michelle.

There was nothing he could have done. As far as he knew, she was not leaving any motherless children behind, at least. With this thought, he ran out the main gate, his mind quickly relativizing the experience into an unpleasant incident.

His thoughts racing, he didn't see the skater of mature years approaching at speed from the right. The two of them reached the area in front of the stone gate at almost exactly the same time. The collision might have been prevented if at least one of them had been paying more attention. Both men went down hard. The skateboard catapulted against the wall, lifting several centimeters off the ground and rolling over a couple of times before disappearing into the bushes. The skater was on his feet first. Furious, he reared up in front of George, who was lying on the ground. "You idiot. Are you blind?" he roared, yanking on George's lapels and dragging him to his feet. George was aware of being set upright and looked into his adversary's face. The latter had a fist raised, ready to hit him—but he stopped abruptly.

"George?" he asked, visibly taken aback.

It took George a few seconds to recognize him.

"Martin?"

Martin grabbed George's shoulders with both hands and gave them a gentle shake. A friendly grin suddenly spread across his face. "George! It's really you! What are you doing here?"

Martin! It was Martin! George remembered that as students, they had shared an apartment for a few months.

"Martin?" he repeated, still in shock, trying to clear his head.

"Yeah, it's me," replied the skater with a smile. "How are you, old buddy?"

"Good, good." George stammered, not responding to the friendly inquiry. "Martin, listen to me!" he went on urgently. "You have to go home, right now! Get as much food and water as you can on the way!"

Martin's smile faded. "George? Are you okay?" His worried tone betrayed his doubts about George's grasp of reality.

But George simply reached out and squeezed Martin's shoulder. "Yes, I'm absolutely fine. And it's nice to see you again after all this time." The two college friends looked at each other, but George couldn't feel any joy at the reunion. He was shaken to the core.

"But Martin, I meant what I said. Call as many people as you can—warn everyone! Friends, family, coworkers! Tell them to stockpile supplies and get to safety. Not tomorrow or sometime this week. Now! Right away! Do you have kids?"

Martin responded, narrowing his eyes. "Yes, a son. I was just going to collect him from his after-school care. What's going on, George?"

It was not the first time someone had asked him that question today. His brain was still working overtime. Even bumping into his old friend could only be a short-lived distraction. He pressed the folder firmly against Martin's chest.

"What's that?" Martin asked, visibly irritated.

"Read it but get going now. Please, Martin! We don't have much time!" George stepped in and pulled Martin into a tight hug. Then he turned and limped to his car. Without even fastening his seat belt, he sped out of the parking space, tires screeching. He merged directly with the moving traffic, not pausing to check for a space. As he rocketed away, he clipped the vehicle parked in front of him, but paid no heed and did not look back.

Martin watched George go, seeing him run the red light at the intersection, forcing several cars to collide with each other.

"What in hell is going on?" he muttered into his beard, bewildered. He fished his skateboard out from the bushes and read the report. Then, breathing faster and faster, he took photographs of the documents, sending the pictures to his contacts and posting them on all the social media channels he was registered with.

As he hastened to his son, the rising spring wind caught the top-secret papers and blew them carelessly away.

CHAPTER 1

BACKUP

I could hardly breathe, let alone control my movements. Wedged in the crowd, which covered the entire area of the port, I couldn't move in any direction. My suitcase was long gone.

Children cried. People were constantly complaining that someone was elbowing them in the ribs or stepping on their toes. Close behind me, someone had to endure a torrent of abuse for trying to clear a little space for themselves. The general level of dread was rising. The mob that had ingested me surged randomly back and forth. I tried to adapt my breathing to the movement of the crowd, managing at least to get enough air into my lungs to stay conscious. Depending on the direction of the wind, I smelled burnt diesel or cold sweat.

A few minutes before, I had managed to turn my upper body halfway around and look back about three hundred meters to the gigantic bridge that connected the mainland with the artificial pier. A desperate battle was raging there. The last of the soldiers who were supposed to protect us were doing everything they could to stop the advancing horde.

Surprisingly, they held out for a long time. Fearfully, I pictured how the infected on the mainland had swept over the last barricades before the bridge, their sheer numbers making them unstoppable. Now they were on the verge of destroying the final human barricade. The rifle fire grew fainter and fainter. My gaze was fixed longingly on the passenger ship floating a few meters away in Barcelona's harbor.

Behind it, way up in the sky, a violent storm was approaching from the north. Thick, white clouds foreshadowed its imminent arrival, the sharp, jagged line of them standing out grotesquely from the blue and losing all light toward its center. Brutal lightning stretched kilometers across the sky, illuminated the interior of the gray-black supercell, casting harsh black-and-white contrasts into the eye of the bora. Seconds later, muffled thunder rolled overhead, ramping up the fear.

Boarding proceeded agonizingly slowly. Armed mercenaries checked the tickets of the fleeing passengers who had managed to secure one of the last seats on the ferry to North Africa, hoping to escape the European madness. The ticket for the crossing had swallowed up all my savings, but anything was better than staying here. I held it crumpled in my cramped fist.

The mammoth evacuation had begun a few hours ago. We were crammed into buses, driven across the city, and deposited at the harbor. The first ship had left sixty minutes ago, full to bursting. The one in front of me was supposed to be taking the rest of us out of here—soon, hopefully.

The decks were connected to the mainland by only four gangways. The people on them pushed and shoved, while the armed guards on the ship surveyed them grimly. The first wave of passengers surged onto the upper levels and rushed toward their cabins. Hundreds of doors with rounded corners were set all around the ship's steel walls. Its once-white paint was peeling everywhere. Rust was gaining ground.

The sounds of the fight behind us died away completely. For a moment, the waiting crowd seemed to be caught frozen in time, the stench of the infected carrying to us on the wind. I was scared that the monstrous grimaces, which I had so far only seen in various amateur photographs and videos online, might be about to come straight at me through the crowd. If they did, I'd have no chance of running for it. The pressure increased.

Then, I heard them! We all heard them, the guttural, greedy screams from deep within the chest, that bloodthirsty sound that had lost all humanity. They were far behind us, but they were closing in fast, driven by the lust for human flesh. Could anything have stopped them? I saw the guards raising their weapons as the horror, which I still couldn't see, came into view.

Fearing for their lives, the people in the back rows crushed forward blindly. The guards fired. Bullets buzzed close to my head. The huge pressure from behind forced the passengers up the walkways onto the decks. They effortlessly overran the guards, although many were shot in the process. Those on the edges of the gangways fell screaming into the water. Barely three meters behind me, another gun clattered loudly. The people around me flinched. Then I was shoved forward again, this time more brutally than ever, and found myself suddenly by one of the narrow bridges leading to the deck. I tried not to stumble over the dead bodies. Seconds later, my upper body slammed against the wall of steel.

The ship began to move. We can't leave; the ferry's still docked, I thought. The idea foundered in the chaos of the human stampede.

My world mutated into a deluge of bellowing. I was carried along on the wave, and catching sight of some stairs, I struggled up them.

On the upper deck, I hurried to the first cabin I could find and pushed down the door handle. Locked. I pounded on the door, but there was no response. Everything was swaying and shuddering. I almost lost my balance as the ship strained against the ropes.

Four or five meters ahead of me, a man opened the door to the next compartment. The jolt made him stumble backward. Blood-encrusted hands appeared as if from nowhere, grabbing him and pulling him away from the cabin. I lost no time and jumped toward the open door. A heartbeat later, I was inside, sliding the bolt into place.

Something big gave way with a loud bang: the ropes, the gangway moorings, or both. The ship lurched and eased away sedately. Lying on the dank floor, I tried to keep the paralyzing fear at bay. But I couldn't get my breathing under control. I sucked in air faster and faster, barely exhaling. My eyes bulged. A burning sensation crept up my skin from my chest to my throat. The buzzing in my ears got louder and louder until it drowned out every other sound. I flailed around in panic. My fingers cramped; my vision blurred. Suddenly I stopped struggling, and the world went black.

I must have slept for two or three hours. Pale light was filtering in through one of the portholes, so I could at least make out the outlines of objects in the room. The only sound I could hear was the low hum of the diesel engines, although I wasn't sure if this was an after-effect of my panic attack. The steady motion of the ship told me we were on the open sea.

I needed to pee. The rest of my body was feeling the aftershocks of my seizure. Escorted by a headache, swaying and groping, I stood up. My leg muscles were numb from my convulsions. Fumbling, I found the door to the toilet in the shower cubicle. It stank abominably in there, and it didn't smell any better when I was finished.

I had done it! I had escaped Barcelona with my life. The ship would take me to North Africa, which was not in the grip of the pandemic—and I would survive. In a silent gesture of gratitude, I clenched my fists and pressed them against my forehead.

A rumbling began outside the cabin. A soft voice was pleading with someone. Another rumble followed. The footsteps fell silent. I hardly dared to breathe. With every heartbeat, the voice became higher, more desperate. Cautiously, I crept to the porthole, pulled aside the threadbare curtain, and peeked out.

The passageway in front of the compartment was dimly lit by a single light bulb. I craned my neck, trying to see what was going on. In the dying light, barely three meters away, I saw two silhouettes crouching by the railing. They were of a petite woman holding a man's head in her lap. He seemed to be asleep. She was rocking him back and forth, begging him not to leave her. The less responsive he became, the shriller her voice became.

Looking back, I wonder why on earth I gave up the safety of my cabin. Was it curiosity that urged me into yet another nerve-racking situation? Or was I driven to help them by a sudden surge of compassion?

I don't have a clear answer to those questions.

Anyway, I unlocked the door and looked out through the narrow gap. Except for the two figures, nothing was moving. To the left, the path was in utter darkness. Adrenaline surged through my veins, and I could feel my heart beating in my throat and my fingertips tingling as if they were infested with ants. I took the plunge. Peering around the door to the right, I stepped out onto the deck.

In three steps I was with them. The man's arm had now gone limp. I saw a bite wound on his hand that was getting darker and darker. The woman was sobbing. She must have realized that he was dead.

"There's nothing more you can do for him," I said irrelevantly, putting a hand on her shoulder. "We have to get out of here; he'll be back soon." She didn't respond. But I pressed on. "Come on! Come with me! Now!" But she only cried. I tugged at her and talked to her. She didn't even seem to notice me. She had given up on herself.

And then it happened. I'd never seen it with my own eyes before. The flaccid body twitched. Once, twice. Involuntarily, I took a step backward, unable to avert my gaze. A breeze came up, but enthralled by the resurrection, I barely felt it. The infected hand shot up searchingly, found the woman's flowing hair and grasped it. The man opened his eyes, his face contorted into a mask of rage. His skin had turned completely gray. I thought I could make out a fine network of black veins. His irises had disappeared. In their place I saw only milky white eyeballs staring into the darkness.

With one fluid motion, he pulled the woman's head down and bit into her throat. She cried out in pain and tried to tear herself away. With another jerk, he bit out a piece of her neck. Blood shot from the injured artery. The dying woman struggled to sit up. She clutched the wound with both hands, but her brain quickly failed her from lack of oxygen. Before her head hit the rusty metal, she was dead.

The night was lit up suddenly by a fork of lightning that struck the sea a few hundred meters from us and was followed almost instantly by deafening thunder. Barely a second later, the rain began to lash down. I was instantly soaked to the skin.

Behind me, I heard a gust of wind slam my cabin door shut. I turned around and faltered. Two figures were staggering through the darkness, cutting me off from the cabin. They were close, but the thunder seemed to have irritated them. They looked out to sea, snuffling in the rain. The one who had just arisen gulped down the chunk of meat he had been chewing on. Then he straightened up and sniffed the air.

I found myself face to face with three infected. They seemed to be searching for me, although I was standing only an arm's length from them.

The thunder crashed again. I seized the opportunity to run for my life. It was hard to get any traction on the slippery deck. The storm became more savage. The ship rocked from side to side. Lightning and thunder crackled and boomed at the same time.

Suddenly, I was in real trouble. A whole group of staggering figures was coming toward me. I just managed to climb the stairs ahead of them.

Then I slipped in a puddle and fell headlong. Through the angry bora, I heard them yelping. They had followed me up. The screams echoed all around. I didn't understand why there were suddenly so many infected on the ship. What had I missed while I had been lying unconscious in the cabin?

Escape was no longer an option. They were coming at me from both sides. Scarcely five minutes earlier, I had been filled with elation at having made it. But now I was suddenly facing the end. I dearly would have loved to fight for my life. But what was the use of trying to stand up to creatures that would emerge victorious after a single scratch? Supporting myself against a cabin door, I stood up. The beasts were so close that I could smell them despite the wind. The sweet putrid stench made me want to gag. I only hoped they would kill me before I became one of them.

Out of the blue, something hit me in the back. I turned around halfway, surprised, looking down at the handle in the sparse glow of the deck lights. The next moment, the door exploded, smashing into my shoulder. I flew through the air as if I'd been rammed by a vehicle and instinctively tried to reach for the railing. But my wet hands couldn't get a grip. My hip slammed against the handrail.

Another flash of lightning lit up the night. Had I imagined an armed woman, dressed in black, in the doorway? Was the panic making me hallucinate? There was no time to think about it because I was too busy falling off the ship. I continued spinning as I flew through the air, twisting into the blackness.

Cold saltwater pressed into my nose and mouth. I tried to swim to the surface, but I no longer knew where that was. I flailed around like a mad thing, until a flash of lightning showed me which way to go. The crest of a wave tossed me up into the air.

The raindrops clattered down in a piercing roar that hurt my ears. The ship chugged past me, tossed by the storm, and disappeared quickly into the night. I swam after it in vain. It was taking all my strength to battle the churning waves. I lost my sense of direction. I swam, dived, coughed, and choked until I could take no more.

A gentle splashing sound reached me. I tried to sit up but was too exhausted. My stomach rebelled, and I vomited a gush of seawater. It was warm and smelled like stomach acid.

Something sharp was pressing against my ribs. I twisted my upper body to relieve the bruises, pushing my hands under my torso and staying in this position while I gathered my strength.

First, I opened my salt-encrusted eyes and looked around. Yesterday's storm had torn my clothes to shreds, and my legs were floating in the water. Meanwhile, my shoes lay deep at the bottom of the Mediterranean.

The rest of my body was on stony ground that seemed to be part of a long, steep coastline. The higher I lifted my head, the more of the cliffs I could see soaring into the sky. A blue, almost cloudless sky.

On the horizon, off at an angle, I saw the storm receding.

And then it all came back to me.

I was alive! But where in God's name was I?

Then I threw up again. After that, I washed my face with seawater and stood up. The sea stretched endlessly behind me. The mountains of the mainland towered in front of me. I had to get away from here.

The barren landscape, interspersed occasionally by dry shrubs and leafless bushes, offered little by way of concealment. Barefoot, I made my way inland. The stony, uneven ground was difficult to walk on, and soon my feet hurt like hell. After what felt like half an hour, I reached the top of the first hill. I looked down over the ridge and saw another mainland, from which I was separated by a wide channel of water. I estimated that at its narrowest point, the strait was about one kilometer across. I wondered again where I had landed up. If my geography wasn't deceiving me, I must be on the Balearic Islands. But which one exactly?

Ibiza? I didn't remember there being a strait like this near Ibiza. And as far as I could recall, Formentera was smaller than this island.

Might I be on Cap de Formentor, looking down on Menorca? Unlikely—they were a good fifty kilometers apart.

Dragonera? I could only be standing on the island of Dragonera, to the southwest of Mallorca. And the mainland opposite must be Mallorca, with its high, rugged cliffs to the northwest. The small island beneath me, which, seen from the east, looked like a sleeping dragon, was a natural refuge. There were no human settlements here. If I were stranded on Dragon Island, I could assume that I was safe. That is, as long as none of the infected had been washed ashore along with me.

I was increasingly tormented by thirst and forced myself to keep going. I reached a man-made path on which it was easier to walk, and shortly after that, the road forked. There was a small hut on the right, with a sign indicating that it was a toilet. I hoped I might find water there.

And I was not mistaken. Clear, cold water gushed from the tap. My spirits revived as I drank greedily and washed the salt from my skin. After a short break, I marched on. I looked all around, across the waterway to the neighboring island, and discovered a village there, nestled in the mountainside, tumbling down to the shoreline. In the harbor there was absolute chaos. The storm must have been brutal. Sailboats and fishing boats floated around like scattered toys, some of them half sunk.

People were nowhere to be seen, but I was not sure I could have spotted anyone at this distance.

At the end of the path, I discovered another hut, bigger than the one with the toilet. Inside was a kind of small museum dedicated to the island's flora and fauna. The doors were locked. Fatigue crept up my legs. How had I even made it this far after last night's ordeal? I needed to rest. If I broke into the museum, they would understand completely and not hold it against me—after all, I was shipwrecked. Or would they? I didn't really care. After everything that had happened to me in the last twenty-four hours, trespassing charges were the least of my concerns. The door looked neither strong nor particularly well secured, but I had to summon all my strength to gain access, all the same.

The room was mostly given over to an exhibition of various tubers, roots, bird feathers, and fossils. To the right was a small office. In the tin cupboard, alongside chaotically piled-up files, I discovered a rain jacket and a poncho, which you would only need in the colder months here. After barricading the front door with the desk and several of the exhibits, I spread the clothes I had found on the floor and lay down on them. Despite the hunger that was raging inside me now, I managed to fall asleep.

I slept until the next morning but had to get up a few times in the night to relieve myself. Once, I was so tormented by thirst, I even went back to the toilet in the dark to drink.

My body still ached all over. But I felt much fitter and stronger, if hungry. Cautiously, I peered out the door. Bright sunshine greeted me. It was cool this early in the morning, so I pulled on the poncho. Apart from me, Dragonera was inhabited only by lizards and seagulls, and hopefully that had not changed overnight. In the restroom, I answered the call of nature and washed as best I could. If I didn't find anything I could eat on Dragonera, I would have to swim. Over there, on Mallorca, it should be easy to satisfy my hunger. I was confident I could swim one kilometer, but I had little desire to get back into the water. There were hardly any dangers lurking in the Mediterranean, but I thought of Portuguese men-of-war, a type of jellyfish that became active here after storms. In my weakened condition, they could be dangerous to me, as their tentacles, up to fifty meters long, were barely visible.

I would try to avoid the water until I was stronger, hoping to find enough to eat on the island for a day or two.

A large sign in front of the museum described various hiking routes on Dragonera. In the southwest, it indicated a lighthouse. What was hidden inside? Was it inhabited? Might there be something there that could help me?

An hour later, I was standing in front of two stone buildings with a tower rising between them. Here, too, everything was locked. Once I had pulled open the shutters of the first house, it was easy to break the glass pane behind them with a fist-size stone. Carefully, I opened the window and climbed in. Inside, it was dark. My eyes quickly adjusted to the change. All that was here was the lighthouse control system, nothing more. I saw a radio on one of the tables. I had no idea how to operate one of these things, and I soon decided I had done enough snooping. I stepped out through some tall French windows.

The second house was just as easy to get into. I was relieved to find myself standing in a small residential building, with tiny rooms and a half-equipped kitchenette. The two beds were more comfortable than the floor in the museum. The refrigerator held food. There was more in one of the wall cupboards: cans and jars containing beans, lentils, and chickpeas. A packet of pasta. They were probably the basics that were always left there. If I rationed myself, I could probably get by for a whole week. But then what? At least there was running water here, so I was better off than I had expected to be in the next few days.

I spent a total of eight days on Dragonera. In that time, I managed to portion out the food to give myself two meals a day. In the first few days, I was almost permanently starving, because the portions were so small. But after three days, the nagging hunger subsided and didn't mess so much with my state of mind. I began to walk the island every day, climbing the steep mountain peaks and jogging along the level tracks. After a week, my feet were no longer bothered by going barefoot.

The whole time, I was worrying about how I was going to get away from here. There were no boats to be seen anywhere. But then I had an epiphany: I could convert the wooden furniture into a raft. I carried it all to the shore in stages, then tied it together using bed sheets and curtains that I'd torn into strips. "It only has to hold for a kilometer," I muttered like a mantra, careful not to leave anything to the tide. I fashioned a paddle out of a broomstick and an Ikea dustpan to enable me to propel and steer the craft.

My biggest worry was that no one came to Dragonera, as they would otherwise have done. No one was sailing along the coast of Mallorca, either. Had the plague spread there? I didn't doubt it for a second. This lowered my motivation to move, but my supplies were now exhausted.

When I got there, I would have to defend myself. So, on the third day, I built myself a spear. I removed the handle of a kitchen knife and sank its lower end into a slot I had carved in a long stick I found on the beach. The saltwater had made it rock-hard, but it was so dry that it hardly weighed anything. It had taken me hours to soften the wood in boiling water to the point where I could manipulate it. But it was worth it. I put the blade into the slot and wound it around with remnants of wire, fixing it in place. Then I bound it with some scraps of material. To avoid scratching myself on the rusty metal and getting blood poisoning, I wrapped the blade in cloth each time I began to train.

My early shadow fights led to many bumps and bruises. Without professional instruction, my efforts were bungling, but I tried to get the moves as fluid as I could. I twirled the spear in all directions, stabbing, slashing, and slicing the air. Later, I uncovered the blade and practiced on blankets and pillows that I had bundled together into a big ball.

Betweentimes, I sat down at the antique radio and turned it on. It buzzed, beeped, and hummed, but I couldn't get it to work, no matter how often I pushed the buttons and or how long I fiddled with the dials. If only there were a manual!

In the evenings, lying exhausted in bed and listening to the sound of the sea, I thought about my life before the plague. When it had all began, hardly anyone had thought it a threat. So the disease had spread, rapidly. It had infected villages, cities, entire countries. The healthy population was frantically evacuated and moved to so-called safe havens.

These were mostly makeshift districts, sealed off by barbed wire and army vehicles. They did not last long. It took a handful of infected people only a few hours to break through the barriers and destroy everything, while the improvised fortresses offered those fleeing them scarcely any escape route.

The diseased seemed unstoppable. I recalled countless blurry shots from the internet. The symptoms were always the same: rapidly rising fever, headache, and shortness of breath, followed by apparent death. The filmmakers told how people who were afflicted by this new contagion died quickly—and then returned to life a short time later as bloodthirsty beasts. Many amateur videos even showed the resurrected corpses throwing themselves dementedly at those standing nearby, biting at them uncontrollably, trying to tear them apart. They ate the raw flesh of the living, and the living became infected.

Secretly, I congratulated myself for having decided to take the ship, even if from my current perspective this had been only a marginally better choice. But at least I was still alive. I hoped that I would still be happy with my strategy after I had crossed the channel.

Too late I realized that the distance from the southernmost corner of the island was almost four times the breadth of the channel. The tabletops that I had placed over each other were a much worse raft than I'd thought they would be. It wobbled precariously with every little wave. For the first thousand meters, my only concern with not to capsize. But eventually, I got the hang of it and paddled purposefully through the strait.

I had tied my spear to one of the skyward-pointing table legs.

It took me all morning to reach Mallorca. It was grim being the sole person navigating a waterway that was normally crowded with boats, yachts, and sailors of all shapes and sizes. Once I was halfway across, I could make out the details of the houses built into the cliffs. Some of the windows and balcony doors stood open. The curtains were waving at me in the wind like ghostly harpies.

I docked my raft at the small wooden jetty in the harbor. Suddenly, an ice-cold trickle ran down my spine. Everywhere, it seemed as if people would emerge from the taverns and side streets at any moment, strolling through the village with their purchases under their arms or their phones to their ears. Children would be frolicking on the sandy beach, splashing around and throwing wet sludge at each other.

But there was none of this to be seen. An eerie silence lay over the village, broken only by occasional gusts of wind, which gave the whole place an even more oppressive feel. I would have thought a world facing the apocalypse would be bleak and dying, with withered plants and trees, their branches bending sadly toward the ground, and a sky without sunshine, devoid of any real color. But the end of the world did not seem to be reflected in the weather. The sky above me was the purest blue, and the sun was beaming cheerfully down upon the earth, as if welcoming the decline of humanity. The bright sunshine awoke a deep sadness in me. I questioned my existence. Was it a good thing that I was alive? Would it have made any difference to the planet if I had drowned?

But if I continued to indulge in such musings, I would make myself depressed and that might make me want to end my life. I didn't want to do that under any circumstances. I would survive as long as I could.

I untied my spear and climbed onto the pier. No one came to meet me. The first building I reached was a small restaurant with the left leaf of its door standing open. I gripped the shaft of the spear with both hands, pointing the tip of the blade forward.

As I called out to see if anyone was there, I became conscious of my fear. There was no answer, and I called out again, more to reassure myself than to let anyone know I had arrived. I took one step and then another. At that point, sheer horror seized me, and my knees began to shake. In my mind's eye, I saw the enraged infected, rushing out of the inn to gnaw the flesh from my bones. My heart was beating fast and so loudly that I thought it had climbed up into my head and was pounding against my ears. As soon as I could think clearly again, I realized that I was in the middle of an empty restaurant. Only some of the furniture had been shifted or tipped over.

When one of the refrigerators started up with a loud click behind me, I almost fell over in shock. I wheeled around, cutting only the air with the blade. I stubbed my bare toes on one of the chair legs. If the infected didn't kill me, I would die of a heart attack. On the other side of the bar, I spotted drawers and pulled one open. A fine cloud of condensation arose from it. The drawer was full of juices and sodas.

I drank some orange juice and dropped the bottle back into the drawer. The next one contained alcoholic beverages, which didn't especially appeal at the moment. But I thought I might be able to barter for things with them in the coming days. They would also make good disinfectant.

The bar would be the worst possible place to set up camp, as one of its large walls was made of glass. I decided to try my luck and went in search of a better place to sleep.

Above the inn, I could see an apartment. The door was to the left of the tavern, but unfortunately, it was locked. If I broke it open, like I had done on Dragon Island, I would have to make sure I could lock it again afterward to protect against intruders.

I had to find another way in.

The apartment had a large balcony stretching across the full width of the tavern's dining area and was also well positioned from a strategic point of view. I would probably be able to see most of the town and all of the harbor from there. And there were no tall buildings obstructing the direct view of the approach to the village from the east.

I walked around the restaurant and discovered a point where I could climb up to the balcony. The terrace was large enough for two cars to park on. The sliding doors had been left open. I stepped inside the apartment, spearhead first.

As I pushed aside one of the curtains, it wrapped around the shaft like a sluggish snake.

The living room was clean and tidy, with stylish minimalist furnishings. I walked over the soft carpet to a spacious kitchen. Here, too, there was electricity, and the refrigerator was humming. Behind it, I discovered a small half-filled pantry. The eighteen one-and-a-half-liter bottles of water standing there should be enough to last me a month, I calculated. My hunger kicked in, but I had to inspect the rest of the apartment first. A short, narrow hallway with two more doors led from the living room. Behind the first one, I found the toilet and a shower cubicle.

The next room, the bedroom, had a large bed in the center. Behind it was an enormous closet, whose potential contents immediately sparked my interest. The two doors on the right side concealed the possessions of the former lady of the house. Judging by the style of her clothes, she had been middle-aged and had been trying to recapture some of her youth with fancy styles and bright colors. The same was true of the gentleman's clothes on the left.

Most of the pieces were not to my taste, though at the moment, it was didn't matter in the least what people's clothes looked like. But I was sure that garish colors would attract attention, and that could cost the wearer their head.

I rummaged around in the closets until I found a couple of less obtrusive items: two pairs of gray sweatpants and three greenish T-shirts in a black-and-white print. Underwear would be important, I thought, so I grabbed a half dozen pairs of boxers and a few pairs of socks.

The closet also held a thicker fleece jacket and a light, wide-brimmed safari hat. In one of the drawers, I discovered expensive watches, whose ostentatious sizes made them completely impractical except as weapons. I chose the smallest one, which was black and self-winding and so did not need a battery.

Once I had finished searching the bedroom, I went back to the bathroom and took a long shower. I washed my hair with one of the expensive-looking shampoos. The soap washed away the dirt of the last few days from my skin. I watched the slightly brown wastewater draining away, unsurprised. Afterward I dried myself and exchanged the tattered rags on my legs for clean underwear, a comfortable pair of sweatpants, and an olive-colored T-shirt. In weather like today's, I wouldn't need any other clothing, except for the hat.

Back in the kitchen, I set about examining the refrigerator. Inside I found opened cans and shriveled fruit. I put it in the almost full garbage bag, which I tied shut and dropped from the balcony onto the garbage cans. My environmental conscience immediately pricked me, but what was the point of putting the garbage in the garbage can, even as a matter of form, if no one ever came to empty it?

As the bag slammed loudly into the can lid, an angry wheezing arose. Immediately I heard the footsteps of many creatures, getting faster as they approached the garbage cans. I dropped to the tiled floor. My spear was leaning against the wall next to the refrigerator. Below me in the passage to the courtyard, there was a commotion that I couldn't see but heard all the better.

Garbage cans were pushed roughly back and forth, and one fell over with a clatter. It was a few minutes, during which I didn't dare move, before the infected left. Perhaps they had forgotten what had brought them here in the first place, but here they were!

This was only a small foretaste of what the future held.

I turned onto my back and took a deep breath before sneaking back into the apartment. Carefully, I locked the sliding door and lowered the blinds as quietly as possible. My hands were still shaking some minutes later. Only a deep rumbling coming from my stomach area was able to distract me.

It was time to eat something. After preparing pasta and tomato sauce, a veritable feast compared to my meals over the last ten days, I drank directly from one of the glass bottles. There was tap water, because as long as there was electricity, the basic utilities would be supplied automatically. Following the meal, I started to tidy up the pantry and arrange the food by type and expiration date. I found several packages of pasta, a lot of jars of lentils, chickpeas, and red beans, plus salt, pepper, and other spices. I asked myself what I would want to eat tomorrow—and the day after that. This gave me the illusion of normality amid the general chaos. It even enabled me to calculate how long the food I had would last.

If I portioned everything out and kept myself to minimum rations, I would be well supplied for several weeks, maybe even a month or a month and a half. As far as carbohydrates were concerned, I was covered.

But to stay healthy in the long run, my body needed fresh fruit and vegetables on a regular basis, and not only the juices I found in the taverna. From my previous trips to Mallorca, I knew that some regions of the island produced tons of oranges, tangerines, and lemons. What was more, typical Mediterranean fruit trees such as figs and mirabelle plums grew in almost every garden. Many smallholders in rural areas grew tomatoes, eggplant, zucchini, garlic, and onions. In a situation like this one, I had no qualms about plundering abandoned farmsteads. Perhaps, I might also find supplements in tablet form in pharmacies and grocery stores.

My anxiety calmed a little at the sight of the stores in the pantry. It was clear that I would not stay alive in the long run if I were to rely solely on the food I had already found. But it was a start.

It was late in the evening, and the sun had just disappeared behind the peaks of Dragonera. I didn't dare go out onto the balcony to watch the colors of the setting sun. So, I just peeked cautiously through a small gap in the blinds and watched the sky change in slow motion from orange to dark blue. The stars flickered sedately to life. Another day had passed. My thoughts circled incessantly around how good I had it despite how critical and lonely my situation was in general.

In the days that followed, I visited all the apartments and houses in the vicinity to which I could gain access.

I never parted with my weapon and trained regularly for encounters with the infected, usually within the safety of the balcony. As I practiced, I imagined a horde of them emerging unexpectedly into the open from one of the doors or one of the many side alleys and rushing toward me. I hoped that this would mean I was at least halfway prepared to fight in the event of a confrontation. I slid my spear deep into imaginary eye sockets, quickly pulling out the blade as I turned to face other newly infected. I cut fictitious throats and severed heads until the imaginary streets were full of the dead. As I did so, I was meticulously careful not to come into contact with the bodily fluids that splattered everywhere. Every time I imagined myself in this kind of situation, it became easier to stay calm and level-headed. How this would translate into practice remained to be seen.

The streets and buildings remained deserted. In the houses I broke into, I found more food, water, and even a pair of brand-new running shoes that fitted me well. But my main haul was a sturdy, modern backpack for hiking. I used it to transport the provisions and bottles I unearthed in kitchens, basements, and storage rooms. Sometimes it was so full and heavy after a raid that I bent over as I walked.

The pantry of my "headquarters," as I had christened the apartment, was filling up. Soon I had no room for more food and had to store it in the wall cabinets in the kitchen. I had now increased my initial stocks almost tenfold and added fruit and vegetables from the surrounding gardens.

I frequently wondered how quickly people must have left their homes, since some of the apartments even had cooked food—now rotten and inedible—waiting on the table. In some places, a radio or television was on, but only static came out of it. In the beginning, I had been too busy stockpiling food and water, so I had not thought to keep myself up to date with current events. Now the receivers were just hissing.

On the morning of the twelfth or thirteenth day after I arrived on Mallorca, I had breakfast as usual. My food supplies were now substantial. I figured I was good for six months. Conserving water would be a bigger problem in the long run, but yesterday it had rained heavily all day. I had positioned plastic buckets and shower pans on the balcony, and by late afternoon, they were full to the brim. I filtered the rainwater with a light cloth and a standard household funnel and filled up some of the empty bottles and preserving jars. At an average of two liters a day, I'd be safe from dying of thirst for three and a half months.

I'd fetched pretty much all I could from the town by now, so I decided to try my luck in the next settlement. I walked east for twenty minutes until I reached the first buildings and hotels of the neighboring village. The clock showed ten. The sky was unusually gray, and the clouds were scudding by quickly, as if fleeing some calamity.

The wind abruptly carried a foul smell to me. At first, I thought there must be rotting animal carcasses nearby. With each step, the intensity increased. The stench became abominable.

And then I remembered where I had first smelled it. At the same time, I heard the staccato, guttural sounds that indicated frustration and hunger. They were burned into my memory from the Port of Barcelona. Immediately, the hairs on the back of my neck stood up. I came to a halt as if rooted to the spot, conscious of my bladder and fervently hoping that I wasn't going to wet my pants.

The wind shifted. The rasping stopped for an instant, only to redouble the next minute. I sensed something invisible starting to move and heard the shuffling of many feet. But I could not yet locate where the sound was coming from.

About twenty meters in front of me, the horrific horde suddenly erupted from a side street to the left. Milky white pairs of eyes fixed themselves on me. The noses beneath them snuffled in the wind. Some of the cadaverous bodies were dressed in torn clothing. Others wore only bathing suits. Their skin had burned and cracked in the scorching sun of the last few weeks. A grayish liquid was running from their many wounds. They had yellow and brown stains around their loins, evidence of uncontrolled bladder and bowel activity. The resulting stink, coupled with the foul stench of the creatures' mouths, made my stomach turn.

Two kilometers from headquarters, I had no chance against their superior strength. Gripping the spear tighter, I turned in the direction from which I had come and ran while a storm of indignation broke out behind me. I thought my chances of escaping were very good since the infected moved relatively slowly and clumsily. The last side street of the village was just a few meters ahead, but another stinking group stormed out from it, cutting off my path. Now I was like Schrödinger's cat, although I assumed I was more dead than alive.

There was no way I could slip past them: the street was too narrow for me to pass easily. So, I slowed down, grabbed my weapon in both hands, and stabbed the first staggering creature in the nose with all my might. I was aiming for its eye, but it moved its head to the side. The spearhead entered its brain, and the last spark of life in it went out. Quickly, before the shaft was torn from my hand, I pulled it out. The infected collapsed.

This first small victory gave me new courage. Self-confidence flared up in me, fueled by the sudden rush of adrenaline. As I stepped backward, I turned the spear around, using its rock-hard shaft as a bludgeon. An infected potbellied tourist in a frayed Hawaiian shirt came at me. I smashed the shaft against his left temple as hard as I could. His head snapped under the force of the blow, and something crunched like a dry branch. The fat man fell to the ground like a sack.

The first group was a good twenty meters behind me. At the speed they were moving, it would take them a few seconds to reach me. The vanguard of the second group stumbled, falling over those of their number that were lying on the ground. This bought me some time. I quickly looked around for a way out and sprinted into the narrow alley on the right. But the infected were waiting there, too. My God, where had they all come from? I had only seen them once since the first week. Now the hellish monstrosities seemed to be everywhere. Going right wasn't going to work.

I turned left again, past the long hotel building. The beach had to be somewhere. In the water, I would have the advantage of being able to swim. Instinct told me to turn right again. But there was only another large modern hotel, blocking my view to the south.

If I had thought I had a lot of infected to deal with, I was soon disabused. The road bent to the left about seventy meters ahead of me. Too late, I caught sight of the hundreds of people stumbling in my direction. My last resort looked as if it would be the alley between us, which led to the right and must lead directly to the beach. But I would never manage to reach it before them, no matter how fast I ran. Behind me, a good twenty creatures were coming toward me, their hands stretched out in front. No matter how hopeless my situation seemed, I would have done anything to reach this one clear path. The rasping horde in the street fixed its attention on me. Before I reached the alley, they finally blocked my way.

Now I was in a very tight spot. They were approaching in extremely high numbers, and there was no possibility of fleeing. I placed myself sideways between the two hordes so that they had to attack my flanks. I resigned myself to dying in the next few seconds—but not before I had fought for my life until the very end. Then I fell into a strange state of mind. Time slowed down, and I perceived the events around me with a strange clarity.

When they were in range, I swung the spear left and right. Since the infected were uncoordinated and clumsy as they closed in on me, I initially managed to keep them off of me, alternately fending off their attacks on both sides. This went well for a while. But then, in the middle of a thrust, I realized that two of the creatures were about the same distance from me. I would only be able to get one of them, leaving the other free to sink its teeth into my flesh. Roaring, I thrust the weapon up into the chin of the attacker to the right, reaching the top of his skull. Then I felt someone clinging to me on the left.

The hungry, sun-scorched creature grabbed and pulled my upper left arm with its clawlike fingers and bent over to sink its rotting teeth into it. The pungent stench of her breath was nauseating and almost clouded my mind. I thought I could literally feel her biting into my flesh and infecting me. Everything went into slow motion. I could not shake the monster off. Her undead incisors were hovering less than an inch from my jacket sleeve when suddenly the beast and several others were caught up in a bluish vortex and hurled across the street.

The bite I had anticipated never came; the swirling entity had saved me. And then it came to a screeching halt a hair's breadth away from me.

A Mercedes 500S, metallic blue, wide, showy. Automated convertible roof that could be lowered into the trunk. A classic car and in good condition except for a few dents. I was still seeing things with unusual clarity, so I took in all the details.

While I was fighting furiously for my life, the Mercedes had driven up from the left, drifting through the crowd of the infected as though they were a flower bed, sending them flying like corn dollies. A fat, bearded man sat at the wheel and was yelling at me. To begin with, I couldn't understand a word he was saying.

The man spoke again, frantically, shouting like a madman. His language was strange, appearing to have an odd dialect. I realized he was speaking English but hadn't mastered the language. The undead were attempting in vain to break the closed window to his right.

"Are you bite?" he bellowed from inside the car. What?

"ARE YOU BITE?"

I corrected his words in my head, finally understanding he was asking whether I had been bitten.

In the heat of the moment, I answered in the same broken language as the question.

"No, no bite!"

"Get in ze car!" he thundered, gesticulating. "NOW!"

The car had no center pillar, and the windows were down on one side. I pulled at the door handle. Locked. The more athletic of the infected scrambled to their feet. Some tried awkwardly to climb onto the hood and the trunk lid. The pressure from those behind them crushed them against the bodywork. The door wouldn't open no matter how desperately I shook it.

The beasts got through the very moment the driver pulled away. Their nails clutched greedily at the air, just inches from my face.

"GET IN ZE CAAAAR!"

I dived headfirst through the window as the vehicle accelerated away, its tires squealing. My backpack was empty and did not hinder me as I rolled onto the seat. Because I had been holding the spear vertically, it got stuck outside. Once I was sitting in a more comfortable position, I pulled the weapon into the car. Since my chauffeur was driving at breakneck speed, careering around every turn, this was no easy task.

"You are no bite?" the driver roared again. He was suddenly holding a gun to my temple. Where had that come from? He must have been sitting on it or keeping it between his knees.

"No! No bite!" I answered truthfully.

He drove even faster without lowering the gun. After we had made three turns, he stopped the car and looked at me.

"No bite?" he repeated the question.

"No, I'm fine," I affirmed without moving.

He waited a while. When I did not transform, he laid the gun aside and took the wheel. Infected appeared in the side-view mirror. I pressed a button in my door to raise the windows. He opened the throttle, thundering through the lanes. We quickly found ourselves behind the larger cluster. I blanched at the sheer number of them. They realized too late that we were making an early exit. Many of them stretched out their claws as we passed them. I kept looking over the back seat until we rounded a bend.

"Where are we going?" I asked, still panting from the fight.

"Safe house." My driver was more relaxed now. He held out his hand. "My name is Nils."

I returned the handshake, introduced myself, and asked, "Where is this 'safe house'?" I wondered what would become of my headquarters.

"There, where it is safe," he said, smiling grimly.

It always took me some time to translate his sentences as he spoke. But my driver was not the talkative type. His taciturnity suited me since I hadn't had any contact with people in the past few weeks and had been out of the habit of dealing with them.

We drove along country roads and through deserted villages. I saw burned out and abandoned car wrecks on many corners. Some stretches of road were barely passable due to long lines of parked cars. Nils skillfully maneuvered us around any obstacles, keeping a careful eye on the road ahead and behind us. It led through the Tramuntana Mountains, over high passes and around hundreds of serpentine bends, past many groves of gnarled holm oak. We saw hardly any other cars, and ours was the only one moving. The weather was still gray and dreary. I was awestruck at having been snatched back from the brink of death yet again. At one of the passes, we turned right and headed east toward the Mallorcan plain of Es Pla.

We were soon passing through endless orange orchards on both sides of the road. The fruit hung lush and heavy from the branches. Ten minutes later, we turned north at the foot of the mountain range. Meanwhile, my hormone levels had returned to normal.

"Thank you for saving my ass back there," I said.

He laughed and waved away my thanks with his right hand, indicating it had been nothing.

"How have you managed to stay alive?" he asked in passing. We were driving on a clearer stretch of road, and he had less need to focus on the route. I gave him a quick summary of my story without revealing too much. He nodded slowly at almost every sentence. Sometimes he looked at me briefly, as if he doubted the truth of what I was saying. I didn't tell him about the stocks in the pantry. How could I know who this guy was? Or what he was up to?

If I had to escape again, I wanted to keep a secret place where I would be able to stay and at least survive for a while.

For the most part, Nils smiled and said nothing.

"Why were you even there?" I asked.

"I often drive around looking for food, water, and survivors. Or fuel for my car. I break into cars, siphon off the fuel, and beat it again right away."

His glasses were slightly tinted. One iris sat a little lower than the other. His oversize shirt hung loosely on his torso, as if trying to hide how stout he was. Massive legs peeked out from a pair of shorts. His feet were in sandals.

"This morning was the first time I saw the large group of the transformed that you came across. That's the biggest group so far. I was curious to see where they were headed. We don't know much about their behavior . . . except that they sometimes form packs. Then I saw you take down the first two stinkers and run off down the back alley. You know the rest."

"Thank you so much for that."

"My pleasure." He raised his right hand, and I grinned back. Suddenly Nils slowed down, inspecting our surroundings more carefully, and asked, "Do you see anyone? Another car behind us? Any stinkers?"

Apart from us, there was no sign of life for kilometers. "No, no one," I replied. After a few minutes of slow driving, we turned onto a gravel road and five kilometers later arrived in front of a massive, two-and-a-half-meter-high steel gate. Nils braked and took a thin section of black plastic from his shirt pocket. He pointed it at the entrance and pressed one of the two yellow buttons. Immediately, it began to move, rolling quietly aside.

We drove into a large courtyard. Nils closed the gate with another push of a button. The driveway was paved with massive, hand-hewn stone slabs. The house itself had previously been a stately villa, surrounded by palm, pine, fig, and orange trees, and only came into view after a short drive down a slight incline over the uneven paving. In front of the doorway stood a grandiose fountain, tasteless and ostentatious, with gargoyles and naked cherubs. We drove around it and stopped in front of the main entrance. Nils turned off the engine. To the left and right of the front door were columns that supported a balcony on the floor above. The semicircular porch was bounded by ornate black railings. Nils unbuckled his seat belt and got out. "Come on," he said.

I followed him around to the back of the house where we came across some people sitting at a large table, diligently portioning and repackaging food.

I counted five other people besides Nils, three women and two men. They were all wearing casual clothes in muted colors. When they saw him, they smiled in greeting. Then they saw me, and their expressions suddenly became more serious.

"Who is this, Nils?" The questioner spoke English with a southern European accent. It was immediately clear who called the shots here. She was dressed in black, and her dark brown hair was gathered into a tight ponytail. Her broad shoulders stretched her T-shirt farther than was good for it. The muscles of her upper arms stood out clearly, and her tight cotton pants revealed the strength of her well-trained legs. She regarded me closely, like a bird of prey observing its quarry, while her body tensed like a cobra about to strike.

I recognized her immediately.

"I'm just here for my next swimming lesson," I responded boldly, before Nils could say anything. I jutted my chin toward her.

She moved her lower jaw in a semicircle while she thought about what I might mean. She looked like she was secreting enough poison to kill me.

The other people at the table noticed the tension and sat up, looking at me.

My mouth filled with saliva. I stopped myself from swallowing. I didn't want them to notice how nervous I was.

"It's all right. We met in the south. The stinkers were about to anoint another honorary member of their country club," Nils said, gesturing to me casually with his thumb. "So, I thought someone who was alive might like it better here with us. Must have killed ten of them with that ridiculous stick before I got involved. Will make a good backup." He sounded almost bored. He took one of the oranges and started peeling it.

Quick as a flash, the woman in black picked up a kitchen knife from the table and pointed it in my direction. She tilted her head slightly to one side, assuming a more threatening posture. Nils rolled his eyes theatrically. She eyed me openly and aggressively without moving the blade. "What swimming lesson?" she hissed, emphasizing each syllable.

Keeping my expression neutral, I answered, "The refugee ship from Barcelona. A few weeks ago. You fell out of a bunk and pushed me over the rail with the door."

Moments later, I saw recognition in her eyes. "Oh, *that*!" She relaxed, grinned mischievously, spread both arms invitingly, and thundered with a mixture of sarcasm and generosity, "Well, welcome *aboard*, Backup!"

The people sitting at the table suppressed their laughter. One of them cautiously pounded the table with his fist several times. Nils shook his head incredulously. He addressed his words to me as if to apologize. "You'll have to get used to this kind of bullshit if you want to stay with us. They're always talking trash to each other! That's Franca. She's kind of the boss here." Then he introduced me to the other survivors. Eva and Patrick were sitting across from each other. She held out a dainty hand to me, and he offered me a seat on the bench next to him.

"Bring our guest something to drink!" cried Waltraud, the Norwegian, watching Jens fill a glass with water for me.

Now I grinned too and took a seat. It seemed like an eternity since I had spent time in the company of other people.

They set freshly baked bread, tomatoes, onions, olives, and olive oil on the table. I dribbled some oil onto the white bread and took some slices of tomato and half a sliced onion.

The first question came before I had wolfed down two bites. "Tell me, who are you and how did you come to be rescued by Nils?"

I took my time and explained in detail how I had ended up here, sarcastically embellishing the moment of my involuntary departure from the cruise ship. Everyone laughed. We sat, ate, and chatted. I didn't mention my pantry. Soon I noticed that the convivial, friendly mood was subtly undermined by the all-pervasive sense of threat. Everyone had that permanently wary look and was keeping an eye on their surroundings. When they laughed, it was never boisterously or loudly. In one way, this made me sad because it would have been nicer to be in the moment, more carefree.

All the same, I was glad that no one brought this up and that everyone was acting as if all was right with the world. We enjoyed the appearance of normality.

Later in the afternoon, the clouds dispersed, and the broad plain was illuminated by the sun's rays. The shadows became longer, the air cooler. The food had been portioned out while this was happening and had quickly disappeared into the cellar of the villa. I offered to help with the cleaning up.

My offer was accepted gratefully, but not before they had glanced at each other, conferring. Franca indicated her agreement with a brief nod.

The cellar, which was accessed through a kind of fire door, had originally been designed as a wine store. There were wine racks everywhere, some of them well stocked. Half of the basement was given over to food storage. It looked similar to my small pantry, only on a larger scale. Cans and jars of preserves farther back, more perishable goods like flour, oatmeal, fruits, and vegetables in the front. I quickly estimated that if it were portioned as I was accustomed to doing, there would be enough to last all of us three months. Several water bottle crates were stacked neatly against the wall.

The darkest side of the basement had no windows and was free of shelves. I saw an old mattress leaning against the wall in the corner. On it was a clumsily drawn target with a lot of different-size holes.

Jens filled me in. "This is our training room. We practice shooting and fighting here. We had to seal the rest of the windows with straw mattresses to muffle the sound. From outside, you can hardly hear it when we're using guns here." I nodded, impressed. Then we went back upstairs.

When it became too cold to continue sitting on the terrace, we collected up the dishes, cutlery, and glasses, everyone carrying their own into the kitchen. Nils explained to me that a few years before he had had a state-of-the-art solar energy system installed on the roof. This fed a large number of batteries that were stored in an adjacent room. When charged, they could supply the key equipment in the house for several days and even operate the steel gate. The gate was also equipped with a device that allowed it to be rolled aside manually in the event of a power failure. Many years ago, before the house had even been planned and farmers had herded goats and sheep there, three wells had been sunk in the three-and-a-half-hectare garden. Today, solar energy powered the compressors that pumped the groundwater up from the wells and passed it through a reverse osmosis filter.

The family who had built the villa in the 1980s—who must have been extremely wealthy—had also built a three-meter wall around the entire property. This wall was now overgrown with bushes and thorny vines. It was almost impossible to gain access from the outside, which explained why there were hardly any guards.

Security, light, heat, water, food—they had everything. Even the company of other people. I shook my head in disbelief. How lucky had I been, first to have been rescued by Nils and then to have been brought here? This troop had it good. They were disciplined and equipped to survive.

When darkness fell, the shutters were closed, and all the doors were locked. The heavy curtains were drawn. In the cool living room, we allowed ourselves to light two candles and sat in the candlelight, done with the day, but not ready for the night.

Franca raised her glass and waited patiently for our attention. Everyone fell silent and looked at her. She made a serious and ceremonial toast.

"Today, our little crew got some reinforcements. From what Nils told us, you'll not only be able to provide backup with consuming our supplies . . ."

Someone chuckled softly.

Franca continued, without reacting, "You're also a dab hand with a homemade stabbing weapon."

Now everyone was looking at me, nodding and raising their glasses. I felt uncomfortable at this sudden attention but met their gazes and raised my glass in turn.

"Even if you almost drowned in the Mediterranean because of me . . ."

Again, the general chuckling.

This time, the corners of Franca's mouth twitched, and her eyes lit up, while I grinned stupidly. "So today we welcome you to our colorful crew!"

Everyone laughed and chimed in, "To Backup!"

"To Backup! Welcome!" Glasses clinked softly as people brought them gently together.

Franca waited for the right moment, then continued. "We've been Nils's guests for a few days now, and even though we all know each other's names now, we only know the bare essentials about each other. I'd like us to take the time to tell our stories every evening, starting tonight. Backup has led the way. For one thing, it would be good if we knew at least a little about who we're sharing the roof over our heads with."

As she said this, the mood seemed to change. Everyone except Franca went back into their shell, playing with empty glasses or intertwining their fingers nervously and then loosening them again immediately. Who had lost family members, lovers, or children in the catastrophe? Who had skeletons in the closet that they did not want to come to light? Who was prepared to reveal—and face—the pain and fear they were hiding?

Franca sighed resignedly. "For another thing, it can be deadly boring here in the evenings. I don't like to go to bed before midnight. There's no compulsion to take part; if you don't want to say anything, feel free not to. But since this is my idea, I think it's my responsibility to get the ball rolling. And if no one wants to listen," she said, shrugging, "that's fine, too."

CHAPTER 2

FRANCA

It was a rainy day, typical for April. Cold wind whistled through the streets. It poured nonstop, and all of Florence had had enough now. Looking down through the raindrops that clung to the window, to the gray roadways six stories below, I thought of all the forks in the road that had led me to Tuscany.

After quitting my job at the Gruppo di Intervento Speciale and then spending a month at a rehab center for alcoholics and drug addicts, I had been looking for a new professional challenge. But what could a woman with my skills do? I was fit for nothing! At least, nothing that could be considered a normal job. I was trained to use weapons of all kinds. My body had been molded into a fighting machine, and I had had to use it countless times in the security services. Do I have anyone on my conscience? If you don't count self-defense, no. All this in the name of the Italian nation, to which I dedicated fourteen years of my life. Now we've gone our separate ways.

Starting a detective agency was the obvious thing to do, so I rented some cheap rooms in a dilapidated office complex. I couldn't afford any big outlay, just an old desk from the flea market. Two well-preserved orange Le Corbusier chairs and a stately but comfortable office chair I bought at an online auction.

The rest of my savings went to three months' rent, which had to be paid in advance. This included the internet and a telephone line, but there wasn't enough money left over to buy myself a proper computer. Instead, I had to make do with my old one, which gave me regular lessons in patience when something didn't work or worked much more slowly than things are supposed to now.

I called in a favor owed to me by a small-time hacker, who had previously worked for me as an informant. He built me a rudimentary website and put it online. For just a hundred euros, one of his mates designed a logo for me, which I saw back to front through the frosted glass window as I sat at my desk every day:

FRANCA PASTORE
PRIVATE DETECTIVE AND PERSONAL PROTECTION

The designer had specifically chosen a 1930s typeface "with strict serifs," he said, "as was customary for detective agencies at the time." He had bent the lower line into a gentle curve, which somewhat resembled a smiley. He babbled something about the emotions that the design would subconsciously evoke in people when they saw it. Although this superfluous information didn't interest me, it stayed with me. I said nothing, put the hundred-euro note on the table and left. Four days later, the logo was emblazoned on my door and website.

My first assignments were deadly boring. I often had to shadow unfaithful spouses and gather evidence for the divorce court. Now and then, I had to give evidence, which was by far the most exciting part of the job. But a woman has to eat, so I didn't have any complaints.

But when one day the agency of a young actress knocked on the door, my daily routine got a bit livelier, and my account got a bit fuller. I was required to follow my client at a discreet distance on her daily jog, to keep a sharp eye on fans during autograph sessions, and to keep the pushy ones at bay.

Due to my constant consumption of alcohol and cannabis and a lack of exercise resulting from the depression, my body had lost a lot of strength, muscle, and tone. I had wanted to regain these for a long time. My new job started in five weeks, so I didn't have nearly enough time to get as fit as I had been before. But since I wasn't going to be getting involved in gun battles or hand-to-hand combat with ruthless human traffickers and drug dealers this time, this amount of time would be enough for now.

Right after the manager of the diva—who I had never heard of, but who half of Italy was talking about—signed the contract and left the office, I turned off the lights and shut down the ancient computer. I swung a leg over my bike and pedaled to the nearest, cheapest gym between my apartment and the office. Thinking that I might start working out, I had left my gym clothes in the depths of the office closet weeks before.

However, I had never got up enough motivation to put the decision into action. Now, I finally signed a twelve-month contract, changed, and in the pale light between the worn-out machines, I tried to remember my old training routine at the unit.

The first few days were so depressing that I almost fell off the wagon. I could barely manage a handful of push-ups. I couldn't even do twenty biceps curls with the five-kilogram dumbbell. And I couldn't do any pull-ups at all! Despite these failures, I went to the gym every morning before work and did my exercises and ran one kilometer farther on the treadmill every day than I had the day before, until the machine read ten kilometers. To warm up and loosen my muscles, I practiced the close combat sequences I had learned in front of the mirror. They were all still there but deeply buried.

I also began to eat more healthily, switching to a completely vegan diet. For breakfast, I ate tons of fruit and some muesli. At lunchtime, I ate large salads. I stocked up on carbohydrates in the evening in the form of pasta and rice and drank at least four liters of water a day. Every now and then I caught myself wishing for a good slug of whiskey. But I pushed such thoughts away. Never again was I going to allow something or someone that much control over my life. The tough training helped distract me from my cravings.

The first week on my new diet was incredibly difficult. But the harder I worked, the more my old self-discipline came through. After a month, I could do thirty push-ups and twelve pull-ups easily, and I had switched to the ten-kilogram dumbbell for the curls. I added to my daily training, alternating between an hour of CrossFit and an evening bouldering session.

My muscles were so stiff in the mornings that I could hardly get out of bed. But it was a pain I welcomed. My stomach flattened again, my legs toned up, and I could see my shoulder muscles beneath my skin again.

While I was fighting my way back to my old self, I noticed how my view of my surroundings and my fellow human beings was changing. The job meant I hardly had any time to think about the past. I was less and less that bad-tempered, grumpy person, wallowing in her misfortune. My stance was upright and confident again, something I had lost toward the end of my career as a colonnello in the elite police force.

I protected the actress for a year, twelve hours a day, six days a week. The first few weeks were exhausting. This time I was the one who was subordinate, and I had to be more of a chaperone than take an active role in what was going on. At least I was used to working in the shadows. After the job was over, contrary to expectations, things began to look up jobs-wise. Sometimes I even gave myself time off, backpacking through Asia, Australia, or South America. I had the office renovated and moved into a larger apartment. So the months and years passed, and my spirit healed. But apparently, nothing good ever lasts.

When the news of the outbreak of the epidemic in Paris first flickered across the screen, I initially planned to increase my daily rates. It was possible that there would be widespread panic in Italy as well, and that my services as a bodyguard would be in greater demand. Weeks passed, and the pandemic spread, but hardly anyone called.

Financially, it was bearable. As far as the business was concerned, I was more bored than worried.

But when the epidemic reached Italy, my optimism quickly fell away.

I continued to train every day, adding in a session of shooting practice. Before the first session, I had to take apart, clean, and oil my somewhat aged Glock pistol. My dexterity had suffered in the absence of routine, but I quickly improved my accuracy and speed at the shooting range. I bought several hundred rounds of ammunition and was soon laying the gun aside only to shower. I kept it under my pillow while I slept.

People on the street became more suspicious, withdrawn, avoidant, greeting each other less. Anyone might be infected; anyone was a potential killer. When France declared martial law because it could no longer cope with the epidemic and the unrest it brought, I realized it was all downhill from there. All the efforts I had made to get my life under control seemed to have been in vain. In Italy, new epidemics broke out from time to time, with the news then claiming that they were under control again. Sandbag barricades went up in the cities, manned by soldiers armed with heavy weapons. Deep inside, I had long had the foreboding that something bad was going to happen, but nothing could have prepared me for the encounter that was looming.

Bad news reports were circulating one after another on the internet. Suddenly, the old despair gripped me again. I detached myself from the dreary sight of the wet streets, went over to my desk, and pulled open the bottom drawer.

A full bottle of bourbon and two whiskey glasses clinked toward me. It took me a minute to gather enough strength to close the drawer with a flourish. I heard the bottle fall over.

Then, footsteps and soft voices sounded outside the office. I made out three diffuse silhouettes through the frosted glass. The Glock was in the top right drawer. I opened it carefully and put my hand on the pistol. My clients usually hired me by email or phone. It was rare for anyone to come here and speak to me in person, and even rarer for them not to at least tell me in advance they were coming. I was more puzzled than concerned, and even more puzzled when my visitors knocked politely. Nevertheless, it did no harm to be prepared for anything.

"Come in," I said, trying to sound busy. The handle turned, and the door was opened carefully by a muscular guy with shoulders twice as wide as mine. He looked as if he were afraid he might rip the door off its hinges. With his short, military haircut, he could have been one of the Special Forces. I could see a gun under his dark pinstripe suit. His jacket was buttoned up, which would make it difficult for him to reach his weapon quickly.

Another heavy waited in the background, his hands clasped over his stomach. The bodyguards stood back in the twilight of the corridor, and an older man came into view between them. Something clicked in my mind. The realization felt like a slap in the face. This *was* the Gruppo di Intervento Speciale!

What the hell did these fuckers want?

As the gray-haired man stepped into the office alone, wearing a tailor-made suit that was almost identical in color to that of his hair, my heart sank into my boots.

It was Judge Roberto Gentile, the corrupt patriarchal asshole who had declared all my official complaints and accusations of sexism against various colleagues and superiors inadmissible. An ancient hatred exploded in every cell of my body. He could be dead on the floor long before his bodyguards even thought of drawing their guns, I reasoned. If the second one was nimble enough, he might be able to take me out before I put a bullet in him. My body was full of adrenaline, and that would enable me to react that crucial fraction of a second faster.

I took a deep breath. My right hand was on the Glock. But one look at the judge's haggard face brought my anger to an abrupt halt. He walked bent over, as if he had aged decades in recent years. His skin was ashen, his cheeks sunken. His eyes sat deep in their sockets.

The suit, which had once fit him like a glove, fluttered like a scarecrow's flannel and overalls. He attempted a guilty smile, and I was overcome by disgust for this man, more strongly than ever.

"Signora Pastore," he greeted me, settling his skinny butt into one of the Le Corbusiers without being invited. Without turning around, he waved off his entourage. They pulled the door shut behind them. My hand was still gripping the gun. We were alone.

"Signore Gentile," I said, my voice cold as ice, emphasizing each syllable. "What can I do for you?"

He shifted in my designer chair. I thought I would need to bring disinfectant to the office next day.

"Signora Pastore . . . I don't want to beat around the bush. Time is short."

Time is short! Exactly the words he had always used when he had discounted my accusations in order to justify the supposedly efficient operation of his court. My hand tensed in the drawer.

"I can see from your face that you still hold a grudge against me."

"Fuck you! You bet I hold a grudge against you, you old prick!" Years of buried anger surfaced abruptly. I pulled my pistol out of the drawer. The judge jumped up, surprised and agitated, which seemed ridiculous considering his physique.

"How dare you . . ." the old man said, outraged, his cheeks starting to redden.

The door behind him burst open. Holding the Glock with both hands, I stood up swiftly and pointed the muzzle at the heavies who had appeared in the doorway. They immediately reached for their own weapons. The startled judge fell back into his chair.

"Move a muscle, and I'll put an extra hole in your skulls!" I thundered.

The two knew exactly who they were dealing with and froze into stone columns.

"Colonnello Pastore! *Colonnello!*" Gentile scrambled clumsily to his feet and positioned himself right in the line of fire. I raised the gun a few inches to give myself space to fire over him.

But hearing him address me by my old rank had got me all choked up.

"You two, beat it. Whatever happens, stay outside! That's an order!" he stammered.

"Hands off your weapons, very slowly!" I heard myself shout with a deep satisfaction. As they carefully pulled their hands back, I heard them both mutter "Yes, sir" to the judge. Visibly annoyed at having to surrender to a woman, they retreated. One of them closed the door again.

"Colonnello Pastore, please!" Gentile raised his hand placatingly. He had become a broken old man again. I lowered the Glock slightly, but neither sat down nor put it away.

"I'd like to ask you a favor."

"Me?" This pile of human garbage, who had helped destroy all my professional efforts despite the sexual and sexist assaults conducted by my male colleagues and officers—he was asking *me* for a favor?

"Yes, you! You see, it's about Roberto Jr., my son."

"Why should I be concerned about your son?" Suddenly, I was enjoying seeing the judge having to ask me for something. He struggled to reply. "Come on, time is short!" I goaded.

At the sound of his own words being repeated back to him, his strength deserted him. He slumped down farther, surprisingly with tears running down his cheeks. I looked away in disgust.

"He's all I have left!"

The once strong and unassailable Judge Gentile sat in front of me the picture of misery and cried his heart out. It could have been comical if it hadn't been so sad. Tears dripped down onto his jacket in dark traces.

"What going on with your son?" I asked, a little more quietly this time. He cried all the harder, his long fingers tightening around the armrests.

"A year ago, he went to Barcelona. He wanted to study law, but it quickly became clear that nothing would come of it. His messages came less and less often, and we could hardly ever reach him on the phone. We didn't hear from him for months at a time."

A quiet foreboding whispered at the edge of my thoughts.

"How could he afford it?"

"We used to transfer money to him. When it became clear that he was going to be deregistered, we stopped the transfers. My wife was against it, but it was my money . . ."

I finished the sentence for him. "And he sought another source of income to help maintain the standard of living of which a rich mama's boy was accustomed."

He nodded in agreement, not rising to my needling. "The Spanish judiciary contacted us three months ago. He was arrested when the Guardia Civil busted a drug ring. The officers identified him as my son and delayed the indictment. I knew some of the judges and prosecutors there from symposiums, and others from the Rotary Club."

There's honor among thieves, I thought.

If I'd said that out loud, it would have been in a voice dripping with cynicism.

Having composed himself somewhat, Judge Gentile continued, "I replied that they should teach him a lesson. As a result, he was put in jail for four weeks. It was all arranged so that he wouldn't get a criminal record. His mother was furious and tried in vain to reach him by phone. She flew to Barcelona. When she got there, he had been released and had disappeared without a trace!"

This time it was my turn to swallow hard.

He continued in a brittle voice, "When the epidemic broke out, she had already gone mad with fear. She had even started hearing voices and seeing angels."

I had an inkling of what was coming.

"Late one night, I found her in bed. She looked like she was sleeping. But the pillbox on her nightstand—" It was all he could get out before his voice failed him. His thirst for power had driven away her only son, and this had ultimately forced her to the most desperate of acts. No court in the world would convict him, even if he *had* basically murdered his wife. He was guilty, and he knew it. And now Judge Gentile was trying to clear his conscience. To exculpate himself twice over by hiring *me* to find and bring home his missing son.

My words were as hard as cold steel. "Why me? Why don't you have your Spanish friends turn him in?"

Another one of those awkward pauses while he squirmed like an eel around the obvious.

"I would prefer—if you accept the assignment—that you keep the matter confidential. On the one hand, the Spanish authorities have their hands full, and on the other hand, it would be, well, undesirable for this to become public."

"Son of the great Judge Gentile arrested for petty crime in Spain"—or something like it—that would be the headline. For the judge, his standing, and reputation, it would be as good as a death sentence.

When he saw that I was hesitating and continued to stare at him coldly, he began to justify what had happened back then. "Listen, Signora

Pastore, I was as unhappy as you about what I had to decide at your trial, but my position meant—"

Disgusted, I cut him off before he could spout any more bullshit. "Spare me the crap, Your Honor!" Bile rose and burned in my throat. I had one last card to play, one that would show me how far he was willing to go.

"Five thousand euros a day, plus expenses!"

To my astonishment, he merely nodded humbly and reached into the inside pocket of his jacket. From it he took out several bundles of fifties. The strap was marked €20,000 in green letters. He gave me four of them.

I wished I'd asked for more.

"This is just an advance. If you need more, call me," he said, placing a business card on the table with his address and a cell phone number.

"Do you have pictures of him? Height, hair and eye color? Last known address, phone number?"

The judge nodded again, this time without looking up, and unfolded some photocopied documents on the table in front of me. I leafed through them quickly.

It was standard police information, but that was all I needed.

He rose awkwardly and staggered unsteadily to the door. He hardly had the strength to open it. One of his associates disobeyed his orders and opened it for him. Judge Gentile, once feared but now a broken man, turned around again. He looked at me and said, "Thank you . . . and I'm sorry!" Then he left the office.

When the door slammed behind him, I slumped into the chair and began to weep uncontrollably. The powerlessness that had seized me during the court proceedings rose up in me again. Since this time the scales of fate were tilted in my favor, I couldn't understand why I was seized by such deep sadness.

It took a long time to get my emotions back under control. And then I began to make a plan.

In Italy, unlike in France or Germany, the number of infected people was still manageable for the time being. Since we had learned from others' mistakes, we could more or less control the numbers at present.

Nonetheless, martial law had been declared in certain areas: airports had ceased operations, nighttime curfews had been imposed, the usual stuff.

One of the advantages of having worked for the special unit was that it left you with certain contacts. I took out an old notebook that I kept in the far corner of a drawer.

Years ago, I had recorded in it the names and numbers of informers and smugglers, slightly encoded in a form that only I could understand at first glance. Some of them were still in my debt.

The first few names didn't pick up. I had expected that, but it didn't stop there. Now and again, a wary voice came on the line, and sometimes the mere sound of breathing showed that someone was listening at the other end. When I spoke, they immediately disconnected and switched off their device. My dissatisfaction rose with every call, and by the time I was halfway through my notepad, it had become downright frustration.

Another half hour later, I had worked my way fruitlessly through almost the entire notebook.

On one of the last pages, I discovered Timo's number. When I had been with the Gruppo, he was still living in Pisa. He was a skilled people smuggler with a social conscience who had transported illegal refugees from Africa and Asia to Europe a few years previously. It had not brought him much money. He used to intercept the overcrowded dinghies that were about to sink, depositing their passengers safely in Sicily, bypassing Operation Triton. And he often got trouble into the bargain. Sometimes he was hired by Tunisian gangs, which helped him boost his finances. We often exchanged information about upcoming raids and smuggling trips. He scratched my back, and I scratched his. What he was doing now, I didn't know.

So, I dialed his old number in the hope that I might still be able to reach him. It rang four times, then he answered. He had never lost his German accent completely.

"Timo here."

As always, it sounded as if he was listening with one ear while, in reality, focusing on a completely different task.

"Franca Pastore." There were a couple seconds of silence.

"It can't be. Franky! How are you?"

I welcomed the tone of surprise in his voice and guessed that he was grinning as broadly as I was.

"Very well again, now. I'm a detective and a bodyguard. Almost like before, only more boring."

He laughed. "I know that; I stalked you the other day and found your website. You're still looking fit!" I could literally hear him winking at me.

"And how about you? How is everything?" I asked.

"Well, the tourists are staying at home this year. With all the crap in the world . . . It looks bad right now. But I'm getting by."

The small talk at an end, he was silent for a moment. "What can I do for you?"

"I have to go to Barcelona, urgently. Someone asked me to bring his kid back. Can you help me out?"

"Weeell. It's difficult right now. And it's not cheap, either."

I stuck to my guns. "The only question is whether it's possible, and if so, how? Money's no object for now."

He thought for a few seconds. "Okay, you'd go by ferry. Takes a whole day. You can't get tickets, I'm afraid, because more than half of the connections get cancelled.

"You might be able to get them on the black market. It'd take two or three days to find them, and then the ferry mightn't leave for another week. Altogether, about two weeks to Barca."

"Crap. I don't have two weeks. The epidemic crossed the Pyrenees a long time back. Don't you have a speedboat that could take three, maybe four, people?"

"Do you know what you're asking? It's over seven hundred kilometers from Livorno."

He emphasized the number as if it represented an impossibility. Then I remembered that Timo liked to think out loud, in detail, and at length.

"If we drove nonstop at a minimum speed of sixty kilometers an hour, it would take us at least eleven or twelve hours," he continued. "If Toulon's open, we could refuel there. That wouldn't even lengthen the crossing much.

"But with this kind of passage, you can't sustain sixty kilometers an hour on the open sea. No human being has the physique for it. And even supposing a superhuman could handle it, at some point the engine would just give up. But if you drove sensibly, and didn't overtax the hardware, broke the journey in Corsica and the south of France, it'd take three or four days, give or take two for the preparations. You could do it in a week. But you won't find anyone to pilot this kind of boat right now."

"What about you?" I didn't understand why he wasn't offering to do it himself.

He laughed conciliatorily. "Can't do it, too risky. The Corsican pirates are absolutely brutal these days."

"Pirates? In the Mediterranean? Are you kidding me?"

"No, they're real," he maintained. "Even if they've only been there a few weeks. People say they're the successors to the hippies from the '80s. And the navy now shoots first and asks questions later."

I said nothing.

"My wild days are over, Franca. I'm married. I've got two kids running around. Irina would tear my head off if I even thought about taking on a job like that. And it's been a long time since I had any contact with the kind of ruffians who would chance it. I can't be much help, I'm afraid. But I wouldn't offer to run that route anyway . . ."

I was hugely disappointed. I suddenly felt caged in, as I always did when I wasn't getting anywhere.

"Damn, Timo . . . What do you suggest I do then?"

"Hey, slow down; let's think! Hmm, how would I do it? There'd be three viable options. First, car: I'd rent a vehicle and drive the eleven hundred kilometers across the Côte d'Azur and southern France to the Costa Brava. I'd be risking getting stuck with an empty tank halfway there, because many gas stations haven't had gas for several days. The power grids aren't reliable, either.

"Or I'd get stuck in the kilometers of traffic jams at the borders, which ultimately amounts to the same thing. In both cases, the infected—or gangs of looters—would get me. I'd be dead, and my mission would have failed. Using the highways would be a stupid plan that would be certain to get me killed.

"Second, speedboat: I'd charter one that would get me across the Mediterranean in one piece. But that—and the appropriate fuel tank— would have to be built first. Rumor has it that life is going on as usual in Corsica, because the pirates are acting as vigilantes and aren't letting anyone through. Unless you have money and can pay your passage, you'll be robbed. You might be able to refuel north of Corsica. Marseille is not a good stopover; the epidemic has already reached there. The biggest problem is the pirates. I wouldn't mess with them. Halfway realistic, but as I said, not doable in a single day. So, of no interest.

"Third, private plane: I'd find someone who was insane or desperate enough, or both, to fly me to Barcelona under the radar. There's an absolute ban on flights in European airspace, including the Mediterranean. Some countries are threatening to shoot planes down immediately. Still, it would seem the safest route to me. Once I reached the location, I would either try my luck and parachute into the city, or I would land farther away on a smaller, rural airfield. After that, I would have to get in some other way, which would involve more risks.

"Plane and chute. If someone would agree to do it, it would be the most viable—and not even the most dangerous—option."

He fell silent for a few seconds, and I didn't dare to speak. Then I heard him say, "Did they teach you to skydive in the Special Forces?"

It cost me tens of thousands of euros in bribes to the military at Galileo Galilei Airport in Pisa to enable us to take off. Around eleven o'clock in the evening, all the lights went out for a short time, just as planned. We took advantage of this window to taxi the modified, fully fueled Cessna Skylane out of the hangar onto the tarmac and accelerate down the runway, which was lit only by the stars. Max Gerlach was an assured pilot in almost complete darkness, even without any of the army's night vision equipment. It had been Timo's idea to bring him aboard, so to speak. The two men were business partners and childhood friends. Max had agreed to fly me over for twenty thousand euros plus kerosene. "Like the back of my hand," I heard him say over the headphones. He accelerated, and the pressure pushed me back into my seat. Seconds later, we were airborne. He had switched the navigation and position lights off. Since we were probably the only people flying over the Mediterranean that night, the collision risk was extremely low, and therefore tolerable. We had one and a half liters of water on board for each of us, two life vests, a small self-inflating lifeboat—hardly bigger than an air mattress for two—and a parachute, which, according to the plan, I was going to use when I jumped out over Barcelona. My weapons also weighed quite a few kilos, but that was a necessary evil. Max had spent the whole day removing unnecessary ballast. Since he wanted to make a turn over Barcelona and fly right back again, it was important to maximize the distance he could cover with a single tank of fuel. In theory, the reduced weight and the fact that he would be making the return trip alone would guarantee him a range of almost eighteen hundred kilometers. We flew low so as not to be picked up on the radar.

When I had confirmed to Timo on the phone that skydiving had indeed been a key part of my training in the special unit, he just said, "Okay, I'll call you right back," and hung up.

Within ten minutes, my phone rang. "When can you be in Pisa?" he asked.

"Depends what train I catch. Noon tomorrow at the latest, I hope. Why?"

"Perfect. Just let me know when you're on the train, and I'll pick you up at Central Station an hour later."

"Can you please tell me what's going on?"

"Talked to Max on the phone."

"Who is Max, and what does he have to do with all this?" I probably sounded like a defiant child.

"Oh man, not on the phone. Get your ass on the first train tomorrow morning. When you get here, we'll explain everything. You got money?"

"Yeah, that's not an issue. How much does he want?"

"He wanted thirty thousand, but I told him I owed you a favor. Now we're at a little over twenty thousand for transportation, and the rest is for fuel."

Now it was my turn to be silent.

"Are you still there?"

"Um, yeah. Just a little speechless that you managed to get back to me so quickly. Thanks a million, Timo!"

"Thank me later; nothing's happened yet. Well, see you in the morning." Before I could say anything back, he hung up.

I stared at the cell phone in disbelief. Something positive had happened in my life! Then I packed my things, locked the office, and went home.

On the way, I biked past the train station and made inquiries about connections to Pisa. I bought a ticket for the first train, which left shortly after six the following morning. On the way to my apartment, I mentally packed my bags. In the closet, neatly stowed in a cardboard box were my old uniform, my combat boots, a bulletproof vest, an assault rifle, and a pistol holster. Unsentimental as I was, I had not been able to part with them. As I put on the black gear in front of the mirror, realizing that it fit me almost as well as it had before, memories of past deployments came flooding back. I sighed, shook off the old ballast, and turned my attention to packing. I refolded the uniform neatly and stashed it with a week's worth of underwear in a large sports bag. For the train ride,

I laid out a comfortable pair of jeans, a black turtleneck sweater, and a dark blue lightweight all-weather jacket. I would put on my jump boots during the ride. I took out the Glock and did some dry-fire drills. Then I disassembled, cleaned, and oiled it, and filled and loaded the magazine.

Throughout the night, I studied the information that Judge Gentile had left me. His contacts in Spain had done a good job. Address, telephone number, apartment number—it was all there. I researched the area where the target was presumed to be staying on the internet. Interactive maps and satellite images were a great help. I printed out a few sheets, marking the relevant properties on them.

I then memorized the details of streets, intersections, houses, windows, traffic lights, and front doors. At 4:00 a.m., I had a shower before brewing myself a strong coffee. At half past four, I called a cab, which dropped me in front of the main train station half an hour later.

Once on the train, I called Pisa. Timo didn't pick up. A minute later, my cell phone rang. He sounded sleepy. "Are you on the train already?" he asked yawning.

"Yes. Are you still asleep?"

"Not anymore. When do you get in?"

"Seven twenty-three."

"Okay, I'll be there no later than seven thirty. See you soon." Again, he hung up without further ado.

Carabinieri, armed to the teeth, were patrolling the train. The oppressive feeling that dominated the streets had spread to the railroad. I set the alarm on my phone for seven fifteen, but I was too keyed up to sleep. My body released stress hormones whenever I thought about the upcoming mission, so when I reached Pisa an hour later, I was wide awake. Timo was waiting for me. His hair was grayer, but he had retained his athletic physique. We walked toward each other, smiling, and hugged.

"It's been a while!" He was wearing flip-flops, a casual T-shirt, and knee-length pants. It occurred to me that this might be the first sunny day I'd seen in weeks.

In the car, he told me about his family, showing me photos on his phone as he drove, and asked how my family plans were coming along. I shook my head. "Not my thing," was all I could think of to say.

He stopped in an alley full of trash. "I'm afraid you'll have to switch seats, or they won't let us on the airfield." He opened the trunk and motioned for me to get in. I hesitated.

"Franca," he said placatingly, "only people with accreditation can enter the airfield. I've been listed as one of Max's mechanics for years, and the guard knows who I am. But with you in tow, we can forget it. You're going to have to trust me on this."

I thought for a few seconds and took the Glock out of my travel bag. Finally, I curled up in the trunk, using my bag as a pillow, all the while looking Timo directly in the eye. He met my gaze without blinking.

The ride was quieter than I had expected. When we stopped, presumably by the gate to the airfield, I heard Timo talking to the guard. It didn't take long. He let us drive on, and we stopped a little later in the hangar. Timo let me out. I stretched out my body under the wing of a four-seater Cessna from which the rear row of seats had just been removed.

"Hey, Max, this is Franca. Franca, this is Max."

Max wiped his oil-smeared hands on an old towel and held out the right one to me. I returned his handshake. The two men hugged each other.

The pilot was of athletic build, a little smaller than Timo. Judging by the oil under his fingernails, he liked tinkering with engines. Although he was probably already in his fifties, he seemed much younger and more agile.

Timo cut across my train of thought. "So, Franky, Max is your pilot. You'll fly to Barca with him tonight. You can trust him like you trust me. I'll come back this afternoon and bring you something to eat." He got into his car and drove off again.

"You don't look so good," Max said, placing a screwdriver inside the Cessna.

"Didn't get enough sleep last night. It's nothing serious, though."

"I have a bed in the room back there. Rest for a while until I'm done here."

Not having anything specific to do, I gratefully followed his advice. After washing my face and brushing my teeth in the small bathroom, I lay down and slept until shortly before 4:00 p.m.

Back in the hangar, I saw that Max had fallen asleep on the Cessna's extended back seat. He was too tall for it, so he had added a chair and made himself comfortable.

I didn't want to draw attention to myself unnecessarily in case soldiers were patrolling here, so I retreated to the back room. I rechecked my weapon and inspected the documents. A little later, I smelled freshly brewed coffee. Max had gotten up and was in the makeshift kitchenette in the corner of the hangar, taking an espresso pot from the gas stove.

"Can I have one, too?" I asked.

"Of course. Sugar, milk? I only have oat milk . . ."

"Perfect. Do you mind if I heat some up? I like it piping hot."

"Sure, help yourself."

We sat down on the freestanding back seat, and Max took out a map of Europe. He told me he knew an officer who was responsible for regulating the power at the airfield.

"He'll cut the power at ten forty-five sharp for exactly five minutes. We must leave in that window. Because the airport has been shut down anyway, hardly anyone will notice. No one's guarding the runway— everyone's focused on the access roads." He gave me a wink.

"Can you do it?" I had no idea how or even if this could be achieved.

He looked at me, almost offended. "We'll be far away over the sea in three minutes! To save on fuel and still get there quickly, we'll be flying at around 130 knots, which is about 240 kilometers an hour. If all goes well, you'll jump at three the next morning. Then I'll turn around." Max gestured along with his words, reenacting the scene he was describing.

"That's the critical point: just before we reach the beach, I'll turn off the engine so that we can't be located acoustically, and I'll pull the crate up. That way, we'll quickly gain a hundred or a hundred and fifty meters. I'll fly in an arc. The radar might pick us up, but only briefly. Hopefully, air traffic control won't pay it too much attention. At the highest point, we'll almost come to a stop for a second or two and kind of hover. And it's at precisely that moment you'll head out. I'll make a short dive, switch the propeller on, and—adios. I'll be back here an hour after sunrise, gliding in from the east with my engine off. The sun will be low, so hopefully I won't be noticed. I might be able to get the plane into the hangar before they arrest me; who knows? Then I can pretend I slept here all night. If not, my officer buddy will get me out of there; it's all included in the price."

"How much does he want?"

"Ten thousand. Five up front, and five when it's all over."

I went back to my bag, took out forty thousand euros, and pressed them into his hands.

"Maybe you can organize some magazines for my Glock. Or one of those little Heckler & Koch fully automatic ones they all carry around here, with enough ammo?"

"Hmm, I'll see what I can do."

We turned our eyes back to the map. "Where exactly do you have to get to?" Max asked.

I pulled out the printouts of Barcelona and showed him the destination. The house where the target had last lived was about one kilometer west of the Plaça de les Glòries Catalanes. Max inspected the map.

After a few minutes, he explained his plan to me. "Okay, theoretically I could land on the beach, set you down, and take off again, but the risk of running into soldiers or the Guardia Civil is too great for me." He shook his head. "We'll fly in at a hundred fifty to a hundred sixty meters. Once we're over the beach, you'll have to jump. You'll only have a hundred fifty meters for the jump at the apex, but then that's your problem."

That was doable. I had done base jumps from much lower altitudes. "Let me see the parachute," I said.

It was military grade and built for precisely this kind of thing. I unfolded it, checked the seams, cords, and lines. Satisfied, I stowed it away again and adjusted all the straps to fit my body size.

Just as I was nodding to Max, Timo turned into the hangar. As always, he was smiling brightly, as if the whole world were in a party mood. "Ready for the big mission?"

"Looks like it," I said.

He took something out of the car and put it in my hand. It was a folded street map of Barcelona and two boxes of Thai vegetable noodles for Max and me.

"Hey, thanks. I'm starving!"

"So, what's the plan?" asked Timo.

While I explained everything to him, transferring the data from the internet printouts to the new map, we ate the food he had brought. Afterward, Max made coffee, handed us two steaming mugs, and added, "The crate is ready, and I've filled her up. We've talked everything through. Now we just wait. I'm going to hit the sack in my bunk for two hours. It's going to be a long night."

The two men hugged and arranged to meet for coffee the next day as if it were a normal afternoon. As if the threat to civilization were on another planet, light-years away.

Timo and I sat together until sunset, drinking coffee and telling each other what had happened to us in the last few years. When the sun disappeared along with all the shadows, he stood up and hugged me tightly. "Take good care of yourself. And let me know when you're back!"

"I will," I said shyly. "And thank you."

He got into his car. We waved to each other until he disappeared around the hangar.

Would we ever see each other again? Under the current circumstances, it seemed less than likely, I thought regretfully.

I went back, lay down on the bench, propped my feet on a chair, and after a while, despite the excitement, I dozed off.

It was 10:00 p.m. when Max woke me up with a light kick against the chair. He was carrying something wrapped in cloth.

"Come on, get up. I brought you something," he whispered. Then he motioned for me to follow him to the back. He laid the bundle on the bed and unfolded it. Inside was a second Glock with several full magazines, an HK237 with six magazines and six packs of loose ammunition, a knife, and a flashlight.

"All that for twenty thousand?" I couldn't believe it.

"Well, for fifteen, the rest is my commission, so to speak."

"You're welcome; it's all yours!"

Max looked at his wristwatch. "You have twenty minutes to get ready. I'll be waiting in the plane."

One hundred and eighty seconds later, I had changed my clothes. I slipped the folded map into my jacket pocket. One Glock was in the holster on my right hip, and I packed the second into my small backpack. I placed a few magazines in the designated pockets and the extra ammunition in the side pockets of my cargo pants. I would put on the bulletproof vest just before the jump. Then I checked the small but lethal HK, shouldered it, and left the room. After a quick trip to the restroom, I was ready. Five minutes behind Max, I climbed into the Cessna.

"Whoa, that was fast. I'll have to tell my wife!"

It probably sounded like a harmless joke to him, but it annoyed the hell out of me. "Save your sexist crap. I'm not the right audience for it."

"What? I was talking about my wife . . ."

"Save it!" I snapped at him.

Irritated, he avoided my gaze, concentrating on the aircraft's control panel. A few moments later, the engine clattered to life, and the propeller spun at a breathtaking speed. We sat in uncomfortable silence until he said, "So, we're about to go."

The next second, as if to confirm his words, all the lights went out. We waited until Max's eyes had adjusted to the darkness, then he accelerated. The propeller spun faster. We taxied out of the hangar onto the runway. Outside, it was pitch-black.

"Can you do it in the darkness?" I asked.

"Of course. I know all the runways here inside out. Like the back of my hand!"

We talked for the next three hours, nothing deep or personal, just superficial stuff. After I had given him a brief account of my reasons for leaving the special unit, he said, "Now I know why you kicked off earlier. I'm sorry, I didn't know. Lousy story . . ."

"It's a sore point for me. It really sucked. Because you're not a man, you're treated like a second-class citizen even though you're performing just as well, if not better. And as soon as you demand justice and equal treatment, you get discredited."

The Mediterranean seemed to spread out endlessly beneath us. Its stoic tranquility gave us a false sense of security. Billions of tiny waves glittered in the moonlight, revealing a multitude of dark silhouettes.

We flew over a small yacht and several freighters, all without position lights. With every nautical mile, my agitation increased. Our low altitude prevented us from seeing the lights of the cities of southern France on the horizon.

As soon as the sickly yellow aura of the Barcelona night came into view, I put on the little backpack and the bulletproof vest, pressing the Velcro tightly shut. Putting on the parachute in the narrow cockpit of the Cessna was a bit more problematic, but I managed that in good time, too.

"Okay, Franky, get ready! Thirty seconds!"

The HK hung in front of my chest, attached to my vest with a small carabiner.

"Twenty!"

The airplane lost speed, climbing. The engine fell silent. I could now see the beach clearly in front of us from a height of eighty meters. A little farther on was the Canaletes Sant Martí sports field, which we had chosen as a landmark in Pisa.

"Ten!"

Before I opened the door, we looked at each other briefly. "Thank you, Max," I called over the sound of the wind.

He looked at me and nodded. "Five, four, three . . ." he said. I opened the door. "Two, ONE!"

At the apex of its climb, the Cessna did indeed seem to hover for a moment. Max had tilted it a few degrees. As soon as the door opened, I fell out almost without doing anything. I let go, and the earth sped toward me. I immediately released the parachute. By the time it opened, I had free-fallen almost fifty meters.

Four seconds later, my face hit the sand. A gust of wind was pulling the parachute out to sea. I searched unsuccessfully for the release mechanism, my mouth filling with tiny salty stones. When I finally found the buttons and ditched the parachute, I smacked headfirst into a knee-high wave. Water went up my nose and into my ears, and salt burned in my eyes. Before I would get completely soaked, I struggled to my feet and fled backward, scrabbling away from the masses of water. I heard Max restarting the engine in the distance, and imagined I could see him, a receding dot against the black sky.

Take care, Max.

A quick glance around told me that my landing had gone unnoticed. Not a soul for kilometers. The parachute was drifting in the shallow coastal waters. I checked my equipment. The Glock was still securely holstered. The matte black HK had gotten wet, but I was much more concerned about it being coated in sand. I was worried even one grain of sand could put the gun out of action and took the time to clean it as best I could, even if only superficially. Then I loaded it slowly, constantly blowing sand grains away. That was all I could do for now.

It was a cloudless night. The stars were twinkling. Behind me I could see the Canaletes Sant Martí club stands. If I went south past them, I would come through a small park. Then I'd need to advance another twelve hundred meters northwest until I reached the multilane avenue named Avinguda Diagonal. I would follow this one kilometer southwest to the Plaça de les Glòries Catalanes.

Crouched in a combat stance, my HK at the ready and the wet balaclava sitting on my head like a cap, I began to work my way between the high blocks of houses. Only a few of the apartments had lights on inside. Curfew had long since become the norm here. The streets were empty and lit only at the intersections, which I quickly scurried across. Otherwise, I moved through the deep darkness and made good progress. Sometimes I heard sirens wailing and listened tensely to see if they were heading in my direction. My body fell into familiar behavior patterns, my brain released adrenaline. My senses became sharper, my vision clearer. The first part of the route held no surprises. I ran, got my bearings, and then ran on.

When the air began to stink, I realized the pleasant part of the mission was over. I heard inhuman grunting and smacking sounds coming around the corner in front of me. Something was dragging across the ground at short, irregular intervals. I shrank deeper into the shadows of the doorway at my back. While I was considering whether it would be wiser to go back and circle the block, I caught sight of some silhouettes shuffling in my direction from behind.

These were the infected the whole world was afraid of. It immediately became clear why. I set the HK to single-shot and waited. From the shadows, I saw the creatures sniffing like animals. They were obviously finding their way by smell, but they were themselves giving off a sickening stench, a mixture of excrement and putrid mouth rot. They came slowly closer, heading toward me.

Shit. Could they smell me?

Fuck. They *could* smell me! When they were ten meters away, they stopped their rigid swaying and fell into an almost normal run, their arms stretching in my direction, and their claws waving greedily in the air.

"Stop!" I yelled in horror, stepping out of the shadows, which only seemed to spur them on. At ten meters, I put a bullet in the chest of the first one. The shot echoed like thunder in the dark street. The man I hit faltered for a moment, then continued to run toward me.

Damn! I couldn't have missed the heart from that distance. Only when I shot him in the forehead from two meters did he slump lifelessly to the ground. The woman behind him stumbled over his body and fell headlong. I gave her a mighty kick in the temple with the steel toe cap of my boot, after which she stopped moving, too. Two other figures appeared behind her. Their heads jerked backward brutally as I put a bullet in each of their brains.

The gunshots woke the neighborhood. Lights went on in the surrounding apartments. People tore open the windows, shouting in

Spanish. But in the confusion, I couldn't understand a thing. I was so distracted that I saw the grotesque face coming at me from the left almost too late. At the last second, I pulled my arm out of the way and rammed the HK sideways between the infected's teeth. Like a madman, he bit down on the metal, breaking his enamel. I took out the Glock with my right hand, put the muzzle against his forehead, and pulled the trigger. A slightly muffled shot splattered what had been his gray matter over his fellows, who had gathered a couple meters behind him. Almost too late, I remembered the warnings not to come into contact with the blood, saliva, and other bodily fluids of the infected.

I pulled the balaclava clumsily over my face, unintentionally covering my left eye. Cursing, I ran back. As I was running, I holstered the pistol and adjusted the balaclava until I had an uninterrupted view again. At the next corner, I peered quickly but carefully to the right. The path was clear. I sprinted two blocks. Having made sure no stinkers were waiting for me at the next intersection, I turned right again.

Police sirens came closer. I saw the blue lights flaring, hid in the nearest doorway, and stayed there until the vehicle passed. Not far away, shots rang out. When I had worked my way back to the intersection, I looked cautiously around the corner and saw two police officers had gotten out of the car. They were shooting at the hungry beasts, the open car doors as shields in front of them, aiming as best they could at the heads of the undead. From the darkness behind them, another dozen staggered toward them. The police officers were hard at work dealing with the frontal assault and did not notice the danger approaching from behind. I stepped into the middle of the street, aimed the HK, and pulled the trigger. First two, then three, fell to the ground as my bullets pierced their skulls. Four or five noticed me and changed direction, coming directly toward me. I seized this moment to take a quick look around. The immediate area was safe. I shot the newcomers and continued to cover my Spanish colleagues. They got the last of their group themselves. Then they heard the noise I was making and looked behind them in the direction I was firing. They quickly did away with the remaining ones.

But suddenly and without warning, the officers froze.

At least fifty infected ran into the light of the intersection. The officers tried to get into their vehicle. They didn't stand a chance. The horde fell upon them and tore them to pieces. Their cries of agony were quickly silenced by the throng of attackers. Sheer horror overcame me. Without inspecting the area again, I fled. I did not wait for my eyes to adjust to the darkness, but bolted northwest with my gun at the ready. It wasn't until five blocks later that I allowed myself a brief respite and retrieved the folding map from the front pocket of my Kevlar vest.

The area around me was silent. I carefully trained my flashlight on the street sign above me, searching for it on the map. Four blocks straight ahead, then left.

Numerous shots rang out behind me. Belated reinforcements had arrived and were engaged in a huge battle with the sick. Volleys of machine-gun fire, mighty explosions of shells, and the blasts of individual pistols rang out through the night. A block ahead of me, another mob wandered by, seemingly attracted by the noise of the battle. I had noticed that some of them moved slowly, almost with their last ounces of strength, while others moved damn fast. They weren't as swift as a healthy human, to be sure, but they were still frighteningly agile. I only hoped that if I met any more, they'd would be of the lamer variety.

After I had crept crouching through the night for two blocks, I reached the Avinguda Diagonal. A pitifully lit green strip—more a narrow alley with a footpath—ran down the center of the multilane highway.

I decided to follow it because it afforded unobstructed views on both sides and the possibility of better escape routes.

It felt good to be sweating in battle gear again. I felt my rapid breathing and my heart thundering in my chest. At the slightest sounds, I paused, surveying the places they had seemed to come from. Fortunately, the avenue was eerily empty. About fifty meters before the Plaça de les Glòries Catalanes, I lay down in the grass and looked closely at the deserted traffic circle. The clock showed four forty-five. The Plaça was motionless. I consulted the map, waited another five minutes, and hoped it would stay that way.

Keeping to the shadows, I circled the northwestern side of the square. Then I reached the correct street and turned onto it. Two blocks straight ahead, right, three more blocks, left. The target's last known address was an apartment on the next crossroad. I hoped the subject would be inside. If my information was correct, I needed to turn right. I did so, checking the house numbers as I went. I was eight houses from the target.

Another siren blared out, approaching swiftly from the south. I ducked deep into the nearest building entrance. The vehicle drove by at breakneck speed. Half a minute later, the siren was swallowed by the distance. Seamlessly, the noise was replaced by other sounds, growing louder and louder. I peeked out cautiously, looking down the street. My heart skipped a beat in terror. At least two hundred infected were coming. They flooded the street and squeezed past the parked cars. Their stench reached me on the wind.

I had to fight not to hurl. At the same time, I wondered if any of them were the ones who could run fast. If I ran for it now, they would be bound to chase me, either until I shook them off or became too exhausted to go on. At best, I would have to find a new way in by moving in a large circle. But I no longer had any desire to run. I pulled the lockpick set from my pants pocket and took out two of the picks to use on the door behind me. In the pale light of the streetlamps at the intersection, I found the serrated hole and inserted the instruments. My hands were shaking. The smell was now overpowering. The moans of the infected were near. Then the keyhole turned halfway, and the door opened with a click. The shuffling throng immediately began to yell.

I felt a slight breeze as the mass of air moved toward me, then I squeezed quickly through the door, slamming it shut in the nick of time. Immediately, fists started pounding on it. The door was made mostly of wired glass and was reinforced from the outside with a stylishly curved steel grille. This alone would have held them up for quite some time. How long the lock would withstand the immense pressure, I did not know.

The glass cracked earlier than I expected. Only the wire mesh embedded in it held it together. I saw it bending inward, as if it were made of flexible plastic. Then I ran up the stairs, fishing out the small flashlight and tremblingly lighting my way as I ran. One of the apartment doors was ripped open. The occupants were stupid enough to look for what was causing the noise.

"¡Puerta cerrada! ¡PUERTA CERRADA!" I yelled in my terrible Spanish, taking three steps at a time. The glass at the bottom was cracking loudly now. If they pushed it far enough inward, they might be able to reach the door handle . . .

I ran faster.

Third floor. Downstairs, the entrance door banged against the wall. The thudding of many feet, rushing after me, flooded the stairwell. The infected screeched. I hoped the apartment doors themselves were better barricaded and tried not to think about how many people I had just condemned to death.

"¡PUERTA CERRADA! ¡PUERTA CERRADA!"

The inhuman moaning intensified.

Fifth floor. My breathing was coming in rapid gasps, but I did not let the rising panic overwhelm me. On the sixth floor, the stairs ended at a locked steel door. I didn't have time to break it open. So I went down to the next landing, which was between two floors. Each landing had a large glass window facing the street. The one in front of me opened smoothly, albeit with a loud squeak.

From the hallway below, I could hear people shouting and slamming doors, and the greedy horde continuing to struggle up the stairs. Holding the flashlight between my teeth, I quickly stepped out through the window onto the ledge, which was the width of a foot, taking care not to catch the gun on anything. Keeping to corners and ledges, I traversed to the left, not only because that was where my target was, but also because the relief in the facade gave the impression that three meters farther on, I might be able to get onto the roof.

I had barely taken four small steps when the first bloody fist shot through the open window. A fraction of a second later, it was followed by a grotesque face distorted by hatred and rage. Her furious scream made me flinch, and I almost lost my footing. A filthy hand snatched at me, missing my arm by a hair's breadth. The creature was abruptly bundled out of the way by those at her rear.

I continued concentrating on climbing, ignoring my panic, not looking down or back. With a few more moves, and I had arrived at a section decorated with ornaments and loops carved from beige sandstone.

I grabbed ahold of anything I could reach and found small ledges with my bulky boots. At the edge of the roof, I heaved my right foot over. Then I pulled my whole body weight up and pushed myself over my heel onto the roof. I had to crawl up carefully for a few meters until I felt safe. I wedged the wide soles of my jump boots into the grooves of the roof like crevices, so that they gripped securely as I pushed myself up.

Behind the low parapet, the slope ended abruptly, becoming a flat roof. I rolled away from the edge and lay still for a moment. The rabid screaming deep below me diminished. Inside the house, I heard panicked screeching. I closed my eyes, but it could not silence the screams of pain.

A few minutes later, I had recovered from the climb and struggled to my feet. I quickly found my bearings and ran on with the flashlight in my hand, jumping over air conditioning units and roof parapets, ducking under low-hanging cables and satellite dishes. Only after I had run over five rooftops did I lean against a door, pull the balaclava off my head, and take several deep breaths. The panic slowly subsided. I checked again that I had everything I needed. The Glock, the HK, the small backpack with ammunition, the knife, the lockpick set, the flashlight, the cell phone. Everything was there, and I had reached the target's building.

This time, I was able to take a little more time getting through the door. I listened through the wood for a few minutes. On the other side, all seemed quiet. Once the lock had given way, I clamped the small, powerful flashlight to the Glock with the designated bracket and directed the beam forward along with the muzzle of the pistol. As expected, I came across a steel door half a floor below, similar to the one at the top of the stairs in the first building. I cracked it without difficulty. My target's apartment was to the left on the fourth floor. Dimming the flashlight, I silently descended the wooden stairs, checking the names on the doors. Roberto Jr. shared an eight-room apartment with two others. I spotted his name on the left-hand door, which had three locks on it. The first two took me just five minutes, but the third was a tougher nut to crack.

It was 5:28 a.m. when I closed the apartment door of Judge Gentile's son quietly behind me. My Glock at the ready, I crept through the grand chambers with grotesquely high ceilings to the state-of-the-art kitchen and the rustic styled dining room with its seven-meter-long table. The pale light of daybreak fought its way through heavy floor-length brocade curtains into a living room furnished with black leather armchairs and sofas, its walls lined with hundreds of books. However, the impact of these stately rooms was undermined by the oafish chaos that was evident everywhere.

Glass pipes, a mirror, metal tubes, credit cards, and other drug paraphernalia were waiting their turn on the massive table, which looked as if it dated back to the colonial era. Next to it, on the floor and on the comfortable upholstered furniture, were lying unwashed dishes, garbage, and empty bottles.

Following the beam of my flashlight, I opened the next door. The opulent bathroom with gold and marble inlays sparkled. There was no one here.

Then I found myself in the lengthy hallway again. In front of me were three massive double doors. I didn't know if whoever lived here was armed. The magazines of the Glock and the HK were full.

I switched off the flashlight and depressed the latch closest to me. The door swung open silently, like the gate of a palace. I saw the bed standing in the middle of the room and vaguely identified two figures in it. Then I turned on the flashlight again and turned it down as low as I could, indirectly illuminating the sleepers. One of them was a young woman, unclothed and covered with a light sheet up to her waist. Her naked breasts were falling and rising. The man lying next to her, who looked just as young, was also asleep.

It was not the target.

I carefully crept out of the bedroom and found the judge's son in the next room. He was not alone, either. On the bedside table there was a hopeless mess of cigarette paper packets, lighters, and overflowing ashtrays. All over the room there was evidence of drug use. There were assorted plastic bags, some containing pills and white powder, others marijuana. A tall glass bong, half filled with brackish yellow water, stood on a table in the corner. Disgusted, I turned my gaze back to the target and looked at his pallid face in the pale light, so similar to the one I hated.

The judge's son was a younger replica of his father. I fervently hoped not to wake the woman, but the risk was unavoidable. I put a hand over his mouth and watched him slowly come back to reality from his drug-fogged sleep. The first thing he would see was the muzzle of the Glock. It took him several seconds to take in the situation, and his eyes widened in fright.

"Shh." I tried to reassure him, speaking slowly and clearly. "Your father sent me."

His breathing slowed, and his gaze cleared.

"I'm going to take my hand off your mouth now. You're not in any danger, so please don't scream. I've no desire to shoot one of your drugged-up friends. Besides, the street in front of the house is full of infected. Okay?"

Again it took him some time to process what he had heard, before he nodded cautiously. I took my hand away from his face.

"I'm putting my gun away now. That's not an invitation for you to try something stupid!"

"May I sit up?" he asked quietly.

I nodded and sat down on the edge of the bed. We were both whispering now.

"My father sent you?"

"Yes. He came by my office the day before yesterday and hired me to bring you home."

"What? Why?" His mind seemed far more befuddled than was justified by mere physical fatigue.

"He feels very guilty about the things that have happened between you lately. He wants you to come back with me."

"No way!" He shook his head decisively. "I'm not leaving this apartment," he said firmly. He gestured expansively at the sleeping beauty beside him and at the drugs and paraphernalia strewn around the bedroom.

Stunned, I looked at him. "You want to risk your life for a few grams of coke and some weed? And who is this girl, anyway?"

Roberto looked at the young woman for a long time. It seemed as if he was having trouble recalling her name. Then he got up and, completely naked, went over to one of the tall cupboards. He took out two large packages that were almost too big for his hands. He strode back and threw one of them to me almost contemptuously. I caught it and looked at it.

"This isn't just about a few grams." He swaggered, crossing his pale arms in front of his chest.

The unexpected sight of the narcotics in my hands caught me off guard. The craving to be under the influence flared in me like a bushfire.

As if disembodied, I looked at the huge bundle of hashish. The closer I brought the substance to me, the more intense its sweetish odor became. An inner struggle reignited. Every fiber of my being was suddenly crying out for the drug. I took the knife, carefully cut open the wrapper, and scraped off some of the dark green substance. Its rich scent overpowered me, silencing my reason. On the corner table, I once again caught sight of the apparatus I was so familiar with. It called to me. Its voice sounded friendly. As if I had no will of my own, I rose, carrying over a kilogram of drugs, and went to the table with the bong.

Roberto couldn't know what was going on inside me, but he watched spellbound and with visible satisfaction. Everywhere I could, I bent down and picked up the packages with the various substances. After a few steps, my hands were so full that I could not carry anything else. As if in a trance, I walked across the room to the bong on the table . . . and casually walked past it.

I stopped at the high window with the brocade curtains and put the contents of my right hand into the crook of my left arm. With my free hand I pushed the curtains aside and opened the window.

"Wh-wh-what are you doing?" stammered Roberto Jr. As the first package sailed out the window, he cried out, "No! What are you doing?"

What precisely the second package contained, I will never know. It went after the marijuana in a great arc. I also scattered the individual sachets onto the street. Down below, the infected bawled as if they were happy about the gifts.

Screaming and naked, the judge's son came at me. "Nooooo!"

I pulled out the pistol in one fluid movement and pointed the muzzle between his eyes. Roberto ran impetuously toward it. I hadn't realized his motor functions wouldn't be at their peak in his wretched condition. He hit the parquet flooring with a cry of pain. I commended myself for having kept my finger off the trigger this time and said as he squirmed at my feet, "If you stay in Barcelona, you're going to die. Now get up and look down at the street!" I jutted my chin toward the window.

Bleeding from the nose, he scrambled up, whining. At the sight of the mob outside the house, he put his hand to his mouth in dismay, smearing blood onto his upper lip. The grown man who reminded me of his powerful father had disappeared.

Before me stood a small, frightened boy whose favorite toy had been taken away. He was looking down in terror at a catastrophe unfolding barely a stone's throw away that was threatening to devour him. I saw defiance flare in him briefly and gradually evaporate. Roberto Jr. admitted defeat, his eyes filling with tears.

Two hours later, we were sitting at the breakfast table. Roberto had gently broken the news to his roommates of who I was and why I was in their apartment. The nameless young woman was still asleep, strung out. I told him all about the judge's visit to my office and about his mother's death.

Hearing this, he sat in his chair for several minutes with his head bowed, weeping silently. At some point, he ran out of tears. He rolled a cigarette, lit it with trembling hands, and asked, "Why did he choose you then?"

I saw no reason to withhold the truth from him. So, I told him about what had passed between Judge Gentile and me many years ago.

He said, "Typical Father—he's ruthless when it comes to exploiting a position of power. It's always pissed me off." Then he poured me a cup of coffee and disappeared into the bathroom.

I reached for the cup and went into the living room. Hoping that the connection was operational, I dialed the judge's number from my cell and was delighted when I heard it ringing. He picked up immediately.

"Gentile."

"Buongiorno, Signore Gentile."

I could tell he hardly dared breathe. "Signora Pastore . . . is . . . where is . . . ?" He faltered.

"I've got him. He's fine."

The old judge gave an audible sob of relief. "Grazie, Signora Pastore, grazie."

"I have to get him out of here, though. Can you pull some strings again? Things are pretty crazy in the city right now. There are a huge number of dangers right outside the door." I didn't have the heart to tell him the truth.

"I'm going to call a few people now and get right back to you, Signora Pastore."

"All right. Talk to you later."

It had not taken me long to find Roberto. Nor had it been easy. But getting back home seemed an impossible undertaking at the moment. I stood by the window with my steaming cup of coffee, looking out at the street at the—well, what were they? I had heard a researcher on a science show say that people died from the infection but came back to life a short time later. Because some scientists had initially underestimated the danger posed by the resurrected, many of them fell victim to the subjects of their own experiments. This had delayed the research. The public had been told hardly anything.

Thus, weeks after the outbreak, our level of knowledge was relatively low. The public only knew that the pathogen was transmitted via bodily fluids in contact with open wounds or mucous membranes, and that those affected had only a few minutes, at best an hour, to live before they, well, died. However, they quickly came back as aggressive monsters who would not spare children nor other defenseless people. But they were not interested in animals. Animals, in turn, gave the resurrected a wide berth. Even insects didn't like them, but nobody could tell us why.

According to my own findings during the night that had just passed, they could not be stopped with shots to key organs in the upper torso. I had clearly hit the heart of an infected person, and nothing had happened. They only fell if you shut down the control center of the nervous system, the brain.

I couldn't make heads nor tails of it, but ultimately I didn't care. I now knew what I had to do to take the resurrected out.

A much bigger problem was the speed at which some of them could move. I had been racking my brain over this for hours. Even during my conversation with Roberto, a processor at the back of my mind had been running relentlessly around this subject. The mere memory of the horde that had overrun the two police officers at the intersection made my blood run cold. All the hairs on my body stood up.

While I was lost in thought, the phone rang. I almost dropped my half-full cup of coffee in shock. I had completely forgotten Judge Gentile would be calling back.

"It is indeed somewhat more complicated than I had hoped," he said without introduction. "But I have good news, nonetheless." I tried hard not to let him hear my relieved sigh.

"At exactly 2:00 p.m., a car will come and take you to the port under police protection," he continued. "The only vehicles permitted to leave Barcelona today are two passenger cruisers heading for North Africa. Yours is making a stop in Palma de Mallorca, where someone will be waiting for you. Surveillance there is not as thorough as on the mainland, so you and my son will be able to transfer to a smaller private yacht that will bring you to Italy."

I guessed the judge had provided them with our descriptions.

"Given the circumstances, that doesn't sound too bad. Good, we'll be ready to leave at 2:00 p.m.," I replied.

"Is he there?" Gentile's voice grew shakier. "Can I speak to him for a moment?"

"Hold on."

I looked around and spotted Roberto, who was rubbing his wet hair with a towel on his way to his room.

"Roberto," I called, going toward him. He looked at me questioningly as I held out the phone. "For you."

He seemed to know instinctively who was on the line and at first refused to take the cell phone. Nevertheless, I pressed it into his hand. He stared at it for a second or two but then put it to his ear and gave his full name. A little later, he disappeared behind the room's huge double doors and didn't come out for a long time.

In the meantime, I filled up all the magazines, checked the weapons, and cleared any remaining sand grains from the HK. Now I had to get some rest. After the previous night, I was at the limits of exhaustion and not even increasing my caffeine level could help. I had snuck a pillow and a couple blankets from one of Roberto's roommates. After enjoying a cold shower, I lay down on the longest couch in the living room.

I placed one of the throws on the creaking leather, laid my head on the pillow, cuddled the second throw, and slept soundly until the alarm clock jolted me from sleep at 12:00 p.m. It was time to brief Roberto. The success of our escape depended on how well or poorly he responded to orders. I feared that he would reject an authoritarian approach and thus become a danger on our way to the port.

My concerns seemed to be unfounded. He was fully dressed, wearing sturdy clothes and good shoes. He sat quietly, nodded at all the instructions, and asked occasional questions. Nevertheless, an uneasy feeling crept over me when I studied him more closely.

"Did you take something?" I asked him. At first, it looked as if he was going to play dumb, but then he thought better of it and came clean.

"Yeah. I smoked a little crystal and some dope. Not much, just to keep my head clear and not get the shakes."

I looked him straight in the eye, noticing for the first time that his pupils were dilated. In the dimly lit living room, this had seemed a natural reaction, so I hadn't picked up on it. But there was nothing I could do about it now. He held my gaze, and I nodded.

We spent the final hour packing and preparing snacks for the trip. Shortly before two, we positioned ourselves by the window. The rows of infected outside the door had thinned, and I felt more hopeful. My faith in our mission grew. Right on time, three SUVs bearing Guardia Civil insignia turned into the street, running over some of the stinkers. The convoy came to a halt in front of the building. Two police officers got out of each vehicle and opened fire on the remaining transmuted. A male head wearing dark sunglasses thrust out of a half-open car window and looked up at our building. I pulled the curtain completely aside, opened the window, and waved. He waved back and motioned for us to come down quickly. I showed him my gun so that they would not unknowingly classify me as a threat and shoot me. He gave me the thumbs-up and yelled something to his troops.

"Go!" I ordered in my turn. When the many locks had been opened, we ran out the door, his now ex-roommates locking it behind us. He had said good-bye to them while I slept.

We ran down the stairs. At the bottom, I instructed him to open the door a crack. My HK at the ready, I checked that no biters were waiting for us behind it. But the Guardia Civil had done good groundwork.

"Saldremos ahora," I shouted.

"Bien, bien. Todo seguro," rang out in return.

Roberto and I stepped out into the street. My fellow officers and I greeted each other with silent nods. I got into one of the SUVs with Junior. It began to move even before the doors slammed shut. The daylight revealed the consequences of the city's nighttime massacres. Whole rivers of blood had flowed. The driver crisscrossed Barcelona at breakneck speed, continually dodging large gatherings of infected, but always heading south. He did not drive around the Parc de la Ciutadella, but found a route through the middle of it, and then hit the asphalt. He accelerated, turned left and right a few times, and then we were in the port area. The other SUVs followed. The wide road was dotted with abandoned vehicles. A few hundred meters before the Ronda del Port, we stopped briefly at a barricade of metal fences, buses, trucks, and emergency and armored vehicles that had been erected by the military. Heavy machine guns were trained on us from the roofs of the vehicles. The soldiers stationed at the entrance quickly inspected the automobiles, made a cursory check that everyone inside was healthy and waved us through. At each corner, more barriers secured the road to the passenger port.

When we reached the apex of the bridge connecting the wharf to the mainland, the SUVs stopped. They pressed two tickets for today's ship into my hand and let us out. Roberto thanked them, and I saluted. Twenty seconds later, the convoy disappeared between the buildings leading into the city.

I hid my weapons in my backpack. In combat gear, I didn't want people to see I was armed. We made our way to the ship as the sky darkened to our right. By the time we reached the forecourt, where hundreds of other nervous refugees were crowded, my wristwatch was showing three o'clock. The waiting ship, which was supposed to take us to safety tonight, was, after all that, a rusty old cruiser that I would have expected to find in a ship graveyard in India or South Pakistan, not at sea. The side of the vessel, once painted white, was the color of urine. Large sections of paint were peeling in numerous places. Long patches of rust were visible under the windows and portholes.

I looked back and saw figures coming toward us. My first impulse was to reach for my weapons until I realized that they were not the infected but fugitives like us. Some were dragging massive suitcases behind them as if they dared not leave the country without everything they owned. Others were dressed more for action, with hiking backpacks and breathable rain jackets. They quickly caught up with us. I felt them pushing us against the crowd standing by the ship.

A feeling of claustrophobia swept over me. I grabbed Roberto's arm with my left hand, pulling him closer to me. As I did so, I thought about the weapons stowed in the bag. If the pressure increased and we were pushed back and forth, it would be difficult to reach them.

I let go of Roberto and wriggled in the crowd like a snake shedding its skin, trying to put the backpack down. I ignored the angry looks and sounds from those around me as I jostled them.

With difficulty, I worked it around to my front and opened it, ruthlessly continuing my maltreatment of my neighbors. I pulled out the HK slowly, taking care not to bring it out into the open. Provoking a panic among this mob would only complicate what was already a tough situation.

Before shouldering the bag again, I placed the submachine gun carefully around my neck. I pressed the second Glock into Roberto's hand.

Slowly, time passed. The ominous tension in the crowd increased by the minute. Roberto and I were in the middle of the group, and people were talking softly among themselves, in pairs and in small groups. I tried to turn around to see what was happening behind us. The sky to the north was getting darker and darker. Its shadow was approaching like an evil omen. Thunder rumbled in the distance.

And then we heard shots.

What had so far only been sporadic sounds from the city grew within a few minutes into the constant noise of fighting, moving inexorably closer. When I heard fighting on the bridge, I took the safety off the HK.

"Roberto," I said softly, my mouth close to his ear. "Get ready to follow me no matter what!"

The infected came closer.

It always amazed me how calm my mind became in critical situations, how the noises around me became quieter, more subdued. My sense of sight sharpened, too, automatically blanking out nonthreatening areas from my field of vision. They literally blurred, like in a photograph when you've opened wide the aperture of a fast lens. Only the areas that were relevant for survival were in focus. My hands instinctively wanted to raise the gun and direct it at the focal points, but I forced them to stay where they were.

The screams, cries, and shouts were coming more often. As the threat approached, the crowd surged back and forth more violently like a single gigantic entity, trying to get onto the rusting ship. The frightened people crowded in front of the gangways. These were guarded by scowling, heavily armed security guards, who pointed the muzzles of their submachine guns at the people in the front. I pulled two pairs of handcuffs from my belt, clicked them together at one end, and pushed in front of Roberto. Then I pressed them into his hand.

"Roberto, hook this to the front of your belt and lock them tight. Then do the same to the back of my belt. We might trip over each other, but at least we won't lose each other. And we'll have our hands free. There's a knife by my left shoulder. If I can't reach it, and we need to cut ourselves free, you'll have to do it."

"What do you mean by *need*?"

Was he being sarcastic, or did he really not know what I meant?

"If we fall down, or if I can't move my hands, or if I'm dead . . ." I responded, brusquely.

He understood and nodded.

The shots were now coming from precisely where the Guardia Civil had dropped us off. If they continued at this pace, the infected would be on us in less than ten minutes!

I doubted that they could be stopped by the current numbers of police. The only way would have been to blow up the bridge, but nothing like that happened. Now it was too late anyway.

Why weren't the ship's crew letting us board? What were they waiting for? If they didn't clear the gangways for us right now, we were doomed. With each wave of the mob, I felt Roberto's weight pulling me as his body moved with the crowd. I tried to keep my balance and keep tabs on everything around us. Then I saw the last fighters on the bridge stumbling backward and heard them firing increasingly weaker volleys at an invisible enemy. When they came into view of us—a sea of fugitives that they were supposed to be protecting—it became clear that they were about to meet their end. As soon as they ran out of ammunition, they would be crushed between us and the advancing infected.

First one, then two, four, and more of the officers threw their empty guns to one side and desperately ran the last two hundred meters toward the crowd. Some jumped the forty meters into the cold sea.

Some tried to escape along the stone parapet that separated the access road from the water. No one made it across the slippery wall.

Once again, I smelled them a few moments before I saw them: the vanguard of the infected, reeking of decay and excrement, climbing unstoppably over their own dead and fighting to get at the flesh of living people. Without any possibility of escape, we were almost being presented to them on a platter.

The soldiers rushed headlong down the steep access road in a panicked attempt to avoid the inevitable. The last ones on the bridge did not stand a chance. And then, as the ship opened fire, all hell broke loose among the waiting crowd. We were pushed forward, hard, without being given any chance to decide in what direction to go. With extreme difficulty, I managed to get the HK free and held it openly above my head. We advanced laboriously, meter by meter. Ahead of us, I saw people tumbling from the gangways into the water, screaming in panic and gesticulating wildly. The few who managed to hold onto the railings for a short time were quickly dragged off by those who followed. Some people found their way onto the ship and ran blindly across the decks. I feared I would end up at the bottom of Barcelona Bay along with Roberto if I couldn't disconnect in time when we fell into the water. I scolded myself for not having thought of this and not having planned for this variable.

I was trying—in vain so far—to steer us toward one of the gangways. Roberto was tagging along well, but I could sense his panic at the back of my neck, as he was catching my heels with almost every step. The security guards who had been defending the ship had been swamped or had fled. The increasingly loud thrumming of the ship's engines mingled with the general cacophony of panic. The rusty funnels were spewing ever greater quantities of oily black smoke into the sky. My heart went cold. They were going to leave without us. I squandered a second panicking about this realization, then discarded it and pushed and shoved forward with all my might. People fell to the ground in front of me and all around. I stumbled over abandoned baggage, people who had fallen. They were as good as dead anyway. If they weren't trampled to death by us, the infected would take care of them.

Ten meters from a gangway, I fired a short volley into the air. The crowd recoiled in shock from the loud bang, forgetting for a few moments the danger approaching them from behind. The pressure around me weakened for two seconds. I took advantage of this and moved toward the walkway. I fired again, for a little longer this time, and cleared a path for us onto the ship. Fights were breaking out right by the gangways, with people lashing out in attempts to get themselves and their families to safety. I kept on shooting into the air, swinging my fist, hammering my elbow against noses, laying about me with the gun. My blows met faces, knocked out teeth, and knocked men and women unconscious. I was a wild animal trying to escape from a trap, knowing no reason, no mercy. And then we were right at the foot of the gangway. I was about to set foot on it, finally, but Roberto resisted, forcing me to stay on the spot. I pulled with all my might, the gap I had fought so hard for threatening to close—and only then did I notice Roberto was screaming. I half turned my head in his direction. The sight shocked me so much that I almost fell into the water. An infected man was clinging to him and had sunk his teeth deep into his shoulder. Black saliva stained Roberto's jacket. I tried to grasp what I was seeing.

There was no escape for Roberto, no possibility of survival. A young person who had been placed in my care was going to die. I had not executed my order to the satisfaction of my client, and that meant I wasn't satisfied, either. I put my submachine gun to the infected man's forehead and pulled the trigger. The force of the shot sent him flying backward and tore off a piece of Roberto's jacket. Soft, rosy skin appeared underneath. It was bleeding. I turned around, stepped onto the jetty, and pulled Roberto behind me without a second thought. He screamed and shrieked the whole time. Now he was an infected himself, breathing down my neck.

How long would it take for him to transform? Seconds, minutes? I advanced slowly, feeling the resistance of his body to my movements with every step. We could not afford to fall over, so I took short, powerful steps. Nevertheless, I knocked over people who were getting their bearings on the crowded decks, trying to loosen the belt of my pants. It was a relief when I was able to pull it off and free myself from my dying burden. Directly in front of me, someone pulled open a cabin door and made to go through it. I slammed a fist into his temple, and he went down without a word. Then I grabbed Roberto by the lapels and pushed him into the space that had been vacated.

I followed instantly, closing and locking the door behind us. As I slumped to the floor in the narrow cabin, I realized it was too small for two people. Whatever function it might once have served, I could only guess. The boy fell over, exhausted, wailing weakly and holding his injured shoulder.

"Am I going to die?" He sounded like a small child.

"Let me see," I said, scrambling over and helping him take off his jacket. I took the flashlight out of my backpack and illuminated Roberto's torso. It was amazing that so small an injury could be so final. The few places where the infected man's teeth had bitten through the jacket and superficially broken the underlying skin were turning from grayish green to olive-black under the cool LED light. Starting with a fine ring, the discoloration spread in all directions, the veins just beneath the surface of the skin taking on a darker tone. The skin and the tissue underneath were turning gray. I thought about removing the diseased flesh with my knife, but my fascination for the speed with which the disease was progressing gave me pause.

"Aaaarrgghhh, it's burning!" Roberto tore himself away from me, hunching up, screaming, and pressing his forehead against the dank, scuffed carpet. I wanted to observe the infection-induced transformation closely, so I ignored his anguish and pulled him back into a sitting position. He gasped as I tore his shirt in two so that I could track the changes better. Within moments, the infected area had grown to twice the size of the bite and was spreading inexorably, although the rate slowed somewhat as the virus assimilated additional areas of tissue.

"Help meeee!" he yelled at the top of his lungs, writhing as if to shake off the pain. "Pleaseeeee!" The poison continued to eat its way through and was crawling up his neck. His entire arm, down to the tips of his fingers, discolored rapidly.

Like in anatomy class, blood channels appeared. His cheeks swiftly turned gray. His gums went black, and his teeth turned chalky white as all life drained from him. A gray haze fell over his eyeballs, the irises fading almost to invisibility. Roberto screamed once, long and loud. He fell to the floor and his body went limp.

I shuddered as I saw a translucent grayish liquid, tough as wallpaper paste, slowly trickle out of his shoulder wound. A sweet stench of decay emanated from it. Involuntarily, I backed away, as if I might become infected if I breathed it in. Then I looked at the clock and calculated. No more than five minutes could have passed since Roberto had been bitten. In the last thirty seconds, the virus had spread explosively and rendered its host unconscious.

Outside, the tramping of feet continued. The ship was moving. Slowly at first, then it faltered, then the engines revved, and everything began to vibrate.

Had anyone thought to untie the ropes and loosen the gangways?

As if in response to my thought, an enormous jolt went through the ship. Something—or someone—fell over in the neighboring cabin. Outside, people were screaming again.

I looked at my watch: six minutes since the bite. Roberto's face was covered in a fine, black, wiry mesh. The color of his skin no longer looked anything like healthy. His breathing became shallower, his fingers twitched uncontrollably and curled into claws. The odor from his mouth became more pungent, like someone with poor oral hygiene or who has had a dead, rotten tooth in his jaw for many years.

The ship was moving freely. I could feel it gaining speed.

Eight minutes.

His other arm and torso were now infested as well. I removed his shoes and socks and concentrated hard as, after nine minutes, the life was squeezed out of his feet and the tissue infiltrated.

When the ship crashed into an obstacle, I almost fell over. But Roberto's transformation continued to fascinate me so much that I immediately banished the impact from my thoughts.

About ten minutes had passed since the bite when he stopped breathing. I carefully put two fingers to his neck and felt no pulse.

Ten minutes to die, after a ridiculous bite that had barely grazed the upper layers of the skin. It might go even faster if a vital part of the body was wounded and the spread was accelerated, I speculated.

But how long did it take for the infection to resurrect the dead?

I opened the door to the shower stall where the toilet was located, quickly pulled the lifeless body in by its feet, and wedged it into the narrow space in such a way that he would not find it easy to stand up after he returned. His legs were pointing up into the air, and his upper body was stuck tight between the toilet bowl and the wall.

Eleven minutes.

Out on deck, the situation had stabilized somewhat. I looked through the yellowing porthole and saw gray sea, and behind it was a black sky that reminded me of the discolored skin of the infected.

Eleven minutes and thirty seconds.

In the shower stall, something hit one of the plastic fiber walls.

Less than two minutes! I turned around and saw through the opened door Roberto—or rather, what had once been Roberto—undergoing spastic convulsions in the narrow cabin. He tried to straighten up, which he could not do because of his position, and jerked back and forth in the cramped conditions. Suddenly, he faltered in the middle of his efforts to free himself, sniffing. He couldn't see me because his legs were in the way, but he sensed me. Somehow he knew I was almost within reach, even though I made no sound. Apparently, he could smell, no, scent me! Then the scales fell from my eyes. The virus used and amplified the host's sense of smell to locate food and other suitable hosts.

At that moment, Roberto threw his head back and hit his skull hard against the wall. His face had lost all its human features. It was a mask of hatred and rage, the pure grimace of madness. He struggled convulsively to get to his feet and finally managed to get onto all fours, baring his teeth at me. He looked like a rabid wolf, ready to pounce.

The force of the bullet fired from a meter away jerked back his head in midflight and threw the creature, which had mutated into a beast, back into the shower chamber. Bone splinters, dark blood, and grayish brain matter splattered across the yellowing walls. I sprang away from the doorway before it could contaminate me. Roberto's remains crashed against the plastic toilet and lay motionless, this time forever.

The muzzle of my HK was smoking. I ejected the magazine and checked the ammunition. Half full. Nonetheless, I fished out a full new one from my backpack. It snapped into place with a familiar click. Roberto must have dropped his Glock in the hullabaloo on the pier because I didn't see it here. But even if I had found it, I would have left the gun with him anyway—splattered with blood and secretions as he was. Disgusted and simultaneously filled with pain at the senseless loss of a young life, I slammed the bloodstained door shut.

The last few nights without sleep had taken their toll. I must have dozed off on the worn-out old bunk. When I came to, I began to rearrange my backpack. Kneeling on the floor, I pulled out one item after another and laid them all neatly side by side.

It was now quiet outside. The ship was rocking to and fro almost imperceptibly. When I had stowed everything, I remembered the mobile phone that Judge Gentile had given me.

The instant I took it out of the backpack, it rang and vibrated simultaneously.

The display showed an Italian area code. A cold shiver ran down my spine because I had to break the news of his son's death to him. Would he think I had let him die out of a desire for revenge? I didn't dare pick up the phone and waited until the call went to voice mail.

I took a deep breath. The phone rang again. I answered on the fourth ring. "Hello?" I said.

"Signora Pastore? What's going on?" The judge's voice sounded appallingly strained. I could literally hear him trembling.

"Signore Gentile," I said evasively. "We are on the ship."

"Good, good. Is my son well? Are you well, too?" My throat was failing me, I could hardly swallow, hardly breathe.

Judge Gentile listened to the silence for a few seconds. Then he said resignedly, very calmly, "Did he suffer?"

"No," I lied, hot tears running down my cheeks. "It all happened . . . terrifyingly fast. We were almost at our destination when the infected fell upon us. Roberto . . . he . . . he was . . ."

I couldn't bring myself to say any more, and I wept silently as I sensed Gentile's despair across the Mediterranean.

"Thank you, Signora Pastore," was the last thing he said. His voice sounded matter-of-fact.

"Signore Gentile? Judge?"

There was a muffled sound; he had dropped the phone. Then came a loud bang that not even the distortion on the phone line could mask.

"Hello, are you there? Judge?" I asked, fully aware of the futility of the question. That branch of the Gentile family tree no longer existed. I hung up.

Thunder cracked outside. Anger, sadness, rage, and relief mixed with my hatred for the old man. All these emotions were building up inside me, looking for an outlet that was no longer available. Judge Gentile was dead. He had died unhappily, but what I would once have felt was a just punishment lay heavily in my stomach. Eating through my guts like a lump of molten lead. I felt deep compassion for the man who I had despised, who had taken his own life after I had failed to save his only son. Did that make me his murderer? If not, why did it all feel so wrong?

Another thunderclap.

For years—literally every damn night—I had dreamed of killing him, of making him pay for my anguish. And now, when I could have prided myself upon it, felt some relief, I felt only an endless emptiness.

When I heard a commotion outside the cabin, I decided that someone had to pay for everything that had happened to me. I positioned myself behind the door, unlocked it, and pushed against it. It wouldn't open. Something was lying in front of it, blocking my exit. I took three steps back and ran at it in a rage, the Glock in my hand.

At full tilt, I hit the handle with my free fist and let my shoulder crash against the door with all its force. I felt something fleshy being catapulted away by the impact. Then I stormed out.

A flash of lightning struck the sea a few hundred meters from us and lit up everything for a moment. I saw a person fly over the railing and realized that they were not infected. Their eyes were wide open.

They looked at me accusingly, as if asking why. Another innocent, unnecessary victim on my conscience.

Anger. Despair. Hatred.

Suddenly, I was standing in a tremendous downpour. Instantly, I was soaked to the skin. The door crashed shut behind me. The ship swayed in the rising bora. In the yellowish glow of the overhead lights, I made out several silhouettes moving swiftly toward me. From their shuffling gait, I could tell that they were infected. It was apparently more difficult for them to pick up my scent in the rain. But they now looked as if they were locating me by sound. I fired at the one closest to me. In the muzzle flash, I saw the bullet ripping his head backward and bursting open the eye of another of the living dead a few meters behind him. All the others flinched in unison, fixed their blank stares on the spot the blast had come from, and sprinted toward me, yelping, gurgling, hissing, and reaching out for me. A dazzling flash of lightning exploded, followed scarcely a second later by the deafening crash of thunder.

My internal organs seemed to leap, aghast, within me. I ducked involuntarily. The resurrected faltered, following the sound, which bought me three or four valuable seconds. I holstered the pistol and turned to my left, aimed the HK at the heads of the infected, and pulled the trigger in a longer volley, waving the weapon back and forth. The muzzle flash kept illuminating the scene, enabling me to see the carnage I was creating despite the boat's feeble lighting. Then I disposed of those approaching me from behind. When the HK was empty, I took out the Glock.

I shot much more sparingly with this, taking aim more deliberately. Then I used the combat knife, stabbing it into eye sockets and the soft flesh under chins until the tip of the knife hit the insides of skulls. The rain washed away the blood and secretions staining me. It was pure luck that I had no open wounds on my hands.

I worked my way purposefully up a staircase, speculating that there would be fewer infected on the higher decks and finding time to switch out the HK and Glock magazines in a dark corridor.

The sea became rougher. A massive storm roared through the ship's corridors, wreaking havoc. It almost blew me out of my hiding place, forcing me to seek firmer footing. I continued to run through the dark passageways and pushed down some latches, but none of the doors gave way. I glanced constantly back and forth, my submachine gun at the ready.

The wind whipped rain and seawater into my face whenever I came close to the railing. The roar of the bora was now deafening. The ship rocked precariously in the high swells. I was thrown against walls and slipped several times on the wet floor but managed to stay upright. The wave of emotion that had surged over me at the judge's suicide had long since dwindled away.

An oval door with a pneumatic safety lock was my salvation. Using all my reserves of strength, I turned the handle, which looked like a steering wheel. The door opened with a squeak, and I stepped into the poorly lit engine room. It was incredibly noisy but warm and dry. I closed the door again and looked around. A lamp was burning somewhere, and this gave enough light for me to find a space where I could sit down on the rusty grid floor.

I clutched my knees and sat motionless, hour after hour. The fear of attack meant sleep was out of the question. The engines pounded beneath me, but my thoughts pounded even louder as I racked my brains about what to do next.

Despite the tremendous noise, I dozed off, exhausted.

And then came an unnaturally loud grinding screech from the deepest corners of the hull, the pitch and volume increasing so much that within a few seconds I thought my eardrums were going to burst. The ship came to an abrupt halt, tipping up. The centrifugal force propelled me forward and my forehead hit one of the steel railings in midflight.

At some point, I regained consciousness and straightened up in pain. My head was humming like a beehive, and there were both high- and low-pitched buzzing sounds in my ears. The ship was at a standstill and was listing at an extreme angle. The light had gone out. I had to clamber blindly along the mesh floor to get to the door.

The HK hung around my neck like a dead weight as I pushed the door open with the last of my strength and crawled out into the glaring daylight. It was a hot Mediterranean day, noon. There was absolute quiet, disturbed only by the frantic screeching of seagulls. Crossing the sloping decks of the wrecked ship, whose hull lay among crushed and scattered launches in the harbor, I slowly made my way toward the mainland. I caught sight of Palma, usually a very lively place, but now resembling a cemetery. In my mind's eye I saw crowds of people strolling through the narrow streets of the old town, tourists and locals alike. Everything was bustling, the city was breathing, living. That was how I always imagined Palma. But now the only indication that people had once lived here were the lonely curtains, blowing on the breeze out of the open windows.

Corpses were strewn all over the ship. I crept past them carefully and worked my way to a place where I could slide a few meters down the hull without breaking all the bones in my body. It was on the stone walls of centuries-old buildings that I found the first spatters of blood. Dozens, hundreds even, of the infected must have stormed Palma from the ship at dawn. That was why there were no victims in the immediate vicinity of the port. The city had been asleep when disaster hit. The hordes were presumably working their way through the alleys at the other end of Palma. I found the last full magazine in one of my cargo pockets and slid it into the machine gun.

At an unstaffed kiosk, I moved from shelf to shelf as if on a tactical mission, filling my backpack with drinks and whatever edibles I could carry, careful not to pick anything with packaging that rustled. I discovered the first body in the entrance of the building right next to the kiosk. Gnawed through, dismembered, bled dry. Massacred beyond recognition, more bones than flesh. It was impossible that this person would ever rise again. I grabbed her decomposing remains by the last shreds of jeans not stained by blood and deposited them around the corner in the neighboring side alley. Then I returned to the entrance.

Behind it, up a few steps, I could see through the open door directly into a first-floor apartment. This I subjected to a thorough inspection. Since I found neither dead nor undead, I barricaded the entrances and exits and hid inside.

During the day, I raided the surrounding stores and homes, hoarding food and water. Unfortunately, none of the phones I found were usable. The computers could be booted up, but they always required a password.

At night, the infected came back. I could hear their shuffling feet. Their hungry gurgling robbed me of sleep. Now and then I heard shots, but always far away. So, I survived six days in Palma until Nils drove by on the multilane highway.

At the sound of his car, I jumped out the window, ran, and stood in his path. When I drew my pistol and pointed it at his forehead, he braked carefully and came to a halt a few meters away from me. Then he leaned over the passenger seat and opened the door.

"¿Español?" I asked, approaching the car.

"No, alemán," he growled in a harsh German accent.

"¿Hablas inglés? ¿O italiano?" My Spanish was halfway okay, but my German left a lot to be desired. I could make superficial conversation, but nothing more.

"Sí, inglés esta bien." He rotated his hand back and forth, the international signal for somewhat okay.

"Oh, great. I've got some more weapons and food in that house there." I pointed at the windows. Everything I owned was there, except for the Glock I was holding.

"Okay, go get it; I wait here."

When I hesitated a moment too long, he said authoritatively, "Don't worry. I wait for you, just hurry! Weapons more important; I have much food at home!" He gestured toward the building.

He left the engine running. I hurried away, packed my backpack to the brim—leaving only a small amount of food behind—and was standing by his blue Mercedes-Benz barely two minutes later. The trunk was open. I stowed my bulging bag and slammed the lid back down in one fluid motion. Nils skillfully turned the venerable old whip around. Silently, we sped back the way he had come. When the city had disappeared behind us and we were on the highway heading toward Inca, I found the courage to break the silence. But Nils was taciturn. The only thing I learned was that we were going to his little "fortress." As we drove, I checked and reloaded my pistol, just to let him know I wasn't in the mood for any monkey business, in case he had any planned.

But I wasn't the first person Nils had saved. Jens and Waltraud had arrived here a day before me. They welcomed me warmly, albeit with initial skepticism.

Who could blame them? The infected had arrived on the island a week ago, and since then, they had multiplied maybe a thousandfold, leaving a trail of destruction in their wake. Meanwhile, some of the survivors had gotten into small skirmishes, extending the work of the undead. Even among the sane, anyone might be an enemy. Instead of working together and protecting each other, most people ultimately decided to take the selfish route, which led to the destruction of many resources.

But we soon realized that we would get along splendidly in Nils's fortress. It was in all our interests to maintain, expand, and strengthen our little community. My original mission had been a resounding failure. But fate did not give me any time to wallow in guilt. Our daily schedules were tightly organized. Everything was geared toward survival.

We plundered the surrounding fincas, those that were uninhabited at least. Twice, people drove us off the properties with poorly aimed shotguns. At home, we kept quiet, reinforced the walls, and filled our stores. That's how we have survived until now. And we hope for the same tomorrow.

When Franca had finished her story, we sat together in the living room. We gave her friendly high fives and hugs as if we were in a support group. She smiled at us, tired and weary.

I thought how her supposed failure must torment her. But I was more preoccupied by my own survival and was glad not to have to be alone. One by one we got up, stretched, and yawned. I had gone way past my usual bedtime, and so I was appropriately tired. It was long past midnight, so I asked where I might sleep.

They assigned me a room on the second floor. I took a quick shower, put on the clean clothes they gave me, and went to bed.

As I lay there with my eyes closed, I heard my new friends locking the doors and completing the last rituals of the day. A few minutes later, silence was spreading throughout the house.

Half asleep, I twitched a few times before letting go and sinking into the safe embrace of the familiar darkness.

INITIUM

I sat up, startled. The sun had long since risen, and its beams were slanting into my room. Since I had spent the last weeks as a lonely stranger to civilization, it came as a shock to hear thunderous stomping outside the door. At first, I shrank back against the wall and pulled the covers up to my nose. But then I remembered where I was and pulled myself together. I reached the door in two bounds, stepping out into the hallway and then rushing down the stairs.

The others were standing around the desk in the living room. Waltraud was sitting at it, typing on a laptop. Eva turned around and cried out in shock. The rest of them started, looking at me in amazement.

"What the hell," Patrick snapped. "Damn it, it's Backup! Fuck, we totally forgot you were here."

Eva was green in the face. Franca was holding one of her pistols, ready for a fight. Jens's dark skin had turned a shade paler. Nils took a shaky breath and put a hand over his heart. For a second, I felt guilty for scaring them like that. "Sorry 'bout that," I said, grinning sheepishly.

"I almost peed my pants," Waltraud replied, clutching the edge of the table.

She, who despite her old-fashioned first name was not even thirty years old, had been trying for days to get information from her Norwegian homeland. The title on her business card probably read *computer scientist*, but I later learned she was more of a hacker. Her job apparently served only to earn her an income and camouflage her other activities.

She took a deep breath before speaking in fluent English with a Scandinavian accent while we stared at the screen as if spellbound.

"Our clients use the servers we manage for their email correspondence. One of my tasks is to configure and maintain them." She pointed to one of the cryptic lines of numbers and special characters on the display. "This is a clinic in Stockholm." She moved the cursor and clicked a button. The content changed.

"Here you can see the email addresses that belong to the clinic's domain. Normally this is subject to data protection, and I don't have the right to show you it, but who cares about that now. Anyway, I've been tracking the email traffic for days. Or rather the lack of it, because nothing has been sent for over two weeks."

"Are you monitoring just the outboxes or the inboxes, too?" interjected Patrick.

Waltraud looked at him over her shoulder. "Just the outboxes. I don't want to be look through spam. So, yesterday a few emails were sent from this account here." She pointed her finger at a line. "I logged in to the mail management system—et voilà—two people who are still alive have been corresponding industriously since last night."

She scrolled casually up and down a long list of emails. "They are Professor Ekström from Stockholm and Doctor Koller from Berlin. From their emails, it appears Doctor Koller is a virologist who did his doctorate years ago with the professor, who at that time held a chair at the Charité University of Medicine in Berlin. They seem to have reached agreement on how and what exactly it was that caused the pandemic but not on how to fight it. The institute in Berlin, however, is on the verge of a breakthrough.

"The rest is formalities and small talk." She looked at us again. "I've sent them both an email. Let's see if anything comes back."

"Not bad," Patrick interjected. "Can we eat now, though? Breakfast?"

"Shut up, Patrick!" someone growled.

"Yeah, go eat, you philistines." Waltraud waved us away irritably, probably because we weren't being appreciative enough of her latest achievement, before immersing herself in the laptop again.

The rest of us went to the kitchen. Again, I was amazed at how efficiently the community functioned. Everyone quietly got on with their tasks like a well-rehearsed team. Even the inevitable clatter of cutlery was barely audible. But why was I noticing this now? It was not the first time I had observed a group of people working. The reason was obvious: the continued existence of civilization depended on how well the survivors worked together. Our community was unconsciously modeling it. Anyone who hadn't internalized the importance of cohesion was surely already dead. But could what worked on a small scale be transferred to a larger group? Up to now, every civilization had perished as soon as it had exceeded a certain size. So, wouldn't it be better to live in tribes than in cities? I didn't have the confidence to intrude into the others' workflow, but as Jens walked by, he gave me a stack of plates and nodded toward the table.

It was good to be able to contribute. I took care not to get in anyone's way and set the table almost silently. Waltraud joined us.

We had breakfast. There was coffee, tea, fresh bread (someone had gotten up early and baked it), fruit, and grilled vegetables. Almost normal, like before the outbreak. The only noticeable difference was that high spirits were largely absent from breakfast, too. People talked quietly, without spontaneous interjections. Compared to the calm that prevailed, the little snacks yesterday afternoon had been a real party.

Franca tapped a knife softly against a glass. Immediately, the talk fell silent. All eyes were on her.

"On the agenda today is the mall at Inca. We'll take two vehicles: Nils in the coupé with Jens, and Patrick and I will take the truck. And you're welcome to come too, Backup, if you'd like."

As she said the last sentence, she looked into the faces of the people at the table. A good leader doesn't make important decisions without consulting the rank and file. She wanted to keep an eye on me for the time being. After all, how could they know who I was?

And I would be able to earn my own dinner, which I was pleased about. After having scrutinized me briefly, everyone nodded.

I nodded back.

"Then I'll see you at the door in ten minutes." With these words, she rose, took her dishes to the sink, and set them down. She left the kitchen, and we followed her example.

My room had its own small bathroom with a toilet, shower, and sink. I washed myself and brushed my teeth. Then I put on yesterday's clothes again, took the spear, and went to the front door.

Less than half a minute later, Franca was standing next to me.

She was dressed in black combat gear and carried her pistols like a gunslinger. Her long dark hair was braided into a tight ponytail that hung over her backpack. A combat knife in its sheath was taped to the left shoulder strap. She looked at me and said casually, "So, excited?"

The fabric of her long, tight-fitting sleeves was stretched tight around her biceps.

"Sure. You?" I said, making an effort to sound more relaxed than I was.

She nodded. "Always am before a mission like this. I don't think it'll be dangerous this time, but I still get a bit of a buzz."

I knew next to nothing about the current situation on the island. "Not dangerous? Aren't there any infected there?"

"Hard to say. They're always on the move, and they prefer places where there are, or have been, people," Franca explained. "They're very good at locating us, but we can only guess at how they do it."

Then I remembered that the wandering corpses had noticed me in the street between the hotels yesterday (Had it only been yesterday?) once the wind had started up. I told her about it briefly.

She thought about it, frowning. "As I said, that's quite possible," she said. "They probably don't do so well in places where they can't smell humans. I'm guessing there won't be many human odors in the mall after almost four weeks of shutdown. That'll be a help. The primary thing we need to watch out for is other looters."

"Oh, no problem; I'm armed," I said with exaggerated bravery, holding out my spear.

At that moment, Jens and Patrick came through the door. Each of them carried a pistol in a hip holster. When they saw us with such different statures and equipment, they began to laugh.

Who could have blamed them, given the picture we made? A muscular female fighting machine armed to the teeth and a skinny caveperson in gray jogging pants with a homemade spear in hand.

Franca grinned back provocatively. "What's up, guys?"

"You two are not to be messed with," Patrick replied as he passed us on his way to get the pickup from the garage. Meanwhile, Jens sat down in the Mercedes.

The sky was mercilessly blue, without the slightest cloud. It was going to be a beautiful, sunny spring day. A gentle, refreshing breeze was rustling through the leaves. But any kind of summery outlook was eluding me.

"D'you know how to use firearms, Backup?"

"No. To be honest, I've never fired a single shot."

"Then it's about time. When we get back, you should join in with training."

"Training? What kind of training?" I asked.

"Close combat, firearms, knife fighting—all the things you have to be able to do these days if you want to survive. In return, you can teach us to fight with your spear." She grinned widely.

Was she mocking me, or was I just imagining it?

"Oh, fuck off," I said, pretending to be offended and giving her a flamboyant sideways glance. At that moment, a vehicle drove up from the courtyard, approaching us almost silently. Only the crunch of gravel under its huge wheels could be heard. But Franca would not leave it.

"No, I'm serious! Nils said yesterday that you killed quite a few stinkers just with it. Well, I'm impressed."

I didn't get a chance to say anything because just then Patrick pulled up the pickup truck right in front of us. It was huge, and this model had modifications. Six headlights were mounted on the roof bar, which was the width of an arm. The windows were tinted black. Monstrous tires that reached to my waist dug deep into the gravel. Except for the turning of the wheels, the vehicle was absolutely silent. Its ostentatious dimensions meant it could seat at least eight people.

But the truly bizarre thing about the truck—besides its severe, elongated pentagon shape that made it seem like something you might find on Mars—was its color, which was canary yellow. It shone like a miniature sun. I looked questioningly at Nils, who caught my glance as I passed.

"One of a kind—and I guess it's a stolen European prototype! It was the only thing a guy who owed me a good chunk of dough had left before he had to get off the island. He had other creditors who would have dealt with him differently if they had gotten ahold of him."

"But . . . That's a cybertr—?" My jaw dropped in amazement.

"Yeah, that's right!" He beamed with pride. "Man, this thing is even fully automatic. The solar panels on the roof of the garage charge it fully in an hour. But you can forget about narrow village streets." Nils stroked the front hood of the truck lovingly before waddling over to the blue Mercedes. He squeezed his overweight frame into it and started the engine. Then he hit the gas and rolled slowly up the hill ahead of us.

"People and tech." Franca pushed past me and took a seat in the truck's passenger seat. She slammed the door, rolled down the window, and looked at me. "Do you want an invitation in writing?"

I had barely taken a seat in the back when Patrick pulled away with an almost inaudible hum. No loud roar, no sooty emissions—the machine made only a little more noise than a laptop ventilation system. Only the glowing LEDs in the cockpit indicated that the car was on—those and the sound of the wheels on the road. The digital speedometer whooshed upward as soon as we drove out of the courtyard onto the dusty track. Taped behind the front seats were several firearms, all Velcroed and positioned so that they were within easy reach and ready for use at any time: one black pump-action shotgun per seat, a total of seven revolvers and pistols, even a smaller MP5K—that one I knew something about. A few months ago, I had seen a documentary about the most commonly used guns. The MP5 and all its different models were at the top of the list.

At the sight of the arsenal, I felt a bit pathetic with my spear. After two or three kilometers on the gravel road, I finally tore my gaze away from the weapons, and asked, "Where did you get all this stuff?"

Patrick turned onto the paved road in the direction of Inca. Franca filled me in, looking over her left shoulder. "During the supply trip a few days ago, we came across an abandoned police station. The door was wide open. We went inside and helped ourselves from the armory."

Her gaze drifted forward again, and she lost herself in the Mallorcan plain. A little later, we hummed across the roundabout into a road that took us onto the highway. We were heading south.

I pushed a button and lowered the window, earning Patrick's disapproval. "Heeey, the air conditioning is on." It wasn't hot, though, and the AC wasn't needed. I ignored him and let my eyes roam outside. Out of the corner of my eye, I noticed him smiling approvingly.

Then he turned off the system and lowered the other windows. Wind flowed through the interior, tangling up the now long strands of my hair.

We followed Nils along the deserted road for another ten minutes. Just before he turned off, he flashed his hazard lights twice, signaling to Patrick. Franca sat up straight in her seat and released the safety catch on her gun with a flick of her thumb.

"Let's go!"

We left the highway. The drivers slowed down, and we approached the mall almost at walking pace.

A few cars were parked in the huge lot, their paintwork crackling in the rising heat. The driver's side door of one of them stood wide open, the seat belt hanging sluggishly down to the asphalt.

The coupé and pickup slowly came to a standstill.

Franca climbed agilely out the open window and moved onto the loading bed behind us. Tapping on the window at my back, she gestured to me to follow her. Less elegantly than she had, I opened the door and stepped toward her over the low chrome bar. I took my spear with me.

Close to my ear, she whispered, "You, Jens, and I are going shopping. We'll cover you and you fill the carts. Okay?"

"Yeah, you got it." I felt my palms begin to sweat.

Jens held his gun at the ready in the front car, monitoring our surroundings through the submachine gun's rear sight. Franca was focused on the driver's side and rear of our small convoy. Except for the branches in the wind, nothing moved. And despite that—or maybe because of it— the tension was rising. We circled the parking lot and came to a stop at the main entrance. Jens got out of the Mercedes and came toward us. Franca jumped off the pickup. I followed her immediately.

She raised both hands like a basketball referee, one clenched in a fist, the fingers of the other spread. Fifteen, I calculated. I saw everyone looking over at her and touching their wristwatches. When she nodded, they all returned the gesture and set their timers.

We moved quickly to the entrance. Franca grabbed two abandoned shopping carts as we walked along and rolled them toward me. They made less noise than I had feared but far more than I liked. I tucked them into each other so that I was only pushing one of them. Together, we entered the decaying temple to consumerism. The plague that had descended on the sleeping island early one morning a few weeks ago had spread from its epicenter to Marratxí, ten kilometers away, as Nils had told us one evening. Employees and customers—those who had managed to flee and escape with their lives—had left all the doors unsecured. This allowed us to walk into any of the stores and take whatever we wanted.

But with all the stores, there was only one type that interested us, the one with the food.

Franca stepped forward with her finger on the trigger, scanning everything in front of us. The feeling that we were about to be surrounded by the undead and torn to pieces intensified. The shops were dark. The automatic power control had turned off the lights one evening. It had been a long time since anyone had needed them again in the morning.

The daylight coming in through the glazed side doors and skylights allowed us to make out the most important details. Several of the windowpanes were shattered, some had been destroyed. Overturned shelves and goods lay on the floor everywhere.

Dry stains indicated where bottles had been broken. We ignored the brownish drag marks in some of the aisles as best we could.

The shopping carts squeaked ominously every meter of the way. Jens brought up the rear. The spear lay half in the cart, sticking out over my right shoulder. Franca led us around the disordered interior to the shelves with the nonperishable goods. We helped ourselves to the canned goods, moving from aisle to aisle and collecting anything that would fit in the carts.

The elite fighter looked at her watch and said softly, "Five."

Five minutes. What had seemed like an eternity to me had actually not been long at all.

"Round two?" asked Jens quietly, as if someone besides us might hear him.

Franca nodded. She took one of the full carts and pushed it in front of her like a protective shield, her elbows slightly bent, permanently ready for battle.

A minute later, we were back at the vehicles. Patrick, Nils, and I filled the trunk of the Mercedes in record time, while Jens and Franca wordlessly kept an eye on the surroundings. Then we turned around and went back into the mall.

I had seen some cargo pants in one of the clothing stores the first time we passed it. Since I had practically nothing to wear other than what I had on now, I needed a change of clothes.

As we passed the store in question, I drew Franca's attention with a quiet "Psst." I gestured to her that I wanted to go in.

She rolled her eyes, said tonelessly, "Be quick, though," underlining her instruction with a jerk of her HK.

It took me less than thirty seconds to grab a few pairs of pants and T-shirts in muted colors.

We continued the raid, this time focusing on water and other drinks. When both carts were once again filled well over the brim, Franca looked at her wristwatch again and whispered, "Thirteen!"

We hurried out as fast as we could. Since each shopping cart was carrying almost a hundred kilograms, this time we made slower progress. My gaze darted back and forth as I clung with both hands to the spear, which I had laid parallel to the cart handle. Despite the armed escort, a shiver of fear was trickling permanently down my spine.

Franca's wristwatch beeped softly just as we arrived at the entrance portal. As soon as we stepped outside, the two vehicles pulled toward us and stopped right in front of us. We packed the water bottles into the back of the pickup. I took my new clothes with me into the back seat. We left the parking lot without incident.

Once the door had closed behind me, I exhaled in relief. My hands were shaking. In my mind, I was going over what had just happened. "We could have gone a few more rounds, though. It was all safe, wasn't it?" I didn't understand why we had left so many good things there.

"The longer we stay in one spot," Franca explained, "the higher the risk of being discovered. That's why we limit the time to fifteen minutes. After that, the risk increases exponentially. We prefer to do short trips every two or three days. And we never go to the same place twice in a row." I thought about this as she added, "But it all went great; we have more to eat and drink for a few weeks."

Patrick steered the car out of the traffic circle and back onto the highway. We drove northeast again. The outside temperature had risen, but this time we didn't use the air conditioning.

All the windows were open, and the wind was rushing in my ears when Patrick's voice suddenly put us all on the alert.

"Franca, look behind us!" First, she looked in the side-view mirror. When she couldn't see anything, she leaned her upper body far out the window and trained her eyes and gun at the direction we had come from.

"What did you see?" She almost had to shout to enable us to hear her over the wind.

"Something flashed back there, like it was reflecting the sun."

"Are you sure?"

"Yes, I'm sure."

"It seems to be gone now."

She kept leaning out of the car the whole time. Only when we reached the gravel road did she lean back in. We closed the windows. She would not have been able to see anything in the swirling dust of both vehicles, and, therefore, our driver kept a greater distance from Nils and Jens.

"Okay, we got everything stowed away." Patrick, Jens, and I climbed the stairs out of the basement. Only now did I notice how tense I had been the entire time. My shoulders and back ached, but that could have been from the lugging. I had a slight irritating ringing in my ears. Just as

I was about to kick my shoes off and lie down by the pool, Waltraud and Franca came past.

"Training time!" the Italian announced.

Jens didn't seem to mind, but Patrick and I looked at each other doubtfully.

Nevertheless, we went to the underground training room. A little later, when Eva joined us, I noticed Patrick's posture change. He straightened his shoulders and stretched his back, and he stroked Eva's arm lovingly. She herself was neither short nor petite, but next to Patrick, who was over two meters tall, we all looked a little stocky.

On the other side of the cellar, I saw Waltraud and Jens embracing. He seemed a bit shy as he looked into her eyes. She, on the other hand, was beaming, no doubt because of the fact that we—or rather he—had returned safely.

Franca was inspecting and sorting various training weapons. Over the next two hours, she taught me the basics of firearms handling, starting with the smallest pistol in the range, to enable me to get used to the recoil gradually. Its low penetration meant it would be of little use to me when fighting the infected, she explained, unless I landed a clean head shot.

While the two of us were busy with the handguns, the others practiced hand-to-hand combat with knives. Apparently, they did this a lot; almost all of their movements seemed fluid and proficient.

Maybe it had to do with his height and the length of his limbs, but Patrick's coordination left something to be desired. Even so, I would never have messed with him if he had a knife in his hand.

They trained with wooden fakes instead of real weapons so they wouldn't hurt each other as they attacked, dodged, and twisted their opponent's arms and knocked each other to the floor, some of which was lined with thin mattresses. Many of the exercises looked like a mixture of the judo, aikido, and jujitsu Franca had mentioned were taught in the Italian Special Forces.

After learning everything I needed to know about the front sight, rear sight, trigger, and all the rest, I was allowed to do some dry fire practice. Franca released the magazine and unloaded the barrel. I had to hold the pistol with both hands so that the recoil wouldn't tear it out of them later. The trigger was easy to pull back. As a child, I had sometimes wondered what it would be like to hold a deadly weapon. A quiet feeling of physical superiority flowed through me.

When she felt I had practiced enough, Franca decided it was time to learn knife throwing. Propped against the wall with the sandbags for precision firearms practice was a thick wooden beam with a mattress behind it. The ex-elite soldier retrieved a black roll containing a dozen throwing blades and asked us to gather around. She gave a short lecture on how to handle these kinds of weapons. Then she turned and, her arms moving faster than we could follow, sank four of the blades into the upper third of the beam from eight meters away. All of them landed surprisingly close together.

She then explained in detail how it all worked: how to hold the blade, how to create momentum from the hip, and finally, how to swing the wrist like a whip to generate more power and give the throwing knife the necessary rotation.

Our best attempts to imitate her resulted in us managing to send the blades in the same direction. It was a huge success if we even grazed the beam. Franca watched the whole thing with a horrified expression, trying to give us tips after each throw ("Put your other foot forward." "No, don't push—throw." "Put some power behind it."), but in vain. We were useless knife throwers.

That is to say, all except Waltraud. As soon as she got her hands on the knives and felt their weight, it was immediately clear that she had a different relationship with throwing weapons. She positioned herself elegantly in front of the line, took a quick yet smooth swing, and of the eight projectiles she hurled, five landed deep in the wood. And the others bounced off it. We were speechless. Franca was all smiles; she had found her disciple. She nodded appreciatively to Waltraud and helped her to collect the blades again.

"That was pretty damn good," she commented, without giving us a second glance.

We grinned like idiots. Then Franca stood behind Waltraud and put her left hand on Waltraud's left hip. With her right, she gently took her wrist and went through the throw in slow motion, at the same time turning her hip outward.

"You're doing everything perfectly, but you can mobilize the wrist from here, like this!" Waltraud flung the knives, hitting the mark eight times.

"I hope she never throws plates at me," Jens interjected dryly. She turned to him, came closer, and put her arms around his neck. Gazing at him in mock infatuation and breathing ethereally, she said, "Never, unless you cheat on me! But then plates will be the least of your worries, dearest."

In a flash, she had a blade in her hand and was holding it to his throat. He didn't even flinch. She pulled him to her with her other hand and kissed him passionately. Jens grabbed her buttocks and pressed her tightly against him, ignoring the blade.

They kissed, released each other, and left the basement without a word.

Patrick summed up our collective thought in one sentence. "What the hell did I just see?"

Shortly after, we followed them upstairs. Delicious smells were coming from the kitchen again, where Nils was fiddling with pots and pans. "Where are Waltraud and Jens?" he asked when we sat down at the table. Patrick moved his right index finger back and forth in a large *O* that he had formed with his left hand. As he did so, he gave several high and low whistles.

The lovers joined us a few minutes later. Their disheveled hair and flushed cheeks spoke for themselves. While we were eating, Waltraud said between bites, "I'll check the emails in a minute."

None of us knew whether it would be a good idea to discover that there might not be anything that could save us from the plague. So, we just spooned food into our mouths in silence and waited.

"I've been thinking," Patrick said, "we should go to the discount sports store and see if they have any wetsuits."

"What do you want them for?" I scoffed. "Are you getting cold?"

"They're sturdy, and they'd give us good protection against bites and scratches. The hoods would cover your neck and almost all of your head. I'd feel more comfortable in them."

"But the hoods also cover your ears, which would affect your hearing," I replied.

After a moment's thought, he replied, "You're right. Maybe we should cut off the hood. It could give the stinkers a something to grab ahold of."

I laughed smugly. I didn't think much of his half-baked idea.

Franca spoke up. "The neoprene wouldn't be any use. I've seen infected bite through several layers of fabric, even a thick denim jacket. They can develop incredible strength. A knight's armor would be better."

"It'd be dumb to cut off the hood, too. If you wanted to hear things, you could just cut small holes in the appropriate places," I said like a smart-ass, winking at Patrick. He smiled back at me sarcastically, holding up his middle finger.

"YEAH!"

I was practicing with my spear on the patio, working up a sweat. When I heard the exclamation from the living room, I stepped inside, onto the cool tiled floor. Waltraud was glued to the screen. Without looking up, she rattled off the gist of the email: "Sooo, it's looking good, at least as far as combatting the disease is concerned. But as always, there's good news and bad news.

"The pathogen has been identified and isolated. It is more or less certain where the whole thing originated, although they don't say exactly where that was. The disease itself is a kind of mutated rabies. There's no hope for the infected, sadly, but a kind of preventative vaccine is in the works. Since, strangely enough, animals are immune to the pathogen, animal testing isn't possible, so they'll have to test it on humans. Computer simulations can do most of the preliminary work, but to be a hundred percent sure, they think they'll need volunteers. Then there are attachments, tables with different values. Nothing of interest to us, unless one of you is a virologist and understands them."

"Patrick's a biologist, isn't he?" Jens looked at him, grinning mockingly. The latter answered in the negative, shaking his head with a nauseated expression.

Waltraud continued unconcerned, "I've written to them both, asking them to please get in touch with us. Not that we can do anything from here, but as a matter of form . . ."

No sooner had she said that than the computer beeped. "Hey, we're in luck; someone's online. It's Koller. Let's see if she has a Skype account." Waltraud typed an email and sent it off. It was scarcely ten seconds before the beep sounded again. "Okay, Skype it is." She opened the app and entered Ms. Koller's full name in the search box. Three results came up. She clicked on the profile from Berlin.

Then she dialed it and connected. After a few seconds, we had visual contact. The image was slightly pixelated and jerked erratically, but the sound was clear.

"Hello, Dr. Koller. We just wrote to each other. How are you?"

There was a barely perceptible delay. "Hello, Waltraud, you can call me Nadine." She was wearing a white coat, had red hair cut fashionably short, and looked friendly, although you could see the fatigue around her green eyes, even in a low-resolution image.

Like a gaggle of well-behaved schoolchildren, we all said, "Hello, Nadine!"

At this, Waltraud turned around and looked at us in bewilderment before turning her attention back to the Skype call.

"Hi, Nadine. I'm sorry for hacking into your personal account. There's no one else outside of our group that we have contact with. And as I wrote you, we are a handful of survivors in Mallorca." She introduced each of us in turn. "And me, you already know."

"That's all right. I'm glad you wrote. We have hardly any contact with anyone outside the Charité, either. Here in Berlin, we're working day and night to stop the plague, but many of my colleagues have also fallen victim to it." Her gaze clouded, and she looked away for a moment. "Unfortunately, there aren't many people who haven't been carried off by the plague. I had hoped that at least the islands off the coasts would remain safe, but that seems not to be the case."

Waltraud answered, equally gloomily. "No, Mallorca has also been overrun. Unfortunately, a month ago, a passenger ship full of infected was wrecked in the port of Palma. Because of a bora, and because the bridge was overrun quickly, the news about the infection on board wasn't transmitted properly. So, the city was taken unawares. And now, almost a month later, the island is full of the walking undead—"

"Zombies!" interjected Nadine. "We call them zombies here."

I saw Waltraud's eyes glitter damply as she heard the word. Jens also straightened his shoulders. In awe, the Norwegian repeated, "Zombies!"

"Yes, zombies," the virologist replied resignedly, then continuing her explanation. "Derived from the North African nzùmbe, which is a term still used in voodoo today. However, we chose this name on medical grounds. It is an aberration, and it is composed in German directly from the pathway of infection. Central nervous system—zentral in German—ophiocordyceps mutation bite invasion elimination. Z-O-M-B-I-E!"

It sounded incomprehensible and arbitrary, but they presumably had far bigger problems in Berlin than the terms used by the public.

But Patrick took a different view. "You researchers always go out of your way to make the obvious as cryptic as possible. Why? To boost your credibility as nerds?"

The Berliner hesitated briefly but didn't take the remark lying down. She raised one hand and began to count off the tips of her fingers. "When the infection is transmitted, it attacks the central nervous system: zentrales nervensystem, so *Z*. Ultimately the pathogen, which we first thought was a virus, focuses its attack on the victim's brain. It is neither a virus nor a bacterium, but simply a fungus, to be precise *Ophiocordyceps*—this is what the *O* stands for. The fungus has mutated, which gives us *M*. Transmission usually occurs through a bite (*B*). Then the pathogen invades (*I*) the host's body, eliminating (*E*) its vital processes and taking over. Then, technically speaking, it reawakens them."

Franca interjected, "Okay, infected, undead, stinkers, zombies—I don't care what you want to call them . . . But how do we stop them? What about the vaccine you were talking about?"

Nadine looked at the spot on her screen where Franca's image must be. "Unfortunately, there is nothing that can be done for the infected except to give them a rapid, merciful death. The best and quickest way to do that is to damage their central nervous system, which I'm sure you all know by now. Our DNA studies have shown the mutation of the fungus was assisted by increased gamma radiation. There were also traces of DNA from a dog that carried clear markers of rabies."

Nadine paused, as if she had to recall the facts. "More than three months ago, we received a message from Paris asking us to take a closer look at the strange case of Ethan Boileau, now known as patient zero. He was admitted to the hospital because his condition had deteriorated rapidly one afternoon. What initially looked like the flu was just the prelude to something much worse."

INITIUM

Abel was shouting his name. "Ethan! Ethan, look at this!"

But Ethan Boileau did not want to look.

He hated everything to do with Abel. He hated Abel's croaky voice and the repulsive sounds his toothless mouth emitted. Yes, he even hated himself for having to work with him.

He hated himself for having not gotten further in life than driving dented excavators through the stinking mountains of waste at the landfill with the moronic Abel, shifting garbage according to an inexplicable logic, while pigeons, seagulls, and other birds crapped on their heads and neon green overalls.

"ETHAN!"

He did not turn around; he wouldn't do Abel the favor of looking at his dirty mug. This time he would ignore him. This time and at all other times in the future. He was fed up with Abel and his stupid antics, most of which ended with Ethan being covered in foul-smelling garbage. He drove the digger away from Abel, away from his repulsive form, focusing doggedly on keeping his anger in check. He never got as angry as he did with Abel. Now, even the mere presence of the blockhead was enough to infuriate him.

Ethan pushed a pile of decomposing plastic waste ahead of his excavator. The machine came to an abrupt halt. His self-control wavered, but still he controlled his anger. He hoped the vehicle had not hit another container of illegally dumped radioactive waste. All you had to do these days was grease the right palms, and then you could bury the waste from one of France's many nuclear power plants deep under a pile of normal garbage, so deep that the Geiger counters couldn't pick it up. Ethan looked over his front right fender and, as expected, spotted the black trefoil symbol on a yellow background. The colors were somewhat faded, but the logo was unmistakable. Did this tank have a leak like the others?

He would have to call the office and tell them. The landfill would be closed for weeks, as it had been three times in the last year and a half. Ethan turned on the engine and tried to drive on. Just as he was about to sit down, the excavator swayed violently. He tried to grab ahold of the wheel but failed. Before he fell headlong to the ground, he knew what had happened.

Abel had rammed him. He had rammed him because he couldn't stand it when Ethan didn't pay attention to him. He had rammed him because he was a dumb, obnoxious asshole who did nothing but get on other people's nerves. Ethan's anger flared.

"Eeethaaaaan!"

It seemed like Abel's mouth was right next to his ear. He could smell his fetid breath over the stench of the landfill. Anger overcame Ethan with such ferocity that he knew he was about to do him an injury.

Behind him, Abel was stomping through the trash. Ethan got up and looked at him. His rage was accelerating his perception of time; everything around him seemed to slow down. The shapeless dark shadow that stood between them, hiding Abel from view, grew larger. But Ethan couldn't move quickly enough to dodge it. So, he just had to watch helplessly as the object advanced toward him. Abel laughed like a lunatic, drumming his hands on his thighs.

Ethan felt no pain when the object hit. It was not large, heavy, or hard, just a small black plastic bag that would take centuries to decompose. But the constant rearrangement of the landfill and the chemicals and fumes of decomposition that it had been constantly exposed to had made it porous. When the bag smacked into Ethan's face, it ripped, and its contents found their way into his half-open mouth. It took him a second or two to figure out what had just happened. He realized what was on his tongue, and his indignation turned to disgust as suddenly as if someone had flipped a switch. Ethan retched and vomited, spewing out his half-digested breakfast and spitting out the decades-old dog shit that had been sitting around the landfill in a plastic bag, boiling in the sun in the summer and freezing into a block of ice in the winter. The stench was rank, sweetish, and putrid at the same time. The pulpy consistency stuck to his teeth and disappeared into the spaces between them. Ethan tried in vain to get rid of it. He reached for his bag under the seat of the excavator, took out his thermos and poured the hot tea directly into his mouth. He rinsed and gargled, not noticing how he was scalding himself. Ethan consumed the entire contents of the bottle and still had the feeling that there were bits of dog feces in his mouth. At least his stomach had calmed down a bit and he wasn't retching anymore.

Abel laughed and laughed, maniacally, his eyes bulging. Ethan half-heartedly threw the empty thermos at him. He was so exhausted, disgusted, and in shock that the bottle flew harmlessly past Abel, missing him by a meter.

Abel laughed even harder.

Ethan pulled himself together, climbed back into the driver's seat, and flipped the toggle switch. The engine hummed to life. He shifted some of the levers and maneuvered the vehicle past his laughing colleague, driving back to the office complex to report the radioactive waste incident.

As soon as he had put the vehicle in the garage, he went to the sink, washed his face, and rinsed out his mouth again for a long time.

Only now did he realize he had scalded himself, but the cold water eased the pain. He would have to suck ice cubes the rest of the day.

"Hello, Helene," he greeted the older secretary as he entered her office.

"Hello, Ethan, finished work already?" Her voice was friendly, but the look she gave him over the top of her glasses betrayed her skepticism.

"Another drum of radioactive waste has turned up." He went over to the large map of the landfill site and put a pin in the point where he had found it. "Here."

"What a load of crap!" It wasn't as bad as it sounded coming out of her mouth, in fact, because it just meant all the staff would have a few extra days off until the container had been disposed of in an environmentally friendly way.

"I'm going to take a shower and call it a day. Will you please let the others know?"

Helene nodded, reached for the radio, and hailed the rest of the workforce. Ethan saluted in thanks with two fingers and went to the locker room, where he took an ice cube from the refrigerator's freezer compartment and popped it in his mouth. He focused intently, remembering to keep spitting out the melted ice. Then he undressed and stood under the cold shower for a quarter of an hour. Each time he thought of Abel and the incident, his stomach turned. He retched again.

He decided categorically that he would think only about the fact that he would have time for his wife over the next few days. They would be able to spend a long weekend at Fontainebleau, wandering the woods all day, admiring the endless boulders. While they were there, they could cheer on the Bleausards as they climbed, or picnic for hours and make love in the open air, or visit the château again.

On the way home, he stopped briefly at the flower store and bought a small bouquet. It was nothing special, but Ethan knew how Annette loved flowers. The first thing he would do when he got home was have a coffee with her. They had moved into their new apartment a few weeks ago, and she was furnishing it while he was at work. At some point, she was going to look for a permanent job again. But first they would drink coffee together. He smiled at the thought, even though he felt unusually weak. That would surely be because he had thrown up. He gagged again. No, he wouldn't think about the incident with Abel.

Annette. Weekend. Fontainebleau. Coffee!

As he arrived at the apartment door, he had to lean against the door-frame. Why was he suddenly so unspeakably tired? And why was he so cold? It was a sunny day in March, and spring was clearly on the way. Besides, he was wearing his thick jacket. And yet he was shivering. Was he experiencing a drop in body temperature after the shower? That hadn't happened in months.

Ethan could not put his key in the keyhole, no matter how hard he tried. The door soon opened as if of its own accord, and Annette was staring back at him. "You look awful." Her expression and tone of voice told him she was worried.

"I'm not feeling well." He staggered into the apartment, Annette supporting him and walking him straight to the bedroom. Then she helped him into bed. As she undressed him, he mumbled, "Hit a barrel of radioactive waste. I hope I wasn't exposed to radiation for too long. But it didn't seem to be damaged."

He kept quiet about the fact that his vision had now blurred. "I drove right on in and reported it." Ethan didn't want to worry Annette unnecessarily.

After he had lain down, she took off his socks and pulled the covers over him. She wanted to kiss him, but he turned his head away. "Don't! Abel . . . he . . ." he began but couldn't finish the sentence.

Annette tensed at the mention of the name, clenching her fists. "What has that crétin done now? Did *he* kiss you?"

Ethan screwed up his face. "No, not quite that bad. He threw dog shit at me, and it hit me right in the mouth." He was too exhausted to feel any disgust at the thought of the incident. "Do we have any ice cubes?"

"Yes, I'll get you some," his wife said, and went to the refrigerator.

When Annette returned to the room with the ice cubes, he was fast asleep. She decided to wait and see how his condition developed. He was lying peacefully in bed, breathing a little more shallowly than usual, but she put that down to the flu or whatever was affecting him. Then she set about unpacking the last of the moving boxes.

It was late afternoon when she entered the bedroom with some fresh broth. Ethan was pale and asleep.

"Ethan. Ethan!" she said. But she could not rouse him. His breathing was barely perceptible, but his pulse was racing. She lifted the blanket to wipe away his sweat. When she saw his body, she took a few steps back in horror. Beneath his ashen skin was a dark web that hadn't been there two hours ago.

Annette looked again. She was not mistaken. As if cast by some demonic fisherman, a gray-black net was encircling his body. She watched the spiky offshoots of the web working their way millimeter by millimeter down his neck and shoulders toward his torso. Then she dropped the blanket and rushed to the phone.

About twenty minutes later, sirens blaring and blue lights flickering, they were speeding toward the hospital. The paramedics had allowed Annette to ride along. Her throat felt constricted. Tears burned hot trails down her cheeks. Ethan was being given saline intravenously and oxygen through a mask. She watched his condition deteriorate rapidly as the veiny web reached his temples and continued to spread. His neck, throat and limbs were enmeshed in it. In less than an hour, it will have engulfed his face.

Ethan was barely breathing. Annette watched closely as the paramedics examined him. One look into his eyes revealed that his irises had largely disappeared and had been replaced by a milky white substance.

When a paramedic shone a flashlight into his pupils, they did not respond. A test for radioactivity was negative, Annette had been told. So, the only possible cause of his condition was poisoning, assuming he hadn't been carrying the strange disease for some time, the young woman in a Croix-Rouge jacket told her. Every now and then his body twitched.

He was taken to the emergency room's intensive care unit. The hospital staff took blood and tissue samples while Annette watched through a window. He was then isolated. She was also quarantined for the time being. It was conceivable that she had been infected. She was given her own room, but she vehemently resisted all precautions and joined Ethan in his.

A hastily assembled medical panel asked her whether her husband had been to any unusual places lately, where he had vacationed in recent years, and whether he had traveled to any exotic countries.

She cried her eyes out as she answered, watching Ethan's chest rise and fall more and more weakly. Something told her that there would be no salvation for him. Still, a last vestige of hope remained, fueled by the desire for a shared future.

At 11:04 p.m. Central European Time, Ethan Boileau's heart failed, and the doctor on duty pronounced him dead after having tried to resuscitate him for a half hour. They removed his oxygen mask and pulled the needles out of his body. Annette stood by, staring into space. She was vaguely aware of her and Ethan's relatives being notified. Half a dozen family members had gathered outside the room where his lifeless body lay. Because of the possible risk of infection, she was the only one allowed into the room with the deceased.

After a while, Annette let them know through the glass that she was doing reasonably well, albeit devastated. She pulled a chair up to Ethan's bed and sat down. Then she took his hand in hers and began stroking it absentmindedly. She was infinitely tired and rested her head on his rigid thigh for a moment.

She must have dozed off for a moment. When she awoke, her wristwatch showed 1:20 a.m.

She looked around and saw through the glass that family members were still sitting in the hallway. Some were crying silently under the cold fluorescent lighting.

Suddenly, she became aware that it was an impulse that had awakened her, but she was too dazed to remember exactly what it had been.

Then, as if in a dream, Ethan's fingers moved slightly. If she hadn't been holding his hand, she wouldn't have noticed. She couldn't believe her senses and stared at his face, spellbound. His eyelids were flickering! She was not imagining it.

His fingers twitched noticeably, and he began to breathe again.

Startled, she shot to her feet, knocking the chair over. She put her hand on the place where his heart was and felt it beating. Joy and shock mingled inside her.

Ethan's arm moved. His fingers rested awkwardly on her forearm.

"Ethan, dearest," she put in.

His fist twitched. Suddenly, his fingers gripped her tightly, digging painfully into her skin. Annette cried out. His eyes opened and she saw that they were completely white.

He sniffed. His features changed, his muscles tightened, but his coordination was all wrong, as if he didn't know how this body worked. He tried to sit up but failed.

Ethan bared his teeth, revealing dark gray gums behind bloodless lips, and he stared blankly at his horrified wife.

He pulled her arm roughly, brought it to his mouth and bit into it. Annette didn't know whether her scream was one of pain or fear.

In the nocturnal silence of the hospital, a scream rang out like an alarm from one of the emergency treatment rooms in the intensive care unit where Raphael was working his shift. He was so startled that he dropped his tray of freshly rinsed cups and glasses. It dropped, clattering to the kitchenette's tiled floor, shattering glass and china.

The young nurse ignored the chaos of dented sheet metal and broken glass. He quickly stepped out into the corridor and looked around.

Someone roared again, but this time it was more intense, louder, more desperate. It shook him to the core. Through three glass walls separating two patient rooms from the corridor, he saw a woman trying to break free from the grip of the patient lying in front of her. Her forearm was red with blood. She was struggling with all her might to free herself.

The man, who Raphael had heard had been pronounced dead an hour before, had bitten into it like a wild animal. His whole body was twitching and rearing, as if in enormous sexual excitement.

The woman screamed again. Raphael sprinted off. He ignored the quarantine warning and pushed open the security door. Without thinking, he threw himself between her and the patient. From the other side of the shatterproof glass, the horrified relatives watched on. The nurse tried to push the man's head back into the pillows with his elbow and at the same time free the woman's arm with both hands. Her screams paralyzed him. After a jerk, the biter let go his victim, who, suddenly free, staggered back and fell into the corner of the room. Dark blood was running from her fingers onto the floor. Raphael watched the woman stare stunned at her wound. A large chunk of flesh was missing, white bone and sinew standing out clearly against the red, blood-streaked tissue.

On the assumption that someone's name refers principally to his personality, then Ethan Boileau could not be said to have existed since 11:04 p.m. the previous day, the time of the patient's death. After his resurrection, he existed less than ever. The personality that inhabited the body from then on had nothing in common with him. In addition, some of his DNA had changed. His distorted facial features were the only remaining testament to Ethan's former existence.

He would go down in the annals as patient zero, the unfortunate individual who had brought the black plague of modernity down upon humankind. Hardly anyone was interested in the fact that he was completely innocent. And the fact that his wife, whom he loved above all, became the second victim of the epidemic would only be a note in the margins of the story.

The fact that Raphael, the nurse who had rushed to her aid, could have prevented the spread of the epidemic if only he had kept the door locked—no one remembered that. Because hardly anyone who might have testified to this survived day zero.

The short glance Raphael gave Annette was his undoing. The sick creature took advantage of his lapse in concentration, seizing the nurse's full hair. He tore at it and brought his bloodied mouth to the neck of his next victim.

Blood splattered again as he caught the carotid artery. Raphael managed to tear himself away. He felt warm blood soaking his green uniform, and his will to survive overcame his panic. He quickly jumped to one of the cabinets in the side room, rummaging through the shelves until he found what he was looking for.

The nurse tore open the package, opened the bottle inside, and dripped the viscous liquid generously over his wound. In an instant, the blood flow dried up.

Then he turned to the woman who had stumbled after him to safety, away from her wild-eyed husband. Raphael treated her with the drug as well. She screamed even louder as the disinfecting liquid burned and closed the open strands of nerve and blood. When he turned back to tie the rabid patient to the bed, he realized with horror that it was empty.

The infected man's attack on Annette and the nurse had lasted less than a minute. Ethan's body, now a host organism, fell out of the hospital bed. The viruslike mutation of the fungus continued extending its control over the host. It quickly learned to control the limbs of the body it had taken over, but it would be several minutes before it mastered walking semi-upright.

So, Ethan crawled out of the room on all fours, in search of food and driven by the desire to reproduce. If it had been known at the time that the radioactive radiation in the landfill had facilitated the mutation of a fungus that had previously attacked an ant and used its body to reproduce, we would probably have understood immediately why patient zero was able to crawl away in the first few minutes after turning. But because no one in a hospital expected to be attacked in the middle of the night by someone covered in blood crawling on all fours, there were further casualties. Fortunately, the incident at the landfill had been noted in Ethan's medical records, so in the days that followed, investigators were able to reconstruct the incident with a certain amount of accuracy.

On day one, they tracked down Abel. However, his incomprehensible speech meant they got scarcely anywhere. The fact that Ethan had marked the exact spot on the map where he had come across the illegally dumped canister enabled the forensic scientist to identify point zero. Fortunately, work at the landfill had ceased when the radioactive container turned up, so the waste had not been moved around any farther.

Ethan's vomit and the torn black bag containing dog excrement—they were both found in the marked area. The finds were shipped to the Pasteur Institute in Paris, which specializes in virology, for examination, but analysis was temporarily delayed. A whole weekend passed, followed by a mass epidemic and countless deaths in Melun, before the researchers began to study the evidence.

Meanwhile, the epidemic spread rapidly. It extended outward in a circle, reaching the capital only a few days after the outbreak. The greater density of people and the more sophisticated infrastructure of the metropolis accelerated the outbreak, and neither the police nor the army were able to stop it.

In the meantime, the Pasteur Institute's investigation was moving ahead at full speed even though the researchers themselves kept falling victim to the epidemic. They brought in expert colleagues from other institutes, and after the plague had reached Russia and Scandinavia four weeks later and almost completely devastated the rest of Europe, the origins of the disease were known.

The mutation in the fungus was caused by a highly dangerous cocktail in the feces of a dog suspected of having rabies, from which traces of *Ophiocordyceps unilateralis* had been extracted that were then exposed to radioactive radiation for a long period of time. The fungus aggressively tried to take over additional living space. Ethan had no chance against the pathogen, which kept on learning and continued to mutate with each new host. Hence, it was able to gain control more quickly by shutting down the organs that were the most crucial to the immune system. The host body did not die after becoming infected but was shut down as far as possible until the pathogen had absolute power over it. Like a rebooted computer, the body continued to operate, only with different software. In subsequent infections, this information was even passed on in the genome. As a result, each generation was faster and more evolved than the one before, and this made it unpredictable, enabling it to spread.

And so, shortly after his transformation, Ethan roamed the hallways of the hospital like a mangy dog, seeking new victims to help the pathogen thrive. He devoured the pieces of meat he bit off them and had almost made it out of the building when he was challenged by the security guards. After attacking and infecting them as well, he was liberated by a shot to the head.

About an hour later, Annette, Raphael, and all the others whom Ethan had injured also died. Since they had been infected directly through the bloodstream, the incubation period was correspondingly short. In the confusion that reigned in the hospital, their metamorphosis went unnoticed. After another twenty minutes, they returned to life as differ-ent beings. The resulting chaos was repeated millions of times over the days that followed, laying waste almost the entire human civilization of Europe.

CHAPTER 3.2

INITIUM

Holy shit!" Patrick voiced exactly what we were all thinking after Nadine's explanation. "And each generation of zombies can access information about their predecessors in real time?" He smacked the palm of his hand theatrically against his thigh as the realization hit him.

"And that's why some are faster and more upright than others and behave in a more coordinated way."

Doctor Koller replied, "That's what I said. And not only that, the incubation period also gets shorter from generation to generation, as well as the transformation period," she added, continuing before Patrick could conjecture further, "which does not mean, however, that in the generations to come, this will only be a matter of seconds. Even radioactively mutated fungi have to obey the laws of nature." She was certainly a talented lecturer.

"Which are those then?" Patrick continued his inquiries.

We looked skeptically in his direction. "Are you some kind of biologist then?" I asked.

"What?" he replied defensively.

Nadine continued unperturbed. "Like all living beings, zombies are subject to the metabolism of the host body, even if things are different for them. And although the metamorphosis reduces their sense of pain, they still die if you damage the key organs—the heart, for example. However, this does not stop them from continuing their attacks until shortly before they collapse. And, as we have observed several times, they don't only feed on the tissues of healthy people! They become cannibals as soon as a zombie from their own ranks dies. So, they can survive longer than usual."

"Are you sure this scourge didn't escape from a military test lab?" Patrick was on top form, but seeing us staring, quickly added, "Wasn't being serious."

Nadine ignored him. "In uninfected humans, when the central nervous system sustains a shock, it shuts down operations. With zombies, this process fails. That's why you have to move quickly: Destroy their brains!"

"So, the pain that leads to a shock reaction in normal people doesn't have any impact on zombies at all," Patrick summarized.

Now we understood our experiences with the sufferers.

Waltraud reiterated the key question Franca had posed earlier, "What about the vaccine?"

"As I mentioned, once you're infected, there's no going back. But prophylaxis will soon be possible. At the moment, we cannot assume that it will be one hundred percent effective. It'll take us several more weeks to make the serum, and then it'll have to be tested. And that'll have to be on humans . . ."

"Where are you getting your test subjects? Are there enough people living in Berlin who would volunteer?" Waltraud asked.

Nadine seemed to have expected this question. Nevertheless, she looked sheepishly past the camera, as if choosing the right answer from many possible options.

Then she decided it was pointless to lie. "This is a solvable problem. There are a few people we would consider as test subjects. Before the state of emergency was imposed here in Berlin, and you couldn't get in or out, there was a conference of advocates for animal testing. These people are of the opinion that it is permissible to use living creatures for medical purposes, even without their consent. The participants are still in town. And since, as I said, the tests can't be done on animals anyway . . ."

Once again, Patrick spoke for all of us. "Oh, fuck!"

After a short pause, the virologist began cleaning her glasses on a corner of her lab coat and said wearily, "Do you know what it's like in Berlin right now? Can you imagine seventy-five percent of the population being dead or infected? And across the whole of Europe? About eighty percent! And those are just the favorable projections. The future of the entire human species is at stake. So please spare me the moralizing, at least when it comes to pity for people who themselves advocate this way of working."

No one dared to say anything in response. Some of us nodded in understanding, some looked away shamefacedly. The horror that this information would have caused in another time quickly evaporated in view of the global situation. Our moral codes shifted with the social realities, especially since the researchers would not be working against the personal convictions of the—albeit involuntary—test subjects.

"None of us is judging you, Doc." Waltraud shook her head resignedly. "I'm sure you'll do what's necessary to help the survivors! Even though we are thousands of kilometers away, if there's anything we can do, let us know. And please keep us posted on how the vaccine is coming along."

"Thank you, Waltraud. Thank you all. As soon as something comes up, I'll let you know in good time. See you soon."

"See you soon," we called out, one or two of us adding, "thank you!" Waltraud disconnected.

Franca gave us a moment to digest this newfound knowledge. But before we got too caught up in brooding, she brought us back to reality. She would not allow us to become demoralized or lose our will to survive.

"Backup, you and I will continue practicing with the gun in the basement. Patrick and Eva, check the perimeter. Waltraud and Jens, check the shelf life of the provisions. Nils, kitchen?" Everyone nodded and set about complying with their orders.

In the basement, Franca first had me run through again what I had practiced that morning. Then, when she was more or less satisfied, she showed me how to load the pistol.

She noticed my attention was drifting now and then, because she had to raise her voice a few times to ensure I was still concentrating on what she was saying. I was preoccupied with Doctor Koller's report.

But when I was allowed to shoot live ammunition—for the first time in my life—my concentration returned in full.

Before I fired the first shot, I had to stuff my ears with paper rolled into pellets. Franca did the same.

"Unlike dry firing, you're going to have to handle recoil now. It's not a large caliber weapon, and it won't be extreme. But it could still rip the gun from your hand if you don't hold it tight enough. You can't hold your arm too stiffly either, though, because you'll yank the gun and miss your target." I nodded, impatient to be allowed to shoot at last.

"Aim over the rear sight, and fire!"

With the gun in my fist pointed at the wall of sandbags, I took aim at the misshapen dark dot painted on one of the bags.

Bam! As Franca had predicted, the recoil almost tore the pistol out of my hand. A small hole had appeared next to the dot, though. Sand was trickling out of it onto the ground.

"Very good! Fire!" *Bam!* This time I held the pistol tighter. As I stiffened my arm, the recoil distorted my aim, and I missed the target by half a meter.

"Try to strike a healthy balance between flexibility and rigidity. The better you do that, the more accurately you'll shoot."

I landed my next shots directly in the painted area. The feeling of power, of superiority, was nothing like what I had felt in the morning—it was far stronger.

I now had a better understanding of the fascination that firearms exerted over some people. I fired until the magazine was empty. Then Franca instructed me to reload. "Now fire one shot first, wait half a second, and fire two right after each other."

After I had fired three shots in quick succession, my ears were pounding violently despite my improvised ear protectors, but I immediately understood what was behind this approach.

The first shot allowed me to see where I had hit, so that I could readjust the second and third shots as necessary and thus achieve a better hit rate. I fired three more magazines until Franca was satisfied and thought we'd done enough for today. A large amount of sand had seeped out of the opening onto the floor. There was nothing left of the painted dot.

For a second, I was reluctant to hand over the gun.

On their return from their inspection, Patrick and Eva reported that there was one place where the fence could use some reinforcement. However, this sounded more like a job creation initiative than a serious vulnerability. Waltraud and Jens had checked the food and arranged it to ensure we would consume the ripest fruit first. Nils was whipping the kitchen into shape. Franca was going to focus on her weapons, cleaning, oiling, and loading them.

There was nothing more for me to do until dinner. So I got them to tell me the exact spot where the fence needed repairing.

Nils walked with me to the garage and thrust a heavy metal case into my hand. "In it you'll find iron pins the length of your arm and some wire. If you can't handle it, let me know and we'll try the welder," he said, starting to tinker with one of his vehicles.

I hoped this would not be necessary. A welder would only attract the stinkers. However, it turned out the place in question could be easily repaired with the wire. Afterward, I returned the toolbox.

A book in my hand, it took me barely ten minutes to fall asleep by the pool in the shade of the house.

When I woke up in the late afternoon, I noticed Franca dozing on one of the loungers on the other side of the pool. She was, unsurprisingly, wearing a black bikini and had placed her HK on the floor beside her. Her muscular body lay completely relaxed in the early evening sun.

From my berth, I heard movement in the kitchen. Nils was cooking for tonight. I decided to help him. Without making a noise and waking Franca, I went first to my room, took a quick shower, and put on my new clothes. The pants fit well, but the T-shirt was a little too big.

In the kitchen, having consulted with Nils, I finely sliced a few cloves of garlic and halved three handfuls of cherry tomatoes. He had prepared a large pot for spaghetti. The water inside was almost at boiling point.

I picked up the pasta and went to put it in.

"What are you doing?" he snapped at me. "You have to wait until the water is really boiling. Otherwise, it won't taste good." I hesitated. It was preposterous: humanity had been almost wiped out and he was worried about how the spaghetti would taste if I put it into the water eleven seconds too early.

So, we waited an endless minute for it to "boil properly." Nils sprinkled some salt into the bubbling liquid while I took a large pan from the lower cupboard and poured in some olive oil. Once it was hot enough, I tossed the garlic and tomatoes in it until the slices were golden and the tomato halves had shriveled. I then added a fair number of small, dried chilies.

Nils grinned gleefully when he saw how many of them were swimming in the simmering oil. Then he mixed the finished sauce with the pasta.

I set the table. Together we distributed the spaghetti onto preheated plates.

Slowly, the kitchen filled up. "Smells great," Patrick said, sniffing his plate.

Nils spoke, pointing his index finger at me, "I have to warn you: Backup threw a few too many chilies into the pan. It may well be pretty spicy."

"Now don't exaggerate. There are seven of us, it won't be that hot," I defended myself.

"I don't mind," Patrick said, a little too confidently for my taste.

Jens added more to his plate. He picked up an above-average amount—that was putting it mildly—with his fork and began to roll the long noodles into a ball.

Nils said, "How do you manage to eat so much and stay such a bean-pole? Look at me. I only eat about half what you do, but I'm sure I weigh twice as much. And we're about the same size." Jens's portion was so substantial, he couldn't believe it.

"That's because I've been climbing for so long. My body knows that and doesn't put on extra weight. Everything that it doesn't need, it mercilessly excretes."

"Or your metabolism is genetically different from Nils's," Patrick, sitting across from me, interjected.

"There he goes again; our 'biologist.'" I scoffed, putting air quotes around the last word with my fingers. As expected, he raised his middle finger in return.

After just a few mouthfuls of spaghetti, I realized that Nils's warning had been right. Beads of sweat began to form all over my face.

An unusually large amount of water was drunk. The bread on the table disappeared in no time, so I kept on having to fetch more.

"It's good for the digestion," I said between two deep breaths.

"How much garlic did you put in? Are we fighting vampires too now?" Patrick wiped the sweat from under his eyes with a napkin.

Without looking up, Eva turned to him and said, "You're eating a lot of bread with your pasta. What's the matter? Too spicy for you?"

Concealing his faintness, he drew in air between his teeth while also replying, "No, what makes you think that? There's just a little too much oil for me . . ."

The rest didn't join in our conversation, as they were busy trying to avoid becoming short of breath. Nils sat up and took a big gulp of water straight from the carafe. "You can taste something else besides chilies? My taste buds have been burned away."

"Don't be like that; it's just a few little chilies." I was also having to pause between bites, but I didn't let on.

Despite the unusually high spice level, every last bite of pasta was eaten.

We had finished our meal. Outside, the sun had disappeared, and the first stars were flickering in the gathering darkness. Patrick and I checked the access gate. Jens secured the house for the night.

In the candlelight, the living room looked as if it had come from another era. Franca sat at the center of the group, making plans for tomorrow, and listing what was on the agenda.

". . . Food looks good; so do water supplies. Ammunition could be topped up a bit. But I have no idea where we'll find any. Probably in police stations. Or one of the army bases, but only if they've been abandoned. Otherwise, we risk getting shot. I'll head for the northwestern villages tomorrow with Nils and see if we can find something. The Mercedes will do. It's not as conspicuous as the pickup."

The group nodded in agreement, even though no one welcomed the fact that only a small group was going.

We discussed the route briefly, and what to do if Franca and Nils stayed away longer. Then we sat back and fell silent, everyone lost in their own thoughts.

When Jens interrupted the relaxed stillness, everyone looked over at him. "Waltraud and I think Franca's suggestion is . . . very good."

It took us a while to understand what he meant.

"And we also have a story we'd like to tell . . . That is, if you want to hear it."

Everyone nodded.

"Go for it," Franca said encouragingly.

"And don't leave out any details," Patrick added ambiguously.

Waltraud bit her lower lip in an exaggeratedly lascivious manner and gave Jens a come-to-bed look. He grinned. Eva rolled her eyes and folded her arms in annoyance.

Amused, I sat back, but soon realized this story was not going to be a comedy.

CHAPTER 4

WALTRAUD AND JENS

This is the story of Waltraud and Jens, which starts about a year pre ini-tium. They meet at a campsite in Arco, north of Lake Garda. There's an unwritten law encouraging hikers to be especially sociable when camping, and so people make friends quickly, and this ensures they get to know each other on the first evening after their arrival.

Waltraud's friends notice two Dutchmen setting up their tent next door and invite them over for a beer. They shake hands, pass around drinks, exchange glances. Jens and Waltraud are soon engrossed in conversation. It isn't necessarily love at first sight, but it's close, and the two of them are afire with enthusiasm for each other.

Over breakfast the next day, he, an experienced and patient mountaineer, offers to teach her the basics of climbing and to take her on some climbs suitable for a beginner. She, impulsive and self-confident, immediately agrees.

In the early morning, they go to an easier climbing area. Jens instructs Waltraud on how to use slings, nuts, quickdraws, and the like until she is ready to make their first joint ascent. He decides on a multipitch route. The terraced, sloping climb, rated only 5.6 on the difficulty scale, should present no problem, he thinks. The athletic Norwegian should be able to cope with it. But for her, attempting her first vertical climb with a rope, helmet, and other equipment is not so straightforward. At every point where mental effort is required, she encourages herself at the top of her voice.

So, she screams her way over the most difficult sections of the face like a high-end professional. Jens, relaxed and sympathetic, offers well-meaning advice from above, to which she—a typical novice climber—turns a deaf ear, cursing, or to which she is unable to follow due to her inexperience.

On a weekend like this, the climbing areas around Arco are often filled with several hundred rock-jocks. Rarely has a climbing duo given such a likeable and exhilarating performance there, those who witness it claim. From then on, if not before, it is clear they are destined for each other.

After the vacation in Arco, they visit each other at least once a month, in Oslo, where Waltraud lives, or in Jens's hometown of Rotterdam. In July, they begin to make more serious plans for the future. They spend their summer vacation in Sardinia, and their winter vacation skiing in the Dolomites. After that, they decide to go traveling together the following summer. First, they want to hike from France across the Pyrenees to Spain, and then cross over to Mallorca for the climbing. Jens has long been tempted to try some of the difficult deepwater soloing along the rocky coast, where only the questionable safety of the deep sea protects climbers from falls. If this vacation turns out as well as all the previous ones, they will put their money where their mouths are and move in together.

Another thing they have in common is their fondness for eighties and nineties cinema. Hardly a day goes by without Waltraud quoting at least one film that fits the situation.

They tell their employers they want to take a sabbatical year, and both requests are granted. Three months later, they are on their way across the Pyrenees. They have planned a tailor-made route based on photos of the most beautiful places they could find on the internet. They have marked the route on two maps. At the end of May, they meet in Perpignan and take a bus to the northern edge of Andorra. Dressed in their best hiking gear and carrying state-of-the-art backpacks, they begin hiking from Lavelanet toward Spain, on their southwest route.

In addition to their planned sabbatical, they want to treat themselves to some digital downtime, so they switch off their mobile devices, stowing them away in the depths of their backpacks. They deliberately avoid towns and larger villages. Only now and then do they stop in small settlements to replenish their food supplies. Drinking water is not a problem at this time of year in the Pyrenees because they come across crystal-clear lakes and fast-flowing mountain streams. The only concession they make to the digital world is at checkouts, paying for their purchases with a credit card.

They spend the nights, snuggled close together, in their lightweight tent or in remote bivouac huts. Every day, they rejoice in dazzling sunrises and magical sunsets.

About a month after the start of their hike, they get caught in a storm that is supposed to last a week. Having initially been hounded and soaked to the skin by the thunderstorm for half a day, they finally reach a mountain hut where they find the refuge they have been longing for.

It is their fourth day at the croft. Jens takes the pot of boiling water from the hearth and pours it into two soup bowls waiting on the dining table, where it is quickly absorbed by the dry rations. It will take about ten minutes for the contents to become edible.

The fire is crackling in the fireplace, its warmth spreading comfortably through the room. Jens watches lovingly as Waltraud, who has just been outside to fetch firewood, hangs her clothes near it to dry.

There is a good-size stock of firewood behind the hut. Doubtless it is regularly replenished by a ranger from the national park. Nevertheless, they use it sparingly.

Once again, Jens is overcome with happiness at being by her side. Dressed only in a T-shirt, panties, and socks, she stands by the fire and lays a log on the embers. Sparks fly up the chimney. She pulls her hand back quickly, turns around, and looks pensively out the window.

The wood beneath Jens's bare feet has been worn smooth and seems alive. He notices the fine grain of the floorboards with every step he takes. Waltraud sits on the wide windowsill, looking out into the fog. Without turning around, she says, "Where do you think we should live when we move in together? Holland or Norway?"

Jens ponders his answer for a moment before moving over to stand by her at the window. With the back of his hand, he tenderly strokes the skin of her bare thigh. Leaning against the window frame, he follows her gaze out into the gray murk.

"As I said, I would say it depends where the best jobs are. Or we could start our own company, wherever we like best." They have had this conversation many times, and she should know what his answers will be.

But she is skeptical. "I'm not sure it's a good idea to be partners and run a company together at the same time. It's bound to go wrong!"

He knows this isn't what she thinks, but it feels incredibly good to take issue with her when she occasionally pretends to have doubts about their relationship and their future together. It fills Jens with lightness and confidence when she looks at him out of the corners of her eyes and breaths almost ethereally. "Do you really mean that?" Every time she does, he falls in love with her all over again.

"I'm sure it'd work out." Without feeling the slightest twinge of doubt, he shares his thoughts. "If it were up to me, you'd do the technical stuff, and I'd do the creative stuff, in line with our skills. Then we'd hire someone to build and manage the customer base, then someone for the office . . . But ultimately, it doesn't matter. Because no matter what we do together—it can't help but work. Wherever we are."

He feels her gaze resting on him.

"Do you really mean that?"

He leans over and kisses her gently, murmuring almost inaudibly, "I love you."

Her eyes close, and she whispers back, "I know."

A few minutes later they are lying naked in front of the fireplace, entwined in a tangle of clothes and sleeping bags.

"What was that? Did you hear that?"

Waltraud sits up in bed, wide awake. "Jens! Wake up!" Her heart is racing, but she doesn't know why. The reddish light of the dying embers illuminates the outlines of the objects in the hut. Its dwindling warmth is powerless against the fear that is entwining itself around her mind. It is a few seconds before she realizes what has woken her from sleep.

A scream?

A cry, but whether it came from an animal or even a human being, she can't say for sure.

She shakes his shoulder. "Jens! Did you hear that?"

"Hm-hmmm? What?" he mumbles, half asleep.

Another piercing shriek shatters the nocturnal quiet.

"There it is again. You must have heard that!"

"Yes. A pheasant or something . . . Go back to sleep, it's the middle of the night!"

"No, listen carefully!" She glances at the pale display on her wristwatch. It's about an hour before sunrise. The rain isn't drumming as hard on the roof of the hut anymore. She wonders when it will finally stop.

Tensely, she listens to the darkness. She hardly dares breathe. Once again, she hears a cry of pain on the wind. Or is it anger?

Branches crunch close by. It reminds her vaguely of the crackling of the fireplace. But this urgent sound sparks pure horror in her. She takes the initiative. "Come on, we need to pack!" Jens gives a short groan, struggles out of his sleeping bag, and pulls the backpacks from under the bed. Waltraud is grateful he doesn't debate the decision. Quietly, they stuff the still-warm bags inside.

One minute later, they are at the door in full gear.

She reaches for the wooden door handle and unlocks the lock. He places his hand on her shoulder. She hears him whisper, "It'll be lighter in about a half hour. It might not be so smart to set off in the dark, you know." During the storm, she has watched him studying the map over and over to escape boredom, memorizing their planned route. "Let's wait a while," he suggests.

As if disagreeing with his suggestion, lightning flashes outside. An enormous thunderclap crashes, making the windowpanes shake. Waltraud jumps. The scream that follows is clearly identifiable as human. And it is close by, so close that she would probably be able to see the person if it were a little brighter and she looked out the door. Another glaring flash lights up the forest on the mountainside, followed by another terrifying clap of thunder.

And then—absolute silence. Not a sound, even from the rain. Waltraud can hear her heart pounding like a jungle drum.

The door of the hut swings open with a crash and a drenched silhouette comes into view. The shock paralyzes them both for a second. The intruder stumbles over the threshold and falls headlong, grunting. They dodge him, startled, fleeing around the table toward the door. Simultaneously, the figure gets up and throws itself onto the bed where they were sleeping just moments before, shredding the mattress with its bare hands. Waltraud and Jens rush out into the cold together. Another flash of lightning lights up the mountainside. As if in a nightmare, they see dozens of swaying figures staggering toward them up the slope. They are wearing threadbare, ragged shirts and pants. Some are barefoot and others are nearly naked. Their eyes have no irises. Many seem to have injuries, but they are obviously not bothered by them. Their skin is the complexion of the sky on a cold autumn day.

Jens and Waltraud bolt. Over the thudding of their own feet, they can hear the snapping of trampled branches and screams of rage from the horrifying creatures close behind them. Waltraud hopes she won't trip over a stone or a root. Running, Jens holds one of his hiking poles before him like a rapier. It's not clear what will happen if their pursuers catch up with them. But the noises they're making scare her to death. They continue to charge along the trail, sensing rather than seeing it. They flee relentlessly uphill, toward the east, where the sky is slowly brightening. After some time, Waltraud notices that the sounds behind them are diminishing. They are faster than their eerie pursuers. The rain stops completely, and the first rays of sunlight break through the clouds. In the clear air, washed clean by the rain, Waltraud sees the sun dispersing the plumes of mist. The sky is soon a warm orange; even the undersides of the clouds are glowing. The path before them is getting easier and easier to see, not least because there are fewer trees. After a few kilometers, when they think they might be halfway safe, they stop on a straight part of the trail, immediately falling into each other's arms.

"What the hell was that?" gasps Waltraud between breaths. She can't ever remember feeling such fear.

Jens is trembling; she can feel it clearly as she hugs him. Can he also feel her knees shaking? She feels his strength as he holds her more tightly.

"No idea, but nothing good, that's for sure. What the hell did that guy do to the mattress?" he says breathlessly.

She doesn't want to think about what would have happened if he'd found them sleeping on it.

Above them, some stones are kicked loose, clattering thunderously into the depths. Waltraud starts. She looks up and sees a billy goat perched on a rocky outcrop, contemplating its kingdom in the dawning day. He lifts his horns confidently, sniffing the air. Suddenly, he pricks up his ears, listening.

Seconds later, he flees in a mad rush, disappearing at breakneck speed up the steep slope. Waltraud and Jens recognize the signs and take to their heels again. From here on, the path drops slightly.

Three kilometers later, it leads them into a ravine. Larger and larger patches of blue appear between the receding wisps of cloud. The sun rises higher, bathing the stone walls in yellow light. They quench their thirst together at a mountain stream and frantically refill their water bottles.

Despite the coolness of the morning, they are sweating. All at once, the inhuman sounds echo over to them from far away. The Norwegian is confused for a moment, not knowing exactly where the sounds are coming from. But she has no choice but to flee.

The echoes of their pursuers get clearer and clearer, coming at them from both sides of the path.

Waltraud looks around, analyzing their situation. They have minutes at the most before they'll have company. The gorge to the right is a good sixty meters deep and between five and ten meters wide. Farther ahead, the canyon walls seem to be closer together. And something else about this point suddenly catches her attention. She grabs Jens and runs. "Give me the rope! Quick!"

There's no time for formalities. He lets go of her hand, running at full pelt as he takes the lighter half rope out of his backpack. She stops abruptly at the point where the gorge narrows. He hands her the rope. She immediately secures one end tightly around her wrist, tying a thick knot in the other end until it is twice the size of her fist.

Now she can clearly hear the crunching of the pebbles on the path ahead of them. Her fear increases the faster the sounds come toward them. A surging stench of excrement superimposes itself on the fragrance of the natural world washed clean by the rain. She swings the twenty-meter half rope back and forth.

The first figure appears on the path in front of them, with ashen skin and torn feet. It stretches out its arms greedily, beginning its swaying walk. Waltraud continues to swing the loosely wound rope, aiming for the wedge-shaped crevice in the ledge on the opposite wall. She throws. And misses her target by a couple millimeters. Now she must pull twenty meters of rope out of the depths of the gorge.

Jens guesses what she's up to. "FASTER!" he urges, looking back and seeing more of the aggressive creatures coming rapidly toward them. Ten seconds at the most before he'll feel the touch of their claws.

Suddenly, there are so many of them. So many that they are pushing each other off the narrow path into the abyss. The falling ones scream, but, he realizes abruptly, not out of fear. They are shrieking with rage at being cheated of their prey.

Out of the corners of his eyes, he watches Waltraud throw the rope again. It seems to take an eternity for it to reach the other side. All the while, the creatures come relentlessly toward them. Ready to defend himself and Waltraud to the last breath, he secures his footing and raises his hiking pole.

Next to him, she jerks the rope before it even comes to rest. The end with the knot slides deeper into the narrow crevice, catching at last as she was hoping it would. In one fluid motion, she winds the rope around her arm and passes the remainder to him. Jens grabs it and follows her lead. The pale creatures are so close that the pebbles they are kicking up as they walk are bouncing off his boots.

The remainder of the climbing rope is in a tangle in the stones at his feet. If they jump now and it doesn't come free, they might end up hanging over the gorge until they no longer have the strength to hold on. The rope is so thin that it won't be easy to pull themselves up on it. Jens kicks it into the abyss in a desperate attempt to loosen it. It finally comes free, snaking into the depths.

"There is no spoon," he hears Waltraud whisper from her repertoire of movie quotes. Then he feels her kiss on his lips.

One last second. The foremost of the horde fall on their victims with their mouths wide open.

They reek of feces and decay, and their claws clamp tightly onto the pair's jackets and backpacks. Jens's hiking pole is torn from his hand. Waltraud and Jens hold each other desperately, and jump. Their attackers follow in blind fury, staggering into the depths. For several meters, everyone is in free fall. But the jolt, which almost pulls their arms out of their shoulder sockets, enables them to shake themselves free. Horrified, Jens notices more bodies whizzing by close behind him as they swing toward the rutted wall. At the last moment, they lift their feet to absorb the brutal impact of the collision. They slam against it as a single unit, the force of the impact making their joints scream.

Pain races through Jens's body like an electric shock. He loses control for a moment, the rope slipping away from him. Expecting to die, he opens his eyes wide and takes one last look at Waltraud, who seems too dazed to take in what is happening. And then he realizes he is in free fall and has only a few moments to live.

Unexpectedly, his whole life does not pass before his eyes. Instead, he remembers with almost painful clarity how Waltraud and he climbed together for the first time and how he flew to see her in Oslo a few weeks later. He remembers their ski vacation and their first powder snow runs together. He misses all that, and it breaks his heart to be leaving her so soon. They have only just made plans for the future, and he would have loved to see where life was going to take them. In his mind, he says good-bye to everything and lets out a final cry.

Another jolt and the world turns upside down. Jens roars in horror as he sees the wild, foaming river deep below him. How long would it be before he is burst open like a ripe watermelon? Six seconds? Seven?

He screams again and again, and over his despair he hears something else. Even though he has never heard it with such intensity, it seems familiar to him.

Waltraud's voice!

It's Waltraud, screaming, right next to him! No! That can only mean that she's also . . .

Once again, her voice echoes in the narrow gorge, drowning out even the wild shrieks of the creatures.

Waltraud! Now she sounds more aggressive than ever.

"Hang on to something, you fool! Or you'll drag us to our deaths!"

Only then does he notice that the bottom of the gorge is still a long way off and isn't getting any nearer. Confused, he grabs the best rock scale he can get his hands on and pulls himself against the wall.

"Do you want me to pull you up, too?" She's beside herself with anger and effort, her face contorted into a grimace. The left corner of her mouth is drooping, and her distress is clearly visible. She screams again, this time in a strangely deep, almost masculine tone, "Sarah, I got you! Just reach up!" Waltraud sees him rolling his eyes as he recalls the scene from the movie. She's hanging by one arm, the rope sling wrapped around it. Her hand is slowly turning blue as the rope compresses its tissues and blood vessels under the weight of their two bodies. Her free hand is hold-ing one of his backpack straps. When Jens finds a secure placement with his shoes on the steep wall, she lets go of him. Releasing the load on the rope means that she immediately slides half a meter upward. She screams as the jerk rips at the forearm the rope has been wrapped around.

Jens climbs up to her, using his free hand to pull her toward him on the rock face. Here, the wall slopes and is punctuated by large ledges and cracks. She finds a secure foothold beside him and frees herself from the rope. "Can you climb?" he asks, glancing at her arm.

"No, you moron, I let go of the cord because I want to jump down now!"

"This is rope, not cord," he corrects her.

"Well, now I'm going to punch you in the face, smart-ass!"

His shock at her harsh words quickly fades. Just a moment ago, he was convinced they were going to die—*he* was going to die. He immediately replaces that thought with another: They have survived. And he realizes afresh that Waltraud is the person he wants to spend the rest of his life with, because he has now seen her deeply hidden, aggressive side. And he isn't bothered by this, quite the reverse. He's delighted by her sarcastic reaction to extreme situations. And she has just saved his life in one of them!

He laughs, and then leans over and kisses her. "Come on, climb up then!" he says with a grin.

They are nine or ten meters from the path above them. They climb without a belay, but the wall section is easy to handle.

They reach the edge and, relieved, step onto the path that, like the previous one, winds along the mountainside. Their all-weather jackets rustle as they hold each other tenderly.

"What were you thinking, letting go like that? If you don't fancy me anymore, just tell me. No need to commit suicide!" Waltraud half jokes.

"I was just testing you, to see what you'd do in that kind of situation, that's all."

Waltraud widens her eyes theatrically. "Of course, and I'm Mother Teresa. I only saved your sorry ass because I didn't want to carry the rope myself. Luckily, you're as thin as a rake and I could hold you. With one hand!"

He barely stifles a laugh as he expertly coils the half rope and stows it back under the lid of his backpack.

She keeps an eye out for potential dangers, massaging her damaged forearm, to which the blood is gradually returning.

Pretty quickly, her aggressive mood evaporates. Jens straightens up, shouldering his backpack. She suddenly snuggles up to him and whispers in his ear, as if she wants to avoid being overheard by someone nearby, "Don't do that again, okay?" Tenderly, she puts her arms around his neck.

"I don't plan to. Only if you're in the vicinity."

"Shut up, you idiot!" she retorts affectionately, hugging him tighter. They hold the hug for almost a minute, until they have shaken off most of the shock. They turn and look at the other side of the ravine without breaking their embrace. The path there is teeming with bloodthirsty creatures, clutching after them into the void. They have realized there is no way they can get to their prey, so they are lashing out, clumsily, furiously. Their screams gradually fade to guttural hisses.

"Are you thinking what I'm thinking?" asks Jens.

"That's the weirdest thing that's ever happened to me," Waltraud replies, nodding.

"Do you think they'll follow us?"

"For sure. We can only hope there's no bridge farther down. Can't remember seeing one on the map, though."

"Okay, let's go!" he urges.

Following the path a few hundred meters, they enter a dense coniferous forest that shields them from the gaze of the greedy creatures. Jens appreciates its luminous greens more intensely than ever before. "Let me take a quick look at the map. I'm not sure where we are anymore," he explains, pulling out the trail map. He traces an imaginary line with his finger, thinking aloud. "Yesterday we were here in the cabin, today we came this way, crossed the gorge, and now we should be about . . . here. The next village is there, about seven kilometers away." He points to a small circle on the map.

"Are you serious about going back to civilization?" she asks skeptically.

"We need to report the incident to someone. Get help. We've been cut off from the outside world for weeks, and we have no idea what's going on out there. And what if there are more of them?"

He raises his arm, pointing in the direction they have come. "Someone has to do something about them!"

Waltraud nods in agreement. Then she pulls her backpack off her shoulders, rummaging through it frantically. "We still have our phones," she explains, holding hers up triumphantly.

But when she tries to turn it on, it won't work. Her bafflement quickly gives way to realization: "We haven't charged it once in the last few weeks. My battery is dead." Meanwhile, Jens has pulled his out, too. "Mine's at eight percent—but there's no network. How could there be, we're at the ass-end of nowhere."

"Never mind," Waltraud interjects, "we'll walk to the village. Let's see what there is there."

They drink and leave the trail to relieve themselves before heading south again.

After a few sharp turns, they lose sight of the other side. A few minutes later, the screams of rage that have been haunting them for hours also fall silent.

"¡Fiera de mi tierra!" The old Spaniard has his double-barreled shotgun trained directly on them. His green rubber boots are smeared with dark red clay. Under other circumstances, with his graying crown of hair and long beard, he might have passed for an oddball grandfather.

But right now, he is radiating a violence that Waltraud would never have thought him capable of. Just behind him, they can see the tower of the gray Jura stone village church, but the passage to it is being rigorously denied them.

"¡Sí, muy bien!" she stammers, as Jens raises both arms in a conciliatory gesture. The muzzle of the shotgun follows them as they look around for the path near the field.

"¡FIEEEERA!" the old man roars furiously; they clearly aren't moving fast enough for him. They sprint off, away from the village that had almost been within reach and head back into the mountains. The earth sticks to their hiking boots and makes them feel as if they are made of lead. After three hundred meters, they reach the stone wall that borders the field and find the wide path that leads out of the forest. The wind blows the echo of ghastly screams toward them. Dejected, they stop.

"That way," Jens states the obvious, pointing south. They shake off their fear and begin to run. The muddy path under their feet is full of potholes and puddles, forcing them to tread more slowly and carefully. There is no way they're going to risk a twisted ankle. Their fear rises with every scream they hear, driving them onward.

After about half an hour, they reach the village. The detour has cost them a lot of time. Far behind them, they hear a roar and recognize the farmer's voice. This time his shouts are louder and more aggressive. The hungry screaming of what were once human beings is the only response. There is one loud bang, then another, followed by screeches of pain.

To their horror, the village seems deserted. The doors and shutters of the old stone houses are barricaded. Not even dogs or cats are roaming the streets.

They can't see a soul, and yet they feel they are being watched. Standing at the center of the cobbled village square, they look frantically for an escape route. An ancient water trough adorns the plaza, but neither cows nor horses are drinking from it. They don't know which way to turn. The cries edge closer and closer.

A sharp whistle makes them jump. At first, they can see no one, but after a second, they spot a man in his fifties waving at them from one of the narrow alleys.

"¡Venga aqui! ¡Venga!"

Without thinking, they rush toward him, their heavy hiking boots echoing like pistol shots through the narrow village streets and leaving muddy footprints in their wake. When he is sure they are following him, the old man starts running.

He is as wiry as Jens, and a bit smaller. But fast. His smooth scalp shines in the midday sun. The house he is heading for is haphazardly covered with dark slates, like all the others. An ancient wooden door opens with a loud creak, and he holds it open in welcome. They stumble inside. He enters smoothly behind them and lets the door thud shut.

Only when the wave of undead has marched through the village do Waltraud and Jens take the time to introduce themselves and explain what has happened to them that day. Pedro's English is rudimentary, but sufficient for simple conversations.

"This house belonged to my great-grandparents. Now it's mine, but we live over on the island." He jerks his chin toward an aerial view of Mallorca that is hanging on the wall.

The picture is aging a little, but the print is high quality, so it shows a lot of detail. As Pedro explains, he and his partner, Svetla, have two dogs. The animals are on the island where Pedro's son Hector is vacationing. Hector is repaying his parents by taking care of their home and tending to their animals. Pedro and Svetla, in turn, are spending the first of the spring school vacations with their granddaughters in the mountains. The two girls are happy to spend time with their grandparents, but now they're all stuck in the village. The vacation has already been two weeks longer than originally planned.

"We only come here on holidays or when it's too hot in the Balearics." Pedro shakes his bald head as if regretting having decided to come this year. Svetla sits on the opposite sofa with the ten- and twelve-year-old girls, reading to them quietly from a children's book. Her curly gray hair falls over the children's shoulders as they snuggle up to her on each side. Only a little light is filtering into the living room through the tightly closed shutters, but it is enough to read by.

"We have been receiving news from Barcelona for days, each time worse than the one before," Pedro says. "Everything is gradually breaking down. The phone and internet are still working, just about, but no one knows how much longer those will last."

"What actually happened? Why were those . . . creatures chasing us? What do they want from us?"

Jens's curiosity is getting the better of him. But before he asks any more questions, Pedro interrupts. "It started somewhere near Paris. A handful at first, but quickly there were more. The cases soon spread across the whole continent.

Until recently, we hoped we were safe here and that the mountain range would prevent it spreading to us." He looks down at his fingers, shaking his head. "Apparently, we were wrong."

As if to confirm his words, a large number of creatures march past the house. The children look fearfully at the window, their eyes widening.

Svetla hugs them tightly and whispers reassuringly. But the girls are listening to the group shuffling down the alley. Fortunately, it isn't long before the sounds begin to fade away.

"What are . . . they?" Jens asks again, pointing to the window. It takes Pedro a few moments to put what he knows into English.

"They say . . . They say that they are people who have been infected with a virus. They attack for no reason and without warning because the disease makes them very aggressive. Once you've been infected, you die and come back as one of them. Just like on TV."

Waltraud and Jens stare at him, fascinated. They think about their day so far and have no doubt of the truth of his words. "Just don't get bitten or spat on. And if you have open wounds, give their blood a wide berth. As a matter of fact, give them and everything they have touched a wide berth."

He lowers his voice, his tone becoming more conspiratorial. "If there's no other way out, destroy their brains, because that's the only way to kill them. Crush their skulls with a hammer or a stone or shoot their heads off their shoulders."

He looks insistently into their horrified faces. Then he claps his hands together softly. His worried expression changes abruptly and he whispers with a smile, "So, who's hungry?"

* * *

What Waltraud can't know is that meager evening meals will become the norm over the coming months. Since she has by now become accustomed to consuming Spartan rations, this does not represent a serious obstacle for her.

She learns from brief telephone calls to Norway that her family members are safe and well for the time being despite the declaration of a state of emergency. She is relieved when Jens hears similar news from his relatives. A few less things to worry about.

As they sit in the semidarkness at the kitchen table with their new hosts, she watches the girls spooning pasta and tomato sauce into their mouths. "Anyone want the rest of my spaghetti?" Waltraud hasn't emptied her plate. When the sisters both raise their hands, wide-eyed and mouths smeared with sauce, she distributes the remaining pasta between the children. Pedro smiles peacefully, and Svetla nods her approval. She is still waiting for news from her home in Bulgaria. Even though they say the virus has not got to the far reaches of the Balkans, she seems tense.

"When I heard the shots before, I was curious," Pedro says guiltily. "I only made it as far as the town square and at first; I just watched you. Then, when I heard the infected, I decided to bring you here."

"Not a second too soon," Jens says. "We really appreciate it, Pedro!" The latter smiles and waves it off. "But we can't stay here. Our food supply is running low. And more infected will come. If this were winter, they'd have frozen to death in the low temperatures, but the warm weather is just beginning. We have to get out of here as soon as we can."

Waltraud sits down with one of the girls. They play cat's cradle, taking her back to her childhood. "Do you have a plan?" she asks her host, keeping her eyes on her intertwined hands. Svetla is putting her younger granddaughter to bed and can be heard singing soft lullabies in the next room.

Pedro studies the ground thoughtfully. Finally, he says, "I'm afraid! Not for myself, but for the children and Svetla. She may be physically stronger than me"—he interrupts himself with a grin—"but I don't want anything to happen to them. No matter what, my granddaughters must make it to Mallorca to be with their parents. That's the safest place at the moment, so Hector and his wife are staying where they are for now. But there are no more flights, and the ferry tickets are overpriced. As luck would have it, though," he says, winking at them conspiratorially, "a guy who used to work for me now runs a small transport company in Morocco. Several years ago, when he fled from Syria to Spain, I took him into the family and gave him work in the restaurant. When he went to North Africa the year before last, he used his savings to buy a small shipping company. He has secured six seats for us on one of his ships, leaving Barcelona in a few days. He thought my son and his wife would be with us.

If you can help me get the kids and Svetla safely on the ferry and over to Mallorca, you're welcome to the two extra tickets."

Waltraud weighs he options. "Actually, we ought to go back to northern Europe."

Pedro shakes his bald head. "No chance—there's a no-fly zone over Europe, except for military aircraft. And overland . . . I'd strongly advise you against it!"

Jens nods and looks at her questioningly. After a moment's thought, she agrees. "All right, we'll go together." Pedro's face brightens abruptly.

Something like a plan begins to take shape in her mind. "Do we have a vehicle? And are there any weapons here in the house?"

Pedro nods. "Yes, I have a shotgun. It's almost an antique, but it can blow a fair amount of lead into your flesh."

Jens asks, "Was that a trend here once? I only ask because we were greeted with that kind of weapon earlier."

Pedro hesitates briefly at the obvious question. "Everyone has a weapon like that here. People used to hunt in the mountains more than they do now. My grandfather bought the rifle back then. Years ago, I went stalking once, with the hunters from the village. Not knowing any better, I purchased a little too much ammunition." He goes to the dresser and pulls open the bottom drawer.

Jens and Waltraud look wide-eyed at several dozen boxes of cartridges. The drawer is filled to the brim.

"But hunting isn't for me. My heart is too soft," he says, smiling and patting his chest with his hand.

The rifle he pulls out of an old-fashioned cabinet looks terrifying, with blackened barrels twice as long as a human forearm.

The grip around the trigger is finely worked with a relief depicting a hunting scene. The solid dark wood shoulder brace is deeply patinated from years of use. The triggers are shaped like small iron roosters.

Waltraud and Jens nod, impressed. Pedro, however, looks skeptical.

"It's unwieldy and barely serviceable. It needs to be shortened so that we can swing the barrel around quickly at short range. I can't hit anything at longer range anyway; I'm completely out of practice."

Grabbing the long-barreled gun, he leaves the room. A little later, they hear sawing noises coming from one of the adjoining rooms. Waltraud is concerned that the noise will also be audible outside. She follows the sounds and finds Pedro in a small room that smells of old wood, machine oil, and metal.

He is standing at a workbench, with the weapon firmly clamped in it, sawing away at it with a metal saw. Every now and then, he stops what he is doing to pour a little oil over the gun. He is aiming to halve the length of the rifle.

"Don't you think they can hear you out there?" Waltraud asks.

Pedro purses his lips and replies, "This has to be done. But I'm going as fast as I can. Will you help me, please? After every tenth cut, pour two or three drops of oil into the gap. Then it should go faster and maybe more quietly. And pull the door shut, that will muffle the sound a bit."

This makes sense to Waltraud. She closes the door. The room doesn't have any windows anyway. Following Pedro's instructions, she makes sure the area he is sawing stays cool and oiled.

Since the saw teeth are no longer jamming in the workpiece, the work progresses quickly. Oil mixed with metal shavings drip blackly onto the old wood chips covering the floor.

It takes them barely twenty minutes to cut through both barrels. With expert movements, Pedro quickly rounds off the sharp edges with a file. Finally, he looks at Waltraud with satisfaction, handing her the gun for inspection.

She nods in mock awe, eliciting a laugh from him. Then she returns the shotgun.

"That's better. Now we can take it in the car. Have you ever shot with one of these?"

She shook her head.

"It's time you learned," he says in a grandfatherly tone.

At first, she is inclined to reject Pedro's proposal, but then she reaches out her hand curiously for the gun.

"Well, here we go," Pedro says, preparing to slide the first cartridges into the long-unused rifle. He shows her how to load it and lets her dry fire it a couple times.

The gun is very easy to use, and she quickly grasps how to operate it.

The Spaniard nods approvingly. "Unfortunately, we can't practice shooting here for real, but you'll have to really watch out for the recoil. It's quite something! And make sure you don't pull the barrel upward in shock when you hear the bang."

"Okay, I won't."

"You did very well," Pedro says, nodding again. "You should teach your husband how to use it," he adds as they leave the room. She smiles, stroking her hand lovingly over the sawed-off weapon.

Jens passes the night in a restless haze. Even Waltraud, who is lying next to him in her sleeping bag, keeps tossing and turning. Only the children seem to be sleeping through the night without a care in the world. He thinks over the plan they have worked out, which seems more and more absurd with every passing minute.

Not because it is difficult to put into practice, but rather because, for the first time in his life, he is worrying about the safest way to travel a route that one would usually be able to drive in a leisurely two hours. He hopes it won't take them more than twice that.

The radio, as it has done every evening, carries reports about the worsening situation in the north of Spain. The position in central Europe is now so catastrophic that even the media can't play it down any longer.

The world is in chaos, Jens thinks with a lump in his throat. And that fuels his fear.

In the morning, they breakfast together, clear the table, and go through the backyard to the doorless garage made of gray concrete bricks.

As agreed the evening before, Jens gets in first and drives the Renault Espace out. To save space, they first push the small suitcases into the back seat footwells at the girls' feet. Svetla, equipped with some children's books, sits between them. Waltraud is assigned the seat next to the driver. They stow the rest of the bags in the trunk, which also accommodates Pedro. He is the only one halfway capable of handling the gun. Should circumstances require, he can take care of any problems by sneaking quickly out through the tailgate, which Jens can open with one push of a button from the driver's seat, and take care of any problems. They tell themselves that this will expose the other occupants to less danger.

Jens drives off slowly, letting the car roll on steeper sections. They pass through seemingly deserted villages until they reach Balaguer, where they finally leave the Pyrenees behind in the north. They would have preferred to go around the town, but they have to drive right through the center to get over the Rio Segre to the C-53.

There they come across other people. They are a disturbing sight. Armed vigilantes are patrolling with squadrons of police and eyeing every newcomer with suspicion. However, the Renault is neither stopped nor checked. Apparently, the assumption is that the infected are not capable of driving vehicles. At a gas station, Pedro hides the gun under his jacket. The cashier responds in monosyllables when Waltraud tries to start a conversation as she is paying. The woman seems more than relieved when the group moves on.

The radio has been reporting the same news for days as if stuck on an eternal loop. Svetla is keeping the girls busy with stories and games, but they seem tense and unsettled. Waltraud is relieved they are quiet and not given to whining. Jens remembers how he and his brother used to drive their parents crazy.

But these days, that seems like another life, a parallel universe even. Now the adults keep glancing out the windows, watching for danger. In the other villages they pass through, they see fewer people, but here, too, are militias armed to the teeth.

It is late morning, and the sun is shining when they reach the A-2. For the last two or three hundred meters to the freeway exit, they are in a convoy, at a standstill. The cars ahead of them, however, are almost all on the westbound feeder road. Very few of them are heading for Barcelona.

On the highway, a bizarre picture emerges. Their own lane is empty except for a handful of other vehicles, while the opposite lanes are full. The cars heading westward are moving slowly. They look as if they are stationary, while the Renault is speeding eastward at over one hundred kilometers per hour.

Now they are making good progress. If everything continues like this, they will reach Barcelona in less than their four-hour target.

But as soon as they leave the Roques Blances area behind, they see increasing signs of destruction. They had known it was bad, to be sure. But seeing overturned and burning vehicles with bullet holes with their own eyes shocks them all. Jens maneuvers the Renault skillfully past roadside barricades. Svetla tries in vain to persuade the children to take a nap. The girls have horror written all over their faces; they can't take their eyes off it all. They don't understand what they are seeing or how the devastation has come about, but they know it must have been something bad. Svetla pulls up the doors' integrated sunshades on both sides. Jens secretly curses the material's semitransparent mesh.

At an overrun army checkpoint, the adults try to conceal the signs of panic. Empty cartridge cases are lying everywhere. Dark stains on the asphalt bear witness to the latest massacre. The only things missing are the corpses.

It takes them almost two hours to cover the last forty kilometers. Each passing minute reveals new and more brutal images of the catastrophe. The few vehicles in front of and behind them move slowly and carefully around obstacles.

The windows and balcony doors of the buildings next to the highway are closed, the shutters lowered. The Catalonian capital appears in the distance.

"What time is it?" asks Pedro. What he really wants to know, though, is if they will make it to the ferry in time. They can see the port from the hills of the Roques Blances reserve. From this distance, the ships look like toys. To the north, large white clouds are gathering and might bring rain, but they are still far away on the horizon.

"One o'clock." Waltraud flips through the road map she has found in the glove compartment, estimating how far they have to go. "At this rate, I'm guessing it'll take us two hours to reach the port. If there are no incidents."

She has barely finished the sentence when Jens stamps on the brake. The vehicle stops immediately. Although they have been driving slowly, everyone is thrown hard against their seat belts, and Pedro crashes into the rear seats from behind. The children cry out in fright. The road map slips from Waltraud's fingers and disappears into the footwell.

"What the hell . . ." She looks over at Jens in annoyance. Her anger abruptly dries up when she sees that all the blood has drained from his face. His eyes are wide.

"Shit," he says in a low voice, pointing toward the windshield.

She raises a hand to her mouth. As if from nowhere, two dozen figures have appeared, rushing toward the old Kia that is driving barely a hundred meters ahead of them. The driver brakes and brings the car to a halt.

"Step on it, man! Step on it, damn it!" mutters Jens. And then the driver does exactly what Jens was subconsciously worrying about: One of the taillights lights up white.

"Oh no, you idiot!" He watches as the man puts his right arm on the back of the passenger seat and looks over his shoulder. Under the car, the tires spin, smoking. The first of the creatures lands on his hood. The shock of the impact means the driver fails to release the clutch at the right moment; had he done so, he might have been out of danger. The next second, the wheels gain traction, but it is too late.

"No, no, no . . ." Jens shifts back into first gear and looks in the rearview mirror, his breathing fast and jerky.

Waltraud gasps for air. "What are you doing?" she yells at him, but he ignores her; he may not have heard her words at all. More figures are clawing at the edges and handles of the small car, which is moving backward, gradually accelerating.

"Hold on!" Jens, in his turn, steps on the gas and finds the biting point.

The massive Espace rolls ponderously forward, gaining speed rapidly.

"WHAT ARE YOU DOING?" Waltraud yells at him, utterly stunned. There is a lane between the abandoned vehicles, at some points barely wide enough to take a single car. Concentrating fiercely, he drives along the winding path toward the reversing Kia.

"You're going to kill us all, Jens!" Waltraud hisses, keeping her voice soft out of consideration for the children. The girls are crying loudly anyway. In the rearview mirror, he sees Svetla putting her arms around them protectively. Pedro is talking to his grandchildren in soothing tones over the noise of the accelerating car.

The Kia is now almost completely invisible under the carpet of writhing bodies. The two vehicles race inexorably toward each other. Waltraud braces her legs against the floor, pressing herself back into her seat, her eyes widening in panic. When the impact seems inevitable, she screams, fearing for her life.

At the very last moment, Jens swings the steering wheel to the right, into the gap between two smoking wrecks. The Renault's front left headlight grazes the Kia's rear fender. There is practically no space between the two vehicles, which screech past each other, tearing off their mirrors and crushing the legs of one of the undead in the process. The impact causes the Espace to sway. The next half second, Jens slows down a little, and as soon as the Kia is behind them, he steers the Renault out through the gap.

Making a small swerve to the right, he brings the vehicle back into the lane and immediately accelerates. The car merely rocks briefly, then regains its stability and drives on.

Waltraud is still screaming. "Hooooooooolyyyyy shit!"

"I hope you didn't scratch the car," Pedro remarks in mock indignation.

"Nothing that can't be polished out," Jens bellows. He glances briefly in the rearview mirror at the children, who are working each other up to more tears within their grandmother's embrace, their eyes wet. Their adrenaline levels are high with the agitation, but it can't mask the panicked fear they're all feeling.

Then the Kia breaks out of its lane fifty meters behind them, lurches back and forth briefly, only to rocket upward explosively as it turns sideways at full speed. The small car rolls several times, catapulting the few remaining infected in all directions. Jens's view is abruptly blocked by smoking wrecked cars. He forces himself not to think about what would have happened if there had been even a single vehicle between them and the Kia and concentrates on driving on. Next to him, Waltraud's breathing is rapid and jerky. She has stopped screaming. Her eyes are still wide open, her feet braced against the ground. Her right hand has gone white as she clings convulsively to the door handle. Jens accelerates the Renault, but soon has to slow down, as the lane is blocked by more and more wrecked cars. The exits are hopelessly clogged, which is why it doesn't even occur to him to get off the highway. They keep on somehow before finally coming to a halt at the Hospital Universitari de Bellvitge. From here on, the road is completely blocked.

"End of the line," Jens shouts, turning off the ignition. "What do we do now?"

Waltraud looks at the street atlas, tracing potential escape routes with her index finger. "It doesn't look so bad, even if we have to get off here. We're about a two-hour walk from the port. Ahead of us is a large industrial zone, which should hopefully mean fewer people and, therefore, fewer monsters. Looks doable."

"Well then, out we get. We'll take only the bare necessities: water, some food, the rifle, and the ammunition."

Pedro points through one of the windows at the sky to the north and adds, "And our rain jackets!"

"And my cuddly toy!" the older of the children protests indignantly.

Svetla immediately appeases her lovingly. "Of course, your cuddly toys have to come, too!"

More vehicles roll up behind them, stopping some distance away. "Let's go then!" Pressing a button, Jens opens the tailgate. The old

Spaniard immediately jumps out of the trunk, his sawed-off shotgun at the ready, and looks around.

Pedro gives the all-clear. "You can get out!" He hugs his granddaughters and speaks soothingly to them, telling them something funny, making them giggle nervously.

Together they pick out everything they want and can carry before taking the opened suitcases back to the car. Jens locks it unnecessarily and hands the flat wireless key back to Pedro.

Waltraud shoulders her backpack and stations herself at the back of the small column with the Spaniard at its head.

Jens and Svetla, in the middle of the group, take the children by the hand. Both girls hold their cuddly toys close.

Before they leave, Pedro looks at their position. Waltraud had torn out the relevant page from the map. "I think it's best if we leave the highway. Otherwise, we'll be handing ourselves to them on a plate, with little chance of escape if things get tight."

"I was thinking the same thing." Waltraud nods.

The adults climb carefully over the guardrail one after the other. The girls don't want to be helped over and crawl underneath, even though they and their cuddly toys get dirty in the process. Then they leave the asphalt, sliding down a small slope.

They head southeast on a bicycle path. To their right are uncultivated fields and a trickle of brown water. Except for a few seagulls flying screeching toward the sea, nothing is stirring. Nobody is following them. The usual hustle and bustle of a big city is absent. It is extraordinarily warm for late spring, and they are sweating after only a few minutes. The adults try not to drink so much, since they don't know when they will come across fresh water again. Passing under a towering highway bridge, they reach the border of the industrial zone west of Barcelona. All around is evidence that people lived here not so long ago. The few community gardens are neat and well kept.

The group passes deserted warehouses. Waltraud keeps thinking normality will return at any moment, that trucks will head toward their destinations and forklifts will beep as they move heavy pallets around. They take a short break at one of the smaller stores to allow the children to rest.

In the first shop they come across, they scavenge for water supplies, candy, prepackaged bread, and canned fruit. There is an eerie silence all around, suppressing any desire for conversation. On high alert, the adults glance continuously back and forth.

A few moments later, they continue their march. The wind carries the sounds of wailing sirens and gunshots to them, but they are so quiet that they might sometimes be mistaken for hallucinations.

Just as they catch sight of the sea at the end of the long streets and Pedro is raising his rifle in the air with a victorious grin, the wind shifts. Waltraud senses the change. The sweet putrid stench makes her digestive tract want to retch. As she fights against throwing up, she spins around and looks back.

Just at that moment, about a hundred meters behind them, the first booted foot stomps around the corner. Her senses are so heightened that she can make out all the details at that distance: the dirt, the clotted blood, and the torn laces of what was once a black jump boot on the foot of an emaciated figure. Staggering grotesquely, it stumbles around the corner. The stench grows stronger and more overwhelming with every second. The rest of the group can apparently smell it too and stops abruptly. To Waltraud's relief, the children do not make a sound.

Behind them, one undead figure quickly becomes two, four, and then so many that she can't count them. They are grunting sporadically, like predators sniffing the air for prey.

A split second before the hunters locate them, the Norwegian gives the command to flee. They charge off, Svetla and Jens each holding a child by the hand. A chorus of bellowing breaks out behind them.

"Where to now?" asks Pedro breathlessly after a few hundred meters. Waltraud thinks about it for a moment, then suddenly goes cold. To the left, she can see a harbor with some giant tankers lying in ruins. Shit! They should have turned at the last traffic circle, but now they're too late.

SHIT!

If they don't make a wide arc to the right around the infected immediately, they'll hit a dead end. They might be able to swim for it but jumping into the cold sea with the two children is too risky. Her search for a solution is suddenly interrupted, however, when more monstrous human forms emerge from a large courtyard on the right, blocking their escape. "Keep going straight on," she yells, "and turn left at the end of the street!" The children scream at the top of their lungs.

More and more infected are joining the chase. Suddenly, one of the stinkers steps out from an entranceway, blocking their path. Pedro has his wits about him, though, and raises his shotgun, pointing it at the figure's head and pulling the trigger when it is a meter away. The bang is unspeakably loud, and the shot tears the top of the creature's skull to pieces. Svetla urges the children on, trying to block their view of the gruesome corpse. A grayish liquid is pouring out of the shattered skull.

Pedro replaces the empty shell, which falls to the ground. The hungry mob is making such a racket that the fleeing group can hardly take in anything else.

"Holy shit, where did those assholes come from so suddenly?" Waltraud is beside herself with rage.

It seems that in every courtyard and building entrance, the infected have been waiting for a secret sign to emerge.

Their tramping footsteps flood the streets, and animalistic howls issue from their deformed throats. Waltraud can hear them close behind her. She overtakes the group, taking the lead next to Pedro.

"Give me the rifle! And the ammunition!" As she runs, she pulls off her backpack in one fluid motion, holding it out to the older man. He exchanges it for his shotgun and vest, giving her a skeptical look that she can't make sense of. She just yells, "At the intersection on the left! There must be a small jetty there, it's our only chance. We'll swim to the other side; it's not so wide there." At the last few steps before the crossroads, Waltraud yells at the top of her lungs, "Keep running! I'll try to hold them off for a while. Don't wait for me. RUN!" Jens turns around and almost stops, his eyes wide open. But before he can make a sound, she screams, "Run, Jens, run!"

The road that leads left from the intersection is as straight as an arrow. It is deserted, but the jetty in question is only distantly visible amid countless abandoned trucks, a thousand meters away. Waltraud drops back and takes up a position at the narrowest point between two transport vehicles standing diagonally on her left and a high wire mesh fence on her right. She positions herself so that she can see both passages and cocks the triggers.

The infected charge in.

Waltraud's brain is working at full throttle. From second to second, she forces herself to override her all-consuming fear and tries to think about the moves required for survival as a program function with an if-then statement, just as she has done thousands of times on the computer. She mentally types in the lines of code, scans them for accuracy, and racks the rifle.

```
function survive(){
    var rifle = $("#rifle"),
        rifleLoaded = rifle.val(),
        undead = $(".undead");

    if(unDead === true){
            if(rifleLoaded != true){
                    rifle.reload();
                    unDead.kill();
            } else {
                    unDead.kill();
            }
        } else {
            run();
        }
    }
survive();
```

She pictures herself going through this statement like a machine ten times a second. It is the only thing stopping her from going mad with fear. When the first undead figure reaches the narrow point on Waltraud's right, she raises the gun, holding it in both hands, points the barrels at the infected's forehead, and shoots into its eye.

survive();

The force rips him backward, and he falls at the feet of his successor, bringing him down.

survive();

She only sees this out of the corners of her eyes because she has the next attacker in her sights. She raises the gun with her right arm and fires. With her free hand, she takes out two fresh cartridges.

survive();

The shotgun cracks like a thunderbolt. The diseased woman, now liberated, flies backward into her rearguard.

survive();

Waltraud reloads the gun in seconds and repeats the process on the other side of the truck.

survive();

This time, she fires twice, quickly, and the blockade of corpses grows a little bigger. Here, too, the greedy compulsion of the back rows ensures that the way is quickly blocked.

survive();

Empty the weapon, reload. At the last moment, Waltraud rams the sawed-off barrels into the mouth of the monster that has pushed its way toward her.

survive();

The sudden suction created by the shot literally sucks out his eyeballs along with his brain. Only the face remains. The force of the shot is sufficient to kill the staggering figure behind it, but far less spectacularly.

survive();

Waltraud dispatches another with the second shot, reloads, and fires again.

survive();

Now the dead infected, those stumbling over them, and those charging greedily onward are preventing each other from making headway.

survive();

She fires to the right, rewarding the monster that has been most successful at extricating itself from the tangle with a round of lead between the eyes.

survive();

She turns and runs. The whole thing has taken less than eight seconds, she realizes with relief, but she will have to hurry to catch up with the group. A glance at the artificial breakwater looming four meters to her right gives her an idea. Concrete cubes, two cubic meters in size, stacked a few centimeters apart in two rows, form a huge barrier against the sea. "Run to the right, to the stone blocks!" she shouts to the others. She registers Jens's relief at seeing her behind him. Following her command, they all swing to the side, gathering by a small embankment beneath the blocks.

Behind them, the undead are freeing themselves from their trap. They only have a few seconds to catch their breath.

"Good job!" Jens praises her breathlessly, giving her a fleeting kiss without letting go of the child's hand. But Waltraud pays no attention.

She is still in survival mode. No superfluous emotion can get through to her.

"Climb up there!" she says, hoisting herself into the free space between the lower row of blocks. There is only a little room up there, barely enough for one person, so next she reaches into the gap at the side of the blocks, wedging her fist into it, and climbs up.

"Pass me the children!" With desperate strength, she helps up first one girl, then the other. She waits in position until Pedro and Svetla have also reached the top. She knows that the cuboids will not present any obstacle to Jens's skills. Two seconds later, he is standing next to her.

"Your barricade held well," says Pedro.

The infected have only just started to approach. The Norwegian grins with satisfaction, and points to the northeast. "That should be our ferry over there."

"Shouldn't it be leaving around six?" asks Svetla.

Waltraud also looks more closely and sees that the ship is departing. Its big funnels are pumping enormous black clouds into the sky.

"Oh, shit!" she curses. "Come on, quickly!"

She runs, carrying a child. The stone wall comes to an end after one hundred meters, and they have to climb down over a wire mesh fence.

The undead are closing in on the fugitives as they touch the ground, but there is a sturdy barrier between them. The angry mob throws itself against the fence, which holds steady, swaying violently.

The fugitives run swiftly on toward the ferry. It is a hundred meters to the jetty, along long metal pipes that serve as fuel lines. The wire mesh to their left protects them from the infected, who do not fall back this time. A gate secured with thick steel chains and a sturdy lock brings their run to an end. The putrefying figures are trying to break through.

"I hope it holds," Jens whispers to himself, giving voice to Waltraud's thoughts.

"It has to, or all that running will have been for nothing," she replies. "But how we're going to get on that damn ferry that'll be passing us in three minutes . . ." She doesn't finish the sentence because, now that the noise around her has diminished, she notices the cacophony of frenzied and pain-filled screams echoing toward her from the ship. She also hears scattered volleys of gunfire. "What the fuck! WHAT THE ACTUAL FUCK!" On the decks of the lurching ferry, she can see wild movements that presage violence. "The freaks are on the goddamn ship! How the hell did they get up there?"

As if in mockery, the metal gate behind them screeches in agony. "The chain would probably have held easily, but the hinges are starting to give way," Jens notes in horror.

Waltraud does not give up. "Come on, climb onto the cranes! The ship is our last hope."

Arriving at the very end of the jetty, they begin to climb two lonely reloading cranes. The children go up first, but the girls hardly have any strength. Their crying gets louder with every move. Svetla and Pedro try in vain to calm them down. When the gate finally gives way and hundreds of infected pour toward them down the jetty, they cry out as if they are in physical agony. Waltraud realizes that there is nothing now that can save them all from certain death. The ship in which they have placed their last hope will pass by in a few seconds and leave them to their fate.

Defying death, the adults climb after the children. Deep below them, the mob works itself into a frenzy. Waltraud clutches the shotgun in her right hand, wrapping the crook of her elbow around the steel as she reaches up with her left.

"The ship! The ship's heading straight for us," Pedro says incredulously. "It's going to run right over us!"

In fact, the ferry isn't moving parallel to the quayside, but it's heading directly for the jetty. Waltraud looks down to check.

From her vantage point, she realizes that the water might be deep enough to keep the boat from running aground. Her survival instinct is still in control. At lightning speed, she calculates the distance of the ship, its speed, and the time until impact, while combining those data with the required climbing moves.

"The children need to climb to the second rung from the top! Pedro, Jens, when I say so, throw them to me."

"What are you up to?" Jens can't seem to follow what she's saying, and Pedro doesn't even seem to understand.

"JUST DO IT!" Shouting in desperation, Waltraud turns around, climbs onto the arm of the crane that usually lifts the ballast, and concentrates on the ship's imminent arrival.

She senses more than sees Pedro, Svetla, and Jens climbing with the children to the height she has indicated on the side of the crane facing the sea. The vessel is closing in.

Ten meters. Five meters.

When it is only two meters from the jetty, Waltraud sprints along the narrow lattice path on the horizontal arm of the crane. Metal crashes into concrete. She plunges into the air toward the ship, throwing all her remaining strength into this one jump, aiming for the third deck. In flight, she realizes that she has slightly miscalculated and is going to crash into the outside of the railing. If she can't catch the children in the next few seconds, they will die. Desperation mobilizes hidden energy reserves within her. She draws her knees toward her chest, her shoes clearing the rusty railing by millimeters as she flies over it. Then she hits the steel floor hard and rolls away. She drops the gun, which skids across the deck and comes to rest on its edge.

"NOW!" she yells as she stands up, turning to face the crane and stretching out her arms blindly. Then her call is lost amid the infernal screeching of metal.

The moment Waltraud runs off, Jens understands what she is up to and swings over to the older of the children. He does not watch her flight, because he has complete trust in her. His mind is utterly calm, and when he hears the command, he throws the girl high into the air and in the direction of the call just before the ship demolishes the pier and makes the cranes lurch.

As Waltraud begins to move, Pedro realizes that Jens is putting her plan—which, unfortunately, he doesn't understand—into action. But he has no time to ask questions or seek explanations. So, he mirrors Jens's moves on the crane. Out of the corners of his eyes, he sees the Norwegian woman land on the deck; then he hears her roar.

Now it is clear what he has to do. A few milliseconds after Jens, Pedro throws the younger girl toward the deck. Almost parallel to each other, the two children sail toward Waltraud and are caught in her arms. But the force of the impact knocks them off their feet. As the ship plows into the cranes, Pedro lets go.

Svetla, almost mad with fear, reaches for her granddaughter. But the girl is out of reach. She stretches for the little one from the crane and almost loses her grip. The next instant, the ship plows into the lifting equipment. The steel trembles like aspen leaves, and the force of the collision rips the metal rung from her hand. She falls. Her stomach smashing painfully into a section of railing, she turns a somersault and slams onto the deck.

Jens tries desperately not to fall the full fifteen meters to the jetty and into the hands of the infected, and he tumbles onto the deck as it shoots past him. Quick on the draw, or merely blessed by good luck, he manages to grab the railing. Barely a heartbeat later, the rebounding crane crashes into the ferry with full force, almost knocking the bar out of his hand.

The violence of the impact realigns the ship's course just enough to enable it to continue its journey out to sea. Jens wastes no time in climbing up.

Pedro crashes headlong onto the deck, knocking all the air out of his lungs. But he picks himself up immediately and crawls over to Svetla. Carefully, he takes her head in his hands, feels it, and checks her pulse. When he sees no bleeding wounds and feels a slightly elevated but steady heartbeat, he is initially reassured. He lovingly strokes the sweaty hair from her face, kissing her lips and whispering her name softly into her ear.

Waltraud stands up, staggering, with both children in her arms. The frightened girls are crying. Their eyes dart back and forth over the deck and find their kneeling grandfather. She lets them run to him and picks up the shotgun.

"Are you hurt?" asks Jens, taking her in his arms.

"No, it's all good. And you?" She discovers a large bump on his forehead.

"Nothing too serious, I'd say. That was another good pl—"

One of the infected charges around the corner behind her. Jens jerks her out of danger. On high alert, she whirls around. The sudden bang frightens everyone far more than the arrival of the monster itself. One shot with the truncated weapon ends the attack. Waltraud lowers the smoking gun. "Come on now. More of these things are going to show up." She waves her Spanish friends over. Then she steps forward and peers around the corner, taking care not to step on the almost decapitated corpse. She pulls her head back abruptly.

"Crap, the lower decks are crawling with them." She peeks around the corner again. "There's a cabin door a few meters away. Can't tell if it's locked, though."

"How far away is it exactly?" asks Pedro.

"Not far. Three, four meters. But if they see us . . ." She doesn't dare finish the sentence. "After the door, maybe eight, ten meters away, there's a staircase. There's a large group of infected underneath it . . . eating someone. If they see us, we're done for. Our best chance of survival right now is to get to the cabin. Assuming the door is open." Waltraud jerks her chin at the emaciated body at her feet. "We can't stay here. Others will arrive soon."

The adults nod their agreement. It doesn't take her long to come up with a new plan. "Pedro, give me the rest of the ammo. Here's what we're going to do . . ."

A minute later, she steps carefully around the corner, satisfying herself with a quick glance that the corridor is clear. She moves forward with the loaded weapon at the ready, pressing herself close against the side of the ship. The others follow a short distance behind. When Waltraud gets to the cabin, she depresses the latch without any problem. The door moves inward five millimeters, but then jams. The Norwegian curses silently. On the deck just a few meters below her, the sea of hungry creatures surges, angry screams and shrill sounds issuing from their parched throats.

Careful to be as quiet as possible, Waltraud pushes against the door, which will not give way. As she presses harder, it finally moves with a grinding of metal on metal and a loud squeaking. The lower deck falls silent for an instant. The undead lift their noses, sniffing, their eyes wandering aimlessly back and forth, trying to locate the source of the sound. Above them, the fugitives press themselves harder against the wall. Svetla signals to the children to be quiet, putting a finger to her lips. As if turned to stone, they stop moving. At that moment, the door gives way with another groan. Waltraud tumbles in, unprepared. A surprised scream escapes her throat as she disappears into the darkness.

As one, the creatures turn their gazes upward. A heartbeat later, they charge up the stairs, bellowing. Only their sheer numbers prevent them from getting to their prey in an instant. Nevertheless, the hungry ones reach the upper deck before Jens, Pedro, or Svetla can break free from their state of shock.

One of the children shrieks and breaks the spell. Svetla pushes at Pedro's back, and together they push Jens toward the open door. As he reaches it, Waltraud's hand shoots out and grabs him by the collar. Pedro and Svetla enter with the girls.

Quick as a flash, as the Bulgarian is stepping over the threshold, the Norwegian pushes the door shut. Milliseconds before the door slams shut, the first infected crash against it. One or two grimy fingers claw their way around, but Waltraud's rage and despair give her superhuman strength.

She roars at the top of her lungs and swiftly pushes the steel latch closed.

Three tiny body parts land at her feet. Then, with the door at her back, she collapses, exhausted. Fists pound against the outer shell. Jens crawls over to his exhausted girlfriend as all hell breaks loose outside.

"Will it hold?" Svetla clutches one of the girls against her, pointing with a trembling finger at the door and looking doubtfully at Pedro.

Clasping the hand of his elder granddaughter tightly, he replies, "Yes, it'll hold. But we'll put something against it to be on the safe side." He tries to reassure the children, taking them to one of the narrow sleeping cots. Then he looks around the cabin.

The door is juddering repeatedly from the blows on the other side. Right next to it stands an unassuming but sturdy cabinet.

"You two, out of the way," he instructs the young couple, getting an inspiration. They obey without protest, crawling exhausted farther into the room. Pedro pushes the item from the corner and wedges it into the narrow hallway.

It takes him a while to find the best position. When the work is done, he sees that the children have fallen asleep, holding on to each other tightly. On the other side of the cabin, Waltraud and Jens have done the same.

Svetla, who now seems less panicked, puts her arms around him. Her loving touch envelops all his fear and doubt. His breathing calms, and tears of relief begin to run down his cheeks.

Hours later, a thunderclap wakes not only Pedro and his companions, but most of the passengers who are still alive. Flashes of light find their way through portholes milky with age, illuminating the cabins and turning faces into ghostly grimaces. Rain whips against the walls and decks of the ship as it pitches and rolls through the night. Again and again, the bow rises several meters above the surface of the water, only to crash back into the sea. Passengers in the dubious safety of their cabins make themselves as small as possible and hold on to the furniture to avoid being thrown across the room or hit by flying objects. Others, less lucky, are washed off the decks by gigantic waves, sinking by the dozen to the bottom of the Mediterranean.

In the cabinet-reinforced cabin, the girls cling to their grandparents, who are equally helpless in the face of the storm. Svetla and Pedro brace themselves against the walls on the worn mattress and narrow bed frame, the children between them. On the other side of the little cabin, Jens and Waltraud hold on to each other, hoping that their joint weight will be enough to ensure they are not thrown out of their berth. Hour after hour passes. They struggle unsuccessfully against seasickness and take turns throwing up. Just before their strength runs out, they notice the storm subsiding and the swells becoming lighter. They try to get some sleep in the stuffy room that now reeks of vomit. A few hours later, once more jolted from their nervous slumber, this time by a loud and brutal convulsion from the ship, they have lost all sense of time. Even their sense of direction seems to have disappeared. The ferry comes to an abrupt halt, as if it has hit a wall. In the cabin, everything overturns. Waltraud and her companions scream and shout in confusion, coming to rest in a tangle in the corner. The fear they have managed to escape for a short while grips them again.

Jens and Waltraud scramble to their feet, smeared with vomit and smelling of stomach acid. "Is anyone hurt?" she whispers into the darkness.

She hears Svetla's voice replying, "I've got a big bruise, but nothing life-threatening."

"What was that? Are we home now?" One of the girls wants to know.

"I'll take a look," says the Norwegian. She has to almost climb to the door, which is practically above their heads. The cabinet that has been blocking the door is gone. Waltraud slides the lock back and carefully pushes down the handle. The door is stuck. She pulls harder, careful not to let it swing open uncontrolled. No one can know who or what might be outside. But she is greeted only by the blackness of the night and the easing rain. Waltraud breathes in the fresh air greedily.

"There's no one here," she whispers into the cabin. Then, holding the doorframe, she climbs carefully out into the night. Innumerable rapid footsteps sound below them, sometimes accompanied by wild shouting, often anguished and panic-stricken. She can almost feel the sickness spreading toward the city.

"What's going on?" Jens asks.

"Shh, people are leaving the ship. Let's wait until everyone's gone," she whispers, hoping she is right.

As another hour passes, the girls relieve themselves in a corner of the cabin. It is too risky to leave the room. Waltraud keeps watch sitting up, her gun across her lap. But as soon as the sun appears in the east and the noises on the ship have died down, they all climb out of the cabin into the dawn. The clouds are clearing swiftly to the south, giving way to the last of the evening's pale starlight.

Waltraud and Jens pull the girls up one by one and then help Svetla and Pedro. "We were lucky the ship didn't land on this side," the old Spaniard observes.

The early light of dawn reveals a scene of devastation. Countless wrecked boats and yachts are lining the path the ferry has plowed into the harbor. From the nearby town they can hear screams, intermittent police sirens, and even occasional gunshots. They wait another full hour until the violent noises have fallen silent. Waltraud addresses the weary group. "I'm going down. As soon as you hear me call, follow me. But slowly and quietly!"

The adults nod in agreement. She slides a little way down the side of the ship on the seat of her pants, shotgun at the ready to remove the brains of anyone who approaches her without permission. Carefully, she checks the crazily sloping decks before allowing her rear guard to follow. They communicate with hand signals as they search for the best way to descend. It takes what feels like hours before they finally reach the railing at the bottom.

The next few minutes drag. This time, Waltraud glides down the hull until she comes to a stop right by the protruding, sloping mast of a yacht buried under the passenger ship. She beckons Jens over and whispers in his ear, "Wait here for the children, then send them down to me one at a time. It's not deep here, three or four meters at the most."

"Okay," he replies. She slides down the wooden pole and out of sight. Pedro and Svetla join him, each holding a child by the hand. The girls now seem lethargic rather than frightened. They are probably completely traumatized and too tired to object. Jens looks sad because their cuddly toys are lying at the bottom of the Mediterranean between Barcelona and Palma.

Whispering, he points past the hull, "Pedro, can you please tell the kids they need to go down the mast? Waltraud is waiting below."

The old man nods, explaining in a few sentences of Spanish what they have to do. The taller girl remains impassive, swinging herself wordlessly onto it and disappearing into the depths. Her grandfather tries to encourage her sister. "Can you do that, too?" The child nods hesitantly. "Just hold on, you've done this kind of thing a hundred times in the playground, haven't you? Waltraud and your sister are waiting for you."

She grips the mast, then looks at the two figures beneath her and slides briskly toward them. Pedro, Svetla, and Jens follow. A few seconds later, they are reunited.

"What now?" Waltraud is tired and too exhausted to continue making decisions for the group. Tension and lack of sleep are written all over her face. When Pedro takes the floor and the initiative, she is visibly relieved.

The Spaniard clears his throat, saying, "Going ashore now would be pure madness. Outright suicide. We'd have a better chance if we sailed back out to sea." He points south.

"Out there again?"

"No way!"

"I've had enough of the sea for the next ten years!"

"Listen!" he placates them. "We'll grab a small yacht from the harbor, one that's broken its mooring, and sail to Sa Ràpita, keeping close to shore. It won't take long, two hours at the most. I've sailed there many times," he assures them. "The wind is with us."

They look at him, aghast. "Two hours?"

"Yes, three at the most," he replies mischievously.

"I can't believe I'm doing this," Jens complains, and sets off to seize a suitable yacht.

They quickly find what they are looking for. Pedro jumps over the railing onto the unmoored boat and throws a loose rope ashore. Jens pulls up the vessel so they can take the girls across. As soon as everyone is on board, Svetla takes the children below deck, which Pedro has unceremoniously unbolted with a powerful kick.

Meanwhile, Waltraud and Jens follow Pedro's orders, untangling the ropes and setting the yacht into the wind. The sails quickly fill with the morning breeze, taking them rapidly out to the open sea. Pedro maneuvers between the boat wrecks, while the Norwegian, leaning against Jens, succumbs to her need for sleep.

* * *

"By sheer luck, we reached Vilafranca the same day," Waltraud continued the narrative. Two of the candles on the table had burned down. "In Sa Ràpita, which had not heard the news of the contaminated ship at that point, we caught a large-capacity cab. Just like that! After the stress of the previous two days, we simply got into a car, and half an hour later it dropped us at Pedro and Svetla's home. Their son and daughter-in-law cried with happiness to have their children back.

The cab driver eyed us suspiciously at first. We smelled of vomit, sweat, and urine. To compensate, we gave him all the money we could find in the inside pockets of our jackets. He would certainly have taken us for less, because so early in the year there were fewer tourists bringing in business. In the end, he received ten times the amount he should have charged according to the taximeter. But we didn't care. On the ride, we told him what had happened. I'm guessing he then drove straight to his family."

As Waltraud sat back in silence, Jens took up the story. "It took a week for the virus to spread across the island. We were with our friends for ten days before a pack of zombies separated us from them on a scavenging trip near Sineu. Pedro and Hector managed to escape in time. We'd been holed up in the railroad station building for five days. Fortunately, we had looted enough food and water shortly beforehand and carried some of it straight to the upper floor.

"Yes, we wanted to get back to Pedro, but how? Hundreds of corpses were wandering around the area. For a long time, there was no way to leave without being torn to pieces. But on the sixth day, the pack finally left." Jens looked over at Nils, who had fallen asleep in the armchair. "And then he came and collected us."

Patrick stood up and walked toward the quietly snoring Nils, bent over, and started making zombielike noises at his ear.

Nils awoke abruptly and sat up, startled, swinging his right hand as he did so.

His fist caught Patrick on the chin and sent him unceremoniously to the ground.

"What's wrong with you? Are you tired of life?" The surprised Nils opened and closed his fist to relieve the pain.

"Chill out, man. It was just a joke. You don't have to punch my lights out." Patrick reached into his mouth with two fingers, checking to make sure everything was in its place. Jens and Waltraud tried to help him up, but he shook them off.

Eva laughed gloatingly. Franca only grinned in disbelief.

"Well, that's enough for today. I'm going to do the rounds and then go to bed. I'll see you in the morning." She bid us goodnight and was gone. The rest of us sat on in the living room for a few minutes, teasing Patrick about his childish antics.

Later, I took the book I had begun reading at lunchtime to my room with a candle. But before I had even read two pages, I had fallen asleep.

CHAPTER 5

HOTEL 23

What, just you and me?" I wasn't sure if he was actually serious.

"Why not? Are you chicken?"

"Of course I'm chicken! You'd have to be an idiot not to be!"

Patrick laughed mockingly at my objection and went on, "Don't be such a baby. Half an hour there, half an hour back. An hour at the most, and we'll have found and collected the children. So, we'll be back in time for lunch. With guests!" He smacked the back of one hand into the palm of the other.

"I think it would be better to wait for Franca, too," Waltraud interjected.

But he stuck to his guns. "Can't we do anything without the mistress' blessing?" When we didn't reply, he added, "As you wish. Then I'll go alone."

"Patrick, that's a stupid idea! Going out alone—"

He cut her off harshly. "They could be in trouble right now. Every second we waste here could cost them their lives."

Waltraud and I looked at each other, stunned. There was some truth in that. But it was also pure suicide to set out hastily on a rescue mission without Franca's guidance. No sooner had she, Jens, and Nils left after breakfast than the Norwegian had sat down at the computer. Eva patrolled the wall while Patrick and I cleaned up the house.

A few minutes later, Waltraud called to us both. She'd reached Dr. Koller, and we heard the virologist saying, "We can't ask you to do this, but the parents don't know what to do. They're desperate. Their children have been stuck with friends in a hotel in S'Arenal for three weeks. They haven't had anything to eat for days."

Waltraud brought her index finger to her chin pensively. "How do they keep in touch?"

"The mobile network in Germany seems to be down. Absurdly, the landline in their hotel room works from time to time, and they always check in when they can. That is, if there are no zombies around."

Waltraud took a pen and paper out of the desk drawer. "Give me the kids' number, please. We'll discuss it and get back to you as soon as we can." She hastily scribbled down the info.

"Thank you very much. I'll let the parents know."

"I'm afraid I can't promise anything, but we'll try."

"Then at least there's a glimmer of hope. That will have to do for now. Thank you again."

"Take care, doctor."

Waltraud disconnected and looked at us. "Some German brats flew here for a birthday party just before the outbreak. A few days later, their return flight was cancelled. The devils wanted to party for a whole week, and they threw all caution to the wind. We're the only ones on the island who know they're there, apart from the infected outside their door."

I said, "Well, let's wait until Franca gets back and discuss it with her first." This seemed to me to be the obvious thing to do.

Flabbergasted, Patrick blurted, "What are you waiting for?"

The question—or his quick temper—caught me completely off guard. It took me a couple seconds to formulate my reply. These days, you didn't just go to S'Arenal at random. Hundreds of zombies were running loose along the popular party strip. I looked at him skeptically. "Um, reinforcements maybe?"

He looked at me as if I was speaking Aramaic. "What kind of reinforcements? A quick in, quick out mission like that only needs two competent people to do their best. There's no need for reinforcements. The bigger the group, the greater the risk of detection."

He had probably gained his tactical understanding of rescue missions from video games. I shook my head and folded my arms, "You see yourself as one of those competent people, I take it?"

"Yeah, I do. And you're the other one! You and me, we'll pull this off easy!"

Waltraud gave a loud laugh. "That punch to the chin last night did more damage than I thought."

"What's your problem? Backup and I will take care of this in no time!" He seemed to really believe himself.

"What, just you and me?" I asked.

We argued until he turned around, annoyed, and made to leave the room.

Waltraud called after Patrick. "Wait! I'll call the youngsters now, and then we'll find out how they're doing and where exactly they are."

She seemed to be just stalling for time. Patrick took the bait and came back. She direct-dialed the room in the hotel and put the telephone on speaker. The receiver was picked up immediately after the first ring. A girl's voice whispered, barely audible, "Hello?"

Waltraud also spoke softly now. "Hi, this is Waltraud. Who am I talking to?"

The voice suddenly trembled, "Who are you? How did you get this number?"

"You're Hanna from Berlin, aren't you?"

There was a short pause. We heard murmuring in the background, and another anxious voice spoke. "Hello? It's Hanna. Who is this?"

The Norwegian spoke more understandingly: "Hello, Hanna, this is Waltraud. My friends and I are also in Mallorca," she repeated. "Your parents told us where you are. We are planning to get you out of there."

The girl on the other end of the line was evidently close to panic. She sobbed several times before speaking again. "I don't know if you guys will make it in time. We can't last much longer here." A muffled knocking with no discernible rhythm could be heard in the background. "They know we're in the room. They've been trying to break down the door for days."

We'd known who "they" were for a long time. The knocking came again. "The door's cracking. It won't hold much longer."

"Can't you climb over the balcony into one of the neighboring rooms?"

"No, they're everywhere. Everywhere! Next door, in the hallways, on the street, EVERYWHERE!" Fear, resignation, and exhaustion mingled in her voice.

"Where exactly are you?"

The frightened teenager gave Waltraud all the info she needed.

"Okay, we're on our way. And hang a hand towel clearly visible over the railing. Do you guys even have one there? One we'll be able to see from a distance?"

"Yes, we'll hang it out now. Please hurry!"

Waltraud ended the conversation, opened a program with digital maps, and immersed herself in it.

Then she stood up and said in a tone that brooked neither contradiction nor doubt, "Patrick, you tell Eva what's going on and get the pickup. Backup and I will fetch the weapons from the basement. We'll rendezvous at the fountain in five minutes. We're going out for two hours."

No sooner had she finished the sentence than he left the building through the main entrance. Without checking to see if I was following her, she headed for the basement. I was hot on her heels. We collected the pistols and ammunition we needed and arrived at the front door at the same time as Patrick. Almost in sync, we got into the pickup. He had a quick word with Eva through the driver's window. She had only just heard of our spontaneous decision and seemed to be less than happy about it. As soon as she mentioned Franca's name, Patrick stiffened and assured her brusquely that he could take care of himself. And besides, he would have us with him. At this, Eva lowered her eyes and stepped back.

He put the pedal to the metal, and I opened the gate with the remote control. Eva waved us good-bye, shaking her head disapprovingly. A few minutes later, he drove out onto the asphalt, speeding southwest. At Sa Cabana, we left the freeway and continued along the Ma-30, following the eerily empty highway past the airport.

When we reached the end of it, we switched to the Ma-19. En route, Waltraud and I checked the weapons, distributed ammunition, and went over the plan with Patrick. Although the pickup was full of shotguns and automatic rifles, we ultimately decided to go with the lighter and quieter handguns.

"The hotel is located directly on the beach at S'Arenal. On the map, I saw a port in the south and thought . . ." Waltraud outlined her plan in more detail. Basically, it was the same as Patrick's: we'd use a small force and make it a quick in and out. No casualties. However, within a half hour, I would find out just how the whole thing would go down in reality.

S'Arenal had once been a beautiful, long sandy beach that ran along almost half of the Badia de Palma, a huge bay south of the island. When mass tourism began its triumphal march at the end of the 1950s, the small village changed. Hotels were built directly on the beachfront, wreaking havoc on the natural world seemingly overnight. The newly built promenade, which separated the residential blocks from the sea, was lined with hundreds of tropical palm trees, intensifying the bizarre contrast between the exotic and the tasteless.

Two decades and any number of corrupt politicians later, an industrious petty criminal saw potential in the region. He took advantage of the fickle corruption of the people's representatives and intimidated the population and his competitors until five percent of the island's construction sites officially belonged to him. Only at the advanced age of seventy did he finally end up in prison, but not before he'd bequeathed the once sleepy area the worst thing that could have happened to it: the Ballermann. It was a vacation spot for the intellectually challenged and the alcoholically inclined. One might have assumed the money they brought with them would benefit the region. This was not remotely the case. At the start of the new millennium, things became truly horrendous. Guiris, the Mallorcans' mocking name for foreigners, flew to Mallorca on budget airlines, stayed in budget hotels, and spent their cash in establishments that mostly made their income under the table and hardly paid any taxes.

But with the outbreak, everything changed.

The route took us past Aqualand El Arenal. The waterslide paradise was closed this season. We took a sharp right and continued until we saw the sea. Many cars had been abandoned in the middle of the road. The pickup slid carefully past them. After three hundred meters, the Norwegian said, "Stop! Backup and I will get out here and check those boats over there." She pointed at the sea. To our left was the harbor. Hundreds of traditional llaüts, skiffs, and small yachts were rising and falling on the gentle swells. Waltraud and I looked around through the darkened windowpanes. She instructed Patrick to wait for us until we had taken a boat and gone out to sea. Since there was no immediate danger, we got out.

In a few minutes, we had found a dinghy with a ten-horsepower engine and a half-full tank. A full five-liter jerrican was stowed under a bench. The engine started reluctantly after a few attempts, the two-stroke banging in my ears like a machine gun.

Waltraud untied the ropes and signaled Patrick to start the rescue mission.

I steered the little boat, making sure to always keep in his sights. The engine rattled frighteningly loudly, but that was a minor part of their plan. Once we had chugged out of the harbor, I turned my gaze northward, scanning the long beach. Almost immediately, I spotted the infected. There were hundreds of them ambling along the promenade between us and our destination in the late spring sun. Some distance away, they moved slowly and sluggishly, with no apparent direction or identifiable behavior patterns. This changed quickly when the first of the zombies heard the noise the boat was making. They turned their faces toward us. Sluggishly they raised their arms and then moved ponderously toward the sea, getting faster with every step. Suddenly, a terrible noise came from behind them on the street. Patrick had opened the windows of the pickup and turned up the vehicle's sound system to the max.

A monotonous but snappy electro beat boomed out. Immediately, the zombies' attention switched away from us, and they changed direction again.

Meanwhile, Waltraud focused unswervingly on the seemingly endless chain of hotels until she spotted the building we were looking for. She pointed to it—it was one of the rare structures that had not fallen victim to the flames. I drove three hundred meters out to sea, turned, and opened the throttle, aiming the bow at the hotel. Only then did I realize how creatively it had been named. Twenty-three was the number of the building. There was no story behind it. I felt almost cheated.

Once we had picked up some speed, I switched off the engine and tilted the propeller out of the water. That way we would get to shore without making any noise. Waltraud kept visual contact with Patrick as best she could from this distance. At first, I had thought he was a show-off, but he had so far proven reliable. To avoid the large mass of infected, he drove down off the boardwalk onto the beach. The huge pickup made child's play of racing across the fine sand.

The zombies became more and more animated, and the wind carried their angry howling out to sea. When Patrick drew level with them, he drove so slowly that the undead could easily keep up with him. Hundreds of them were following the pickup. Dozens kept blocking his path, but cold as ice, he mowed them down. So as not to lose traction, he avoided driving toward larger clusters, purposefully circling only individuals or smaller groups. He had now closed the windows, but the music was still extremely loud. The infected emerged from everywhere. Many seemed weak—zombies appeared not to be immune to the effects of malnutrition after all. Others tried to jump onto the pickup or banged their hands and heads against the windows in blind rage. They almost looked like they were jumping and hopping to the rhythm of the techno beats blasting from the truck.

I heard Waltraud say, as if to herself, "Hmm. Not sure if they're infected or just Ballermann regulars . . ."

"What do zombies like to eat for dessert?" I asked.

She looked at me, shook her head skeptically, and shrugged. "I don't know, what?"

"Eyescream."

"Oh yeah. And what's their favorite fruit?"

I thought for a moment. "The Adam's apple?"

"Correctomundo," she thundered with mock admiration in an exaggerated American accent. "And at receptions, they serve finger food. With tomb-atoes. Atop a head of lettuce!"

Suddenly, the situation on the beach changed.

Having arrived level with Hotel 23, Patrick floored it for real, making his pursuers move faster. The whole pack ran after him, leaving the field free for us.

The Pied Piper of Hamelin, zombie version.

We continued to glide toward the shore. My heart was racing. Over the last hundred meters, I kept calling to mind the training of the last few days. Waltraud was breathing fast and jerkily. Amazingly, Patrick's distraction took effect at exactly the right time, so we were washed up on the beach unnoticed by the zombies.

The wind was with us. No sooner had the keel crunched onto the sand than we jumped out and ran crouching to the hotel, our guns drawn. Passing only a few meters behind the rearguard of the undead, we ran toward the hotel entrance. The door stood wide open, and we cautiously entered the lobby.

We were almost overcome by the stench of feces, death, and decay. Waltraud put a hand over her mouth. I tried to breathe as shallowly as possible. There was overturned furniture, broken glass, and mirrors everywhere. Dried bloodstains bore witness to the massacre that had taken place here. The room was a good four meters high. The hotel seemed to have been recently renovated. The walls were exposed gray concrete.

A few large-format black-and-white photographs showed landmarks from the world's most famous cities.

The designer lamps above us were out of service. In the twilight of the hotel reception, we found the door leading to the staircase. We gestured quickly at each other, agreeing how to proceed. I bent my knees slightly and pushed against the door, which sprang open with a soft click. Waltraud, her gun at the ready, secured the perimeter. When nothing happened, I pushed the door farther open. The narrow stairway was dimly bathed in greenish emergency light. This floor was empty. We began our ascent. My companion walked ahead, her gaze and the muzzle of her weapon always directed one step ahead of us. I followed her, making sure that no wandering corpse ambushed us from behind. When we reached the fifth floor, she raised her fist in the air with two outstretched fingers and then pointed upward. I nodded.

Two floors later, we stopped at the target level. Waltraud put an ear to the fire door into the hallway and listened. She told me with hand signals that she couldn't tell if there was anyone behind it. We had no way of knowing whether zombies were standing quietly there, so I suggested that she knock on the door. She considered my suggestion, then gave three quick raps with her knuckles. Almost instantly, zombie sounds boomed out through the closed door. I had to get ahold of myself to suppress the panic. My heart hammered in my ears.

This time, Waltraud pulled the door open a crack. Since the stairwell door opened at a right angle, we couldn't visualize the left arm of the hallway for the moment. I pointed my pistol at the narrow gap and looked through it into the right arm. Parts of the hallway were lit by the daylight streaming through the windows at the end and out of some of the rooms whose doors had been left open. There were dark sections in between. In the diffuse light, I made out first three, then four figures charging toward us. Compared to most zombies, these were moving quickly. There was just enough time to warn Waltraud and signal to her to open the door a little wider. I let the stinkers get within five meters. Then I fired.

The first shot echoed violently around the narrow stairwell. The head of the foremost living corpse burst open as soon as the bullet hit its skull. I used up half a magazine of my 9-millimeter liberating the others from their undead state. As Waltraud tried to pull the door open, another infected crashed into it heavily from the other side of the hallway, knocking the Norwegian over. She hit the back of her head, hard. The pistol slipped from her fingers and slid down a few steps.

I started, almost dropping the Glock in my turn, but had enough presence of mind to fire a well-placed, last-second shot at close range. The zombie, once a big-bellied man in his midforties, in blue swimming shorts and with faded tattoos, slumped lifelessly to the ground. Meanwhile, Waltraud had got to her feet again and picked up the gun. We listened intently to see if more undead were coming down the hallway. As we were taking a quick look around to make sure it was empty and safe to enter, a frenzied bellowing reached us from the stairwell below.

"Come on, in you go," I instructed her. I then grabbed the fat man by the arms. With a huge effort, I pulled him out into the stairwell and leaned him against the door from the outside.

"What are you doing?" asked Waltraud anxiously.

I slid into the hallway with her. The obese corpse pushed the door shut. We heard it sliding down it to the floor. Now the way to this floor was barricaded. At least, that's what I hoped. Even if the zombies were intelligent enough to pull open a fire door—which I couldn't imagine—hopefully they wouldn't be able to remove a corpse in front of it first.

Waltraud nodded as she saw the logic of what I had done. "Number 753," she whispered, knocking as soon as we reached the nearly demolished door. It had deep cracks in its hinges. The fat creature, or another one, must have been banging on it and shaking it for days. It would not have taken much more effort to make it give way completely.

When nothing happened, she knocked again. "Who is it?" a frightened voice said, followed by an excited murmur.

"Hanna? This is Waltraud. We spoke on the phone earlier. Come out, the coast is clear."

The door opened, tentatively. A group of skinny teenagers looked out at us. Seven of them had survived the last few weeks in the small twin-bedded room. They had run out of food days ago, as I knew from the phone call. They looked haggard and lethargic, but that could have been due to lack of exercise. One of them was standing in the background watching what was going on as if he didn't belong. He looked fitter and was older.

Some cried with relief when they saw us. But we had no time for emotional outbursts. Waltraud gave instructions: "Put on your shoes, take off any jingling jewelry, and follow us. Oh, and someone get the towel." She pointed to the balcony. One of the boys stepped out and removed it. The absence of the red towel outside was a signal to Patrick that we were on our way down. Waltraud had confirmed during the phone call that there were no other beach towels hanging on neighboring balconies.

"I'll only tell you this once: you must do exactly what we tell you. Is that clear?" The young people were too frightened and exhausted to object.

They made a pitiful picture in their unwashed clothes that had once been expensive. They nodded obediently.

"Okay, now follow us, but in absolute silence!"

The older one, who I estimated was in his early thirties, kept himself at a bit of a distance, but came with us. We walked back together. At the door to the emergency exit, Waltraud turned quietly to our protégés.

"Stay here. We'll check the stairwell." Again, she listened at the door and then shook her head, indicating there was nothing there.

I had to strain to move the corpse behind the door even a little. We listened. The noises from before had ceased. While I was pushing the door open, the Norwegian covered the surrounding area. When the gap was big enough for one person, I slipped through and quickly checked the stairway landings above and below us. They were empty. Then I beckoned the youths to join me. They eyed the corpse in disgust and gave it a wide berth. Waltraud was the last to arrive. Behind her, the door slammed shut. In the absolute silence, it sounded horribly loud. Immediately, there was a roar from a horde of the undead about four floors below, followed by the hurried tramping of feet. They were coming toward us—and frighteningly fast.

After a moment of bafflement, the youngsters rushed up the stairs, screaming in panic. Furious, Waltraud ran after them. It took three or four seconds for the first zombies to come into sight. There were dozens of them.

I began to fire. Even though there were some I didn't hit in the head, they fell down from the sheer force of the shot. Then I turned and ran.

If memory served me right, the hotel had nine floors. I saw no one on the ninth, but I heard the youths farther up. They were screaming and crying in fear for their lives. They had run blindly up to the roof and were now standing in front of a closed door.

I looked down past the handrail. The first zombies were running clumsily after us. Their shadows were flitting around the seventh floor. I fled before my knees gave way in fright.

There was a bang above me. Then I felt a draft. Waltraud had evidently shot off the lock to the roof door. I ran last onto the flat roof, throwing the door shut behind me. We realized too late that we had no further escape route. I changed the empty magazine.

The zombies crashed against the door. Now I would find out whether my theory about their door opening abilities was right or wrong. The youngsters cowered at the edge of the knee-high metal sheet, half mad with fear. Meanwhile, Waltraud ran once around the solar panels, desperately looking for a way out. "SHIT!" she yelled, scaring our charges even more. "Backup, that was the only way out of here," she said frantically, nodding her head toward the door.

Under the onslaught of the zombies, it trembled again. "There are too many! We can't take them down on our own, the two of us!" I replied. A mighty shove burst the door open by the width of a hand. Noise rushed at us for a second, then it slammed shut again. I was sweating with fear. Waltraud turned again and ran to the opposite side of the roof. "What are you doing? They'll be coming through any minute!" I yelled after her. I felt abandoned. Again, the door burst open. Dirty fingers reached through the gap. Apparently not all infected possessed the same dexterity and intelligence, because it immediately swung shut again. But it didn't close completely. A single hand had managed to reach a little farther. I heard the breaking of finger bones. Moments later, a milky white eye looked greedily at me through the gap. Shaking all over, I shot, almost emptying the magazine, but not managing to dispatch the intelligent beast that could open fire doors. Bullets bounced off the door and facade with ridiculous imprecision. "WALTRAAAUD!" I yelled at the top of my lungs without turning around.

My knees buckled in shock as she suddenly shouted, right next to my ear, "ADRIAAAAAN!" Then the door burst open, and the zombies poured onto the roof. Waltraud took aim at the first walking corpse and fired. As this one went down, I spotted the intellectual among them. He sprinted toward us. He did not seem to notice the primary hit.

The second exploded his skull. But for every zombie we killed, five more came at us. That's when I realized I was about to die.

Suddenly, Waltraud grabbed my outstretched arm and dragged me away from the pack. "Run, Backup, run!"

Yes, but where to? I wanted to ask, as we rushed toward the low parapet. There, where seconds ago a bunch of young people had been squatting miserably, three individuals were standing, staring down. "JUMP!" Waltraud shouted at them at the top of her voice. Two of them actually did! She looked at me for a moment and, without slowing down, yelled, "Do you want to live forever?" At that, she grinned, let go of my arm, and dived over the edge.

One step later, I catapulted blindly from the roof of the ninth floor, which was higher than the ferry Franca had once pushed me from. Only then did I realize what Waltraud was planning and that we might not have to die after all.

I just had to hope the pool in the hotel's courtyard was deep enough. Then I splashed into the water, almost at the same time as the hacker.

It felt as if I had crashed into a moving bus. The gun almost slipped out of my hand as the impact hit. An elbow dug into my ribs. My legs buckled as I hit the bottom of the pool. At least it was deep enough not to break anything. With all my might, I pushed myself back to the surface and swam to the edge. Some of the teenagers were just getting out of the pool. I heard screams from above, quickly growing louder on the way down until they ceased abruptly with dull thuds. I ventured a glance behind me. At the edge of the pool, in a puddle of blood and grayish bodily fluids, lay the young man who had been standing on the roof seconds before. His skull was unnaturally flat, and one eye had burst open. The corpses of three liberated zombies were clinging to his lifeless body.

It continued to rain undead. In addition, those that had been lurking in the basement were about to follow us onto the terrace. The glass doors shattered under their onslaught.

We had barely ten meters on them. Waltraud led our headlong flight. Jumping over an overturned plastic couch, she yelled, "That's mine! Someone else had better not put their towel on it!" Then she pointed to the burned-out hotel next door. "Patrick is waiting for us behind there."

We ran as one across the neglected lawn. Garbage lay strewn everywhere. Anthracite-colored tubs held meter-high bamboo plants that had once delineated more private areas of the hotel garden but were now withering. We had to fight our way through a five-foot-high oleander shrub in bloom because the gate next to it was locked. Branches whipped our faces. One of the girls behind me caught her T-shirt in them. She tugged at it in panic but was unable to free herself. Crying, she called on the Gods, but it didn't help. Two zombies grabbed her and bit the flesh from her bones before I could do anything. Days later, her screams still echoed in my ears as if she were standing right beside me.

We burst out of the bushes, our footsteps thundering over the hot concrete. We ran blindly onto the road and were almost run over by the pickup truck. The car screeched to a halt. Waltraud shouted, "Shotgun!" She yanked open the passenger door, threw herself into the seat, and in one fluid motion pointed a rifle out the window—right between my eyes. I watched her finger slide to the trigger and ducked a split second before the bang. The rush as the shot whizzed through my hair felt unreal, like something you think you might have imagined. I roughly pushed a teenager trying unsuccessfully to climb into the back seat into the overcrowded interior of the car, threw the door shut behind him, and almost at the same time carried the last teenager into the back of the car, jumping in after her. At that moment, Patrick drove off at breakneck speed. I slammed hard against something that, unlike my face, would not give way. The sudden pain brought tears to my eyes. Blood shot from my nose. The lurching of the vehicle meant I could barely sit up. When the torment had subsided somewhat, I looked through the windshield, leaning on my elbows. A zombie was trying to jump onto the hood. Patrick took evasive action, flinging us back and forth on the bed of the truck.

This time, it was the area around my kidneys that had to absorb the shock. The force of the impact fired the infected over the windshield, sending it spinning on its axis as it flew through the air. The young woman next to me dropped onto her back and immediately pulled in her legs as the flying corpse eclipsed the sun above us.

The zombie crashed headfirst between us. With full force, the young woman, screaming with rage and desperation, kicked him in the abdomen with both legs. The force of her kick propelled him out of the truck bed. He slapped onto the asphalt and didn't move again. Patrick braked slightly, turned left into a side alley, and took us out of danger.

I noticed my nose swelling rapidly, making it more difficult to breathe. The pain increased with it until my head felt as if it were about to burst. A few seconds later, I lost consciousness.

I came to as we were driving through the gate into the yard that afternoon. Franca had now returned with Jens and Nils.

While Patrick brought the vehicle to a halt, I looked over the edge of the loading area and saw her staring at us reproachfully. At the sight of my swollen face, her expression darkened still further. She walked briskly over to the pickup and helped me down.

The woman who had been sitting next to me the whole time, on the other hand, jumped nimbly onto the cobblestones.

I felt sick to my stomach. I could hardly stand upright. Franca led me into the living room and made me sit down. She alternately held my left and right eyelids open and shone her little flashlight into them. Then she felt my head and bent it back and forth. This intensified the headache, and I groaned. Finally, she told me her diagnosis. "Even though I'm wondering how this is even possible with your thick head, you've got concussion."

I just grinned inanely at her. Someone brought a kitchen towel full of crushed ice cubes. A mattress was placed on the floor next to me, and I rolled onto it carefully. Even more carefully, I put the soothing ice on my painfully pulsating nose.

Then I sank back down into the darkness, away from the pain, away from Franca's reproaches.

In the evening, I came to again. The nausea had mostly lifted, but my eyelids were fluttering with exhaustion. The ice had melted and the mattress beneath me was damp. My swollen nose hurt less. I heard muffled voices and the clattering of cutlery.

As soon as I tried to sit up, the world began to spin again.

Patrick appeared and sat in the armchair next to me. In his hands he held a steaming bowl of soup and a crust of bread. "You look shittier than usual," he said in mock unconcern, pressing the bowl into my hand.

"Meh," I replied between spoonfuls. "I'm trying to compete with you."

He grinned. "How's the head? Still hurting?"

I carefully bit off a piece of bread and drank some broth. "It's more of a dull throbbing. But it'll pass. What happened while I was asleep?"

Patrick glanced furtively toward the dining room, lowered his voice, and slid closer. "Franca gave us a good talking to. She was angry, but not in the traditional way. She didn't scream or anything. No, man. She gave us such a dressing-down, I felt this small, even with my hat on." He held up his right hand, with his index finger at a tiny distance from his thumb. Then he grinned again. "I mean, she's got a point, but we did save five people, all the same."

"We all could have been killed, Patrick." I would have hung my head if the pain had allowed it. "And if we'd waited for her, we might have saved them all."

"Or we'd all have died! What would we have done differently if Franca had been there? Even she said afterward that she couldn't have thought of better tactics." He shook his head again. I couldn't tell whether he felt misunderstood or was fighting against himself so as not to have to accept the accusations.

"No, that's true," I said in a conciliatory tone. "It could have ended badly with Franca, too. Or worse, even."

I squeezed his shoulder as hard as my condition allowed. Then I changed the subject. "What kind of teens are they?"

Patrick relaxed a little and sat up straighter. "Two of the youngsters we rescued are the people we were looking for. The rest are other survivors they had met at the hotel. The older guy is a little strange. They looted rooms together, going over the balconies. Some of the minibars had plenty of nuts and candy bars. Many of the rooms were empty. But zombies were lurking in the hallways, and at some point, they began to break down doors. That's why the kids had to keep running. There was a bit of running water, and they also drank from the cisterns."

I nodded, distressed. From my seat, I saw people leaving the table one after the other. The meal was obviously finished. Then I heard Franca's commanding voice. "Everyone cleans their own stuff here. We're happy to share our food with you, but if you want to stay, you'll have to abide by our rules." She was speaking to the oldest one, who was a full head taller than her and whose muscles were far bigger.

He looked at her condescendingly. "Since when do you tell me what to do?" Everyone else either stood frozen where they were or got themselves out of harm's way.

"Excuse me?"

"Are you deaf or something? If you want the kitchen to be clean, then surely you know whose job it is." With these words he went out of the room, leaving his cutlery and dishes on the dining table. I heard him go up the stairs and close a door behind him.

Jens made to follow him, but Franca waved him back with a barely noticeable gesture. She went to the table, collected his dishes, and washed them herself. No one dared move. Franca dried her hands as if nothing had happened and came into the living area. She looked relaxed, and that frightened me to the core. Unfortunately, she immediately looked in my direction. With an enigmatic smile, she asked, "Backup, what about your bowl?"

"Just finished. I'll take it through in a minute." I'd forgotten the headaches and the concussion.

"Great," she praised me, clapping her hands. I shuddered even more when she asked cheerfully, "So, whose turn is it to tell a story today?"

CHAPTER 6

NILS

The earlier events had hit me worse than I thought. I woke up with an incredible headache. My neck was stiff, my full bladder was screaming to be emptied. The pain didn't permit any quick movements. It took me five minutes to reach the bathroom. My ears rang incessantly.

A stranger looked back at me from the mirror, his face grotesquely swollen and purple. Cautiously, I brushed my teeth, avoiding the area around my nose. The foam I spat out was pink. Evidently one or another of my teeth had come loose. Which one exactly I couldn't say, because everything was numb.

Arriving back at the bed, my skin was suddenly covered in beads of sweat. I shivered and wondered if I had a fever. Frantically, I began to search my body for bite marks. Had I been infected yesterday after all? In my panic I forgot that if I had been, I would have turned into a zombie long ago. There were neither scratches nor teeth marks to be found. With the relief, the pain also returned. Blood dripped from my nose onto the hand that was supporting me on the edge of the bed as I gasped for air. In vain I tried to steady myself on the bedside table with my other hand. Seconds later, I toppled forward.

When I came to, Patrick was sitting next to me with a book in his hand. Much of my vision was blurred, but I recognized his silhouette.

"Whtmsit?" I mumbled. He put the text aside and took the cooling pad from my mouth.

"What did you say?" he asked.

"What time is it?" I croaked out.

"Four thirty," he replied. "Remember yesterday, when I told you how shitty you looked?"

"Yes."

"Well, that was silly of me, because now there's nowhere for me to go." He had a strained and worried expression.

"It is that bad?"

"Yes! It's that bad!"

"Well, I definitely still look better than you. Where did you go today?"

Patrick's face twitched. He gave me a pained look. "The old lady's losing it."

"The old lady? Who do you mean?"

He closed his eyes and ran his hand over his mouth. "We went to Sa Pobla. There are two or three smaller supermarkets there. One of the new ones was with us. The one who acted out last night, remember?"

I nodded cautiously.

"Franca suggested that he come along, and he immediately agreed. I think he wanted to prove to her how tough he was or some masculine shit like that. At first, everything went according to plan. We'd done three rounds and we were getting back in the car when she stood in his way. With one hand, she pushed him away from the car door, putting one of the smaller guns on the ground along with two full boxes of ammo. You know, the ones we keep under the driver's seat." I nodded and immediately regretted it.

"She took the magazine out and put it down a few meters from the gun. Then she told him to fuck off.

"The guy—I don't even know his name—stood there speechless for a few seconds. And then he started to call her names. The usual macho gibberish and insults. He was raging. When she turned her back on him, he went for her." Patrick clenched his fists as if reenacting the scene. "But she had expected it! She knew he was going to do it! She ducked out of his way. He smacked into the car, at full tilt, and earned himself two quick punches. One to the kidneys, the other to the ribs. Then he fell over like a freshly cut tree." Patrick paused and looked guiltily at the ground before continuing. "Franca just leaned down to him, grabbed him by the hair, and said something softly into his ear. You should have seen her face! Ice cold, man, ice cold! The guy tried to get up, but he could barely move from the pain. She got into the car and impatiently motioned for me to drive off. The undead heard the noise and came closer. We left him lying there. And the zombies were coming around the corner!" He took a deep breath. "I was glad they assigned me to be your guard after that. I just wanted to get out of her way. You had passed out by then and knocked over the nightstand. Waltraud heard the racket and came to look. Your nose was bleeding. She kept an eye on you until we came back."

I replied, "Too bad I couldn't be there. My head's throbbing like crazy, I'm afraid. And that guy was an asshole. He would have brought us nothing but trouble. On the other hand, it was a dirty trick to leave him out there," I added, trying to soften Patrick's uncomprehending stare.

"Better if you get some rest first. Are you hungry? Shall I get you some soup?"

"That'd be good. Is there a spicy one?"

"You wouldn't be able to handle it." he scoffed and left the room to get me something to eat.

In the days that followed, I hardly left my room. I slept a lot and had the crew bring me food and water in bed. I was not proud of this, but my physical condition didn't allow me to walk any farther than the bathroom next door.

Franca came and examined me every day. Each time she seemed more distant, almost catatonic.

On the first day, she had said, "Hmm, it's worse than I thought. The swelling is slowly going down, but it'll take you at least a week to recover from the concussion." Then she got up and left. The next day, she said nothing. Waltraud, Eva, Patrick, Jens, and Nils took turns visiting me and told me how well the rest of the young people were integrating or how the day's looting had gone. No one mentioned the Sa Pobla incident.

One evening, Eva came to my room. After I had eaten the stew—the swelling had gone down, and it was good to be able to smell food again—she put a smartphone on the nightstand. "Yesterday we had a long talk with the kids about their time at the hotel. I thought you'd be interested in what they had to say, so I recorded it all," she said. "And in the process, you'll even get to hear Nils's story."

"What, he said more than five sentences at a time?"

"And how! Listen to this, but don't complain if it stops you from sleeping all night. The kiddies have been through some serious shit."

She looked at the painting above the bed and it seemed as if her gaze was lost in the vastness of the ancient panorama.

"But first I'm going to sleep," I replied wanly, sinking deeper into my pillows. She grinned, pulled up the covers in a motherly fashion, and kissed me on the forehead.

"Sleep well and get well soon," she said on the way out.

It was the middle of the night when I woke up again. I tossed and turned restlessly for half an hour until I remembered the smartphone. I switched on the bedside light and picked it up. The screen lock had been deactivated, so it was easy to start the recording. I had to increase the volume to identify all the voices while at the same time being careful not to wake anyone in the house. I groaned inwardly as I braced myself to translate Nils's narrative. Eva had begun recording when the conversation was already underway, so it started midsentence. The whole thing seemed like a radio play.

Unknown girl: ". . . the airport was shut down. We were already on the bus, but then they sent us back to the hotel. The driver was mega annoyed and kept ranting in Spanish. The hotel was in chaos, too, because the staff refused to take us in. They only let us stay when a jeep with soldiers came and a female officer talked to the resort people. She actually threatened them with her gun."

Patrick: "What, does Franca have a twin sister?"

[quiet laughter]

Unknown girl: "We even got our old room back. In the beginning, it was totally cool to be having a longer vacation. We had no idea what was going on anywhere else. So, we just kept partying and drinking. Just having a good time, you know. But then we found out what was happening.

"I ignored my parents all week while they were trying like maniacs to reach me."

[long pause, breathing sounds, and creaking furniture]

Unknown boy: "The longer we were there, the crankier and less friendly people became. We were constantly having to prove our identity when we left or came back to the hotel. Soon there were hardly any services. No one came to clean. There wasn't always food in the restaurant and the waiting staff were long gone. We had some money, so we bought food outside. We heard things were the same in the surrounding hotels.

After a week or so, local youths driving around in battered cars and on old mopeds started harassing us and calling us names. We hadn't seen any cops in a long time, and it wasn't long before the first brawls broke out on the streets. It went on like that for a week.

"All that stopped after a massive storm. I didn't get a wink of sleep that night. The next day, things got really heavy. Screams from the street woke me up in the late morning. At first, I was angry because I thought they were fighting in front of the hotel again. But then I saw them for the first time from the balcony . . ."

Franca: "Zombies!"

[pause]

Unknown girl: "Yes, zombies. I was lying on the balcony in the sun chair, chilling out because I hadn't slept much that night because of the storm. My younger sister was crashing, inside, on the bed. I heard the screams, too, but I was too tired to check what was going on. Then there was a commotion under the balcony. I got really scared. In the second I looked down at the people, a grayish woman jumped on a man's back and dug her claws into him. She bit him in the neck and tore out a huge piece of meat. That was really heavy. Man! The blood sprayed up in a high arc. The guy fell down, and the zombie woman got off him. Then more infected people jumped on him. I screamed like a banshee, which was pretty stupid. Of course, all the zombies immediately looked up at me. They were sniffing around, kind of like dogs. I was scared to death, stepped backward, and fell over the deck chair. And the zombies ran into the hotel. I immediately dashed into the room, locked the door, and drew the curtains. The screaming woke my sister. She was terrified. I told her to stay quiet. Then we heard screaming and footsteps tramping in the hallway outside our door. How long did we spend in the hotel room? One, maybe two weeks? I can't say for sure. We lived on what was left over from the packed lunches they'd been giving out each day. For some reason, I'd been putting a little of it in the minibar every day because I couldn't get the food down at first.

"That, the nuts, and the chocolate bars kept us alive to begin with. After a few days, however, even that had gone. At some point, we were so famished that we had to go find something to eat. We didn't dare step out into the hallway. Sometimes we heard footsteps shuffling and of course got mega panicked again. Even so, we climbed over the balcony under cover of darkness, going from room to room. Wherever we got the sliding door open, we helped ourselves to the minibar.

"Once they almost caught us. The door of a hotel room we were looting was ajar. We didn't notice because it was dark. The undead smelled us and rushed in. Luckily, there were so many of them that they got in each other's way in the narrow entrance. We escaped at the last moment over the balcony. The next morning, we came across other survivors."

Unknown boy: "We did pretty much the same. We couldn't leave the hotel because of the zombies. Every now and then, we met others like us. Some joined our group. But unfortunately, people also kept getting killed when the infected got us. That strange Dutchman was there from the beginning and wanted to play the leader, the asshole. We ignored his showboating as best we could until he started using threats and violence to try and get what he wanted. He kept trying to get a share of our loot. If you hadn't shown up, there'd have soon been bad blood between us and him. I think it's good that we're rid of him now."

[pause]

Jens: "Nils? Are you asleep?"

[indistinct grunting]

Jens: [laughing] "Your turn."

Nils: "My turn for what?"

Jens: "To tell your story. We've told ours, but we haven't heard yours yet."

[Pause. Nils's unmistakable wheezing and the old leather chair creaking as he moves in it can be heard.]

Nils: "I don't like prattling on; it goes against the grain. But okay, since it's you guys. What do you want to know, exactly? How and when I got here?

"Gee, I've been living on the island four or five years now. I had a nose for profit, and I invested in cryptocurrency at the right time. So, I became rich overnight, left Germany, and bought this hut and upgraded it. Then I did nothing in particular—adapted to the local lifestyle and got busy lazing away the days. Sometimes I had visitors from home, family or friends dropped by. That was the sum total of my life. And I liked it that way.

"But then the epidemic came and changed everything. I can remember every detail of the day after the storm. In the late morning, the sun came out, and I saw the clouds moving away to the south. I was looking forward to a beautiful day. As usual, my radio was nothing more than babble in the background, until the music was interrupted by an emergency announcement. At first, I was only half listening, but I got interested quickly when the speaker mentioned the first deaths. There had been riots in Palma, and the police were not getting them under control. Throughout the day, the same reports kept on coming in from other towns and villages. I'd known for a long time what was going on, but I'd been too frightened to act. To organize food and such, I mean.

"I listened to the radio as one island broadcaster after the next fell silent. The few that were still functioning reported increasingly horrific incidents spreading out from Palma. After two days, people were talking openly about the fact that the plague from the mainland had infested the island.

"On the third day, it reached this area. The infected had wandered haphazardly across the plain, looking for food. Were they looking for their own kind so that they could band together, like animals in a herd? This thought crossed my mind many times in the days that followed.

"After a week, I'd run out of food. Because I wasn't used to going hungry, it drove me out of hiding. Fortunately, I have a good water supply, but except for all the orange trees, not much grows on the property. I had to get something to eat. My body was screaming for carbohydrates. It took two days for the hunger to get so extreme that I had to venture out.

"Ten days! It only took ten days to destroy an island like Mallorca. In the beginning, I went out in the truck, but its size was often troublesome, even if it did provide good protection against zombie attacks. The plague had caught the inhabitants completely by surprise. Everywhere on the streets, I came across hastily abandoned cars, some of them burned out. In the residential areas, doors and windows stood wide open. In some places, I discovered human remains that had been gnawed down to the bone. But you know what? I think I heard some hints a few days before the invasion that even here, no one could think they were safe anymore. But I had fallen into the Mallorcan mañana mentality and ignored all that. Ten days later, I drove through ghost towns, cursing myself over and over for my arrogance and apathy. I should have stockpiled more food long ago, should have armed myself, should have installed surveillance cameras . . . should have, would have . . .

"In the first little store, I filled one shopping cart after the next, almost breathless with fear. My knees were shaking like Elvis Presley's did when he danced. Before I left the store, I put one of my credit cards on the cash register. Then I went back, and I saw the zombies up close for the first time. It was a group of fifteen or twenty infected, blocking my path. Before I could even shake off the terror, they charged at me. I don't know what frightened me more, the sight of their white eyeballs or the sickly color of their skin.

"I opened up the throttle, and the truck swerved and almost crashed into a building. But I managed to keep it on track, and I drove right through the group instead. I caught more than half of the undead head-on. The rest of them bounced off the sides like rubber doughnuts. Horror-struck, I tore through the streets like a mad thing until I realized in the afternoon that I had landed at a completely different part of the island. I knew the area, of course, but I hadn't often ended up there. As soon as I stopped shaking, I started the car again and drove to a hill where there was a view of the area. You'd think this day had already been exciting enough, but it wasn't over yet. From my vantage point, I saw an unbelievably large pack of zombies that had moved out of Sineu and was only a few kilometers away.

"I've never been an adrenaline junkie, so my next decision surprised me all the more. The wandering corpses wouldn't be able to harm me in the big pickup truck, I figured, so what could happen? I taxied cautiously to Sineu, following the cluster from a safe distance. My heart was pounding, but this time almost in joyful anticipation of danger.

"I chugged after them at walking pace. The town seemed deserted like the other villages. In the small railroad station, I saw the gray train that had been standing there for weeks with its doors open. A movement on the second floor of the station building made me jump. I looked up at the window and saw two figures waving at me from above. I sat in the truck and thought for a couple minutes about what to do. They watched me the whole time. Then I lowered the driver's window and waved them down. They reeked. But I let them get in and brought them here. The craving for the feeling you get when you save someone's life has driven everything I do ever since. I literally crave the kick it gives me. I've gone out every other day. For places where the truck would have been too clunky and cumbersome, I took the Mercedes. While I was looking for food and keeping an eye out for survivors, I also looked for gasoline for my coupé. One by one, I found you and took you in. Some, whom I met elsewhere, did not want to come. What has happened to them in the meantime, I can only guess . . ."

[pause]

Nils: "Well, that's my story—and now don't bug me about it! Man, I can't remember the last time I talked so long . . . My throat is completely dry."

Almost as if in a dream, I heard other voices mingling with the recording. I was tired again now and couldn't keep listening. Half asleep, I turned off the smartphone, though I don't remember turning off the bedside light.

CHAPTER 7

EVA AND PATRICK

DAY 28 A.I.

No matter where or how well you hide, they'll find you. It doesn't seem to make any difference to them what you do, because they'll find you anyway. They can smell you! They have a phenomenal sense of smell. But only a limited ability to see. The most their milky white eyes can do is sense outlines and movement. But that doesn't stop them from gnawing the flesh off your bones while you're fully conscious, once they've got you in their filthy claws.

Patrick and I have been fleeing them for weeks. At first, we were in a car, but when that gave up the ghost on a lonely alpine road after Grenoble, we kept on toward the Mediterranean on foot. Before sleep overtook us, we made sure to find the most airtight places to shelter, usually abandoned trucks, buses, or vans. We covered the insides of the vehicles with scraps of old newspapers and maps so we wouldn't be seen. We washed whenever we could, using rainwater, herbs, and sand. Never with modern detergents. That attracts them like moths to a flame.

When the outbreak of the disease was officially recognized, we were, crazily enough, on our way to Paris by car. At that time, as we learned later, there were heavily armed military personnel on the streets, as the police couldn't handle things on their own anymore. Near Chessy, we ran into a checkpoint. While we were waiting to be allowed through, the outpost was overrun.

Before our eyes, countless infected emerged from the darkness, mowing down everything that breathed. They smashed the windows of the vehicles in front of us and killed the passengers.

And why am I still alive? When the massacre began, Patrick took the initiative, turned our car around and drove back down the highway, ignoring the speed limits. Shortly afterward, I turned on the radio and tried to make sense of the French news. The few fragments I understood were more than enough to make us panic.

I refuse to write them down again, the details of what I experienced after that. The horror was too much for me. Despondency and helplessness take ahold of me again every time I think of it. You'd think I might have gotten used to it after all these weeks, but I haven't. When we had to leave our car because of engine failure, I left my diary behind. Did my unconscious want to help me escape from my meticulous documentation of the evil, too? Maybe. The simpler and more realistic answer is that in my haste, I just didn't think of it. Patrick told me yesterday that I should set down the events again. Maybe it would help make sense of the madness in my head, he said. Well, okay then, if Patrick says so. So, herewith is a short summary of the experiences that haunt my dreams. As far as I can remember.

We marched for days, over mountain passes and through forests. We avoided roads and towns wherever possible. Our destination was Saint-Raphaël.

My parents had moored their little boat in a berth there for decades, and that was where it was now anchored. Since they were now too frail for sailing trips, they had passed the yacht, and the berth, to us. As we fled, we had worked out a plan. We were going to try to get to Gran Canaria by boat.

If this diary has fallen into the hands of someone who isn't able to ask me for answers, because I'm dead or worse, that person may well want to know: Who is Patrick? In this day and age, I find it difficult to make emotional speeches or even put them down on paper. And I am increasingly losing my enthusiasm for the written word. But when I write about Patrick, I can hardly stop. To say I am in love with him is a paltry understatement.

And the fact that I feel like a teenage girl with a crush when he plays me love songs on his guitar and sings along, well, I couldn't do anything about that even if I wanted to.

We are an odd couple. Patrick, at almost two meters, is three heads taller than me. Whereas I am petite, he is muscular. Not in the modern sense like a bodybuilder, not at all. More massive, like a stonemason whose shirt would stretch over his abs and whose muscular arms could tip over a small car.

His long graying hair contrasts with my dark short style. He is the person who connects me with a spark of reality among all the madness. When I feel his warm hand on my back as I fall asleep, or hear his footsteps beside me, I know that I have something true, something real that I can rely on after all. He is there, real, indestructible.

Having him by my side helps me not to give in to the panic and fear that lie constantly in wait for me like a cat stalking a bird, wishing to break its neck for fun.

We arrived in the evening of the twenty-eighth day A.I. The sun had just set. In the blue hour, we could see Saint-Raphaël and the seemingly endless Ligurian Sea behind it. A salty breeze was blowing toward us at the foot of the mountains, and no man-made sound could be heard.

The plague raged all along the coast. We couldn't walk down to the harbor—we had witnessed too often the horrors inflicted by the infected. We would not take any unnecessary risks so close to our destination. Everywhere in the upper town, we came across abandoned vehicles, most with their doors standing open. Their batteries were now dead. We let one roll down the hill, its keys dangling uselessly from the ignition, until it started. Our few belongings fit in the footwell in front of me. We didn't dare turn on the lights. Behind us, the wind whirled undefinable shreds into the air.

Saint-Raphaël looked like a ghost town. There was garbage everywhere. We found our bearings by the slope of the streets. Again and again, the way was blocked by abandoned cars and here and there an overturned bus, so we had to look out for alternative routes. When our path was finally barred by the infected, we were heading almost straight for Port de Santa Lucia Sud. The permanent fear had left me in a state of detachment, so I wasn't even distressed. Patrick finally turned on the lights, hit the gas, and drove like a demon through the dark alleys.

Needless to say, they chased us immediately. At the Jardin des Corailleurs, we had left them far enough behind to exit the vehicle and run over to the port area.

After all the years I had come here since my childhood, I found the correct jetty right away. The little yacht, which could carry four people, was waiting in the same place it always had. We rushed madly along the jetty and jumped onto the deck. I couldn't immediately locate the key to the cabin and rummaged frantically in my backpack. The undead were closing in. My hands began to shake and no matter how hard I tried, I couldn't put my hands on the bunch of keys. Then, calmly, Patrick took the bag, put his arm inside and took out the keys. No sooner had we disappeared into the cabin than dozens of feet tramped across the landing stage, just a few meters from us. They were sniffing and grunting. We didn't dare breathe. The wandering corpses stomped up and down between the boats for half an hour before disappearing around midnight in search of new victims.

A little later, Patrick and I were lying in bed with our arms wrapped tightly around each other, waiting for the sleep that wouldn't come. Suddenly, I remembered the old sketch books and diaries that lay dormant on one of the shelves above us. In the windowless room, I switched on my headlamp, fished out one of the emptier notebooks and a functioning ballpoint pen, and began to write these lines.

It was early morning. We had slept for six hours, but we did not feel remotely refreshed. Solitary seagulls screeched high above us. Carefully, we untied the boat and used long telescopic tiller extensions to punt quietly out of the harbor. Starting the engine so close to the infected was unthinkable. We didn't do that until we had left the marina well behind. The old well-maintained two-stroke took us out to sea. After a few hundred meters, we felt safe enough, so we switched off the engine and hoisted the sails.

Sitting close together on deck, we breathed in lungfuls of the salty air.

Only once the mainland had sunk behind the horizon did we feel any relief about this small victory. Before, I wrote that our plan was to go to Gran Canaria, but we had just changed it. We figured the archipelago was far enough away to offer us long-term protection from the disease and that we'd be able to reach it by dinghy.

Initially, we had plotted a west-southwest course that would have taken us in a more or less straight line from Saint-Raphaël to Gibraltar. But first, we had to make some arrangements. We had hardly any food on board—two cans of beans—and only three liters of water. So, we decided to head for Calvi, on Corsica, to replenish our supplies.

In the safety of the endless sea and kissed by the sun, my long-ignored tiredness returned. Sitting at the tiller, my eyes fell closed of their own accord. Patrick stroked my skin. I leaned my shoulder against him and let myself gradually fall asleep.

We sighted Corsica late in the afternoon. A ship that looked like a heavily armed naval cruiser signaled us to slow down and pass on their port side. Over the radio, they ordered us to identify ourselves and tell them whether there were any infected onboard. Ridiculous. As if we would have been alive and able to operate the radio.

So, the ship's crew, pointing their fully automatic weapons at us, asked us to come closer. I didn't blame them. A dinghy was launched and five soldiers, who, judging from their armor, would have had no problem surviving a nuclear winter, chugged over. Since our cutter was too small to take them all aboard, three of them stayed in the gray rubber boat. Once the two-man search party had found nothing of relevance, they gave us the go-ahead. After that, my fingers reached for the pen and the notebook of their own accord.

Following my semirestful nap, I became more aware of my emotional state again. The days spent under the threat of the infected, when I could not—or did not want to—process the abominations I was experiencing in writing, had left me emotionally blunted and hard. But the endless horizon, some sleep, and the good weather brought me slowly back to myself again. Sitting at the tiller next to Patrick, I noticed my eyes filling with tears. My chin trembled as I looked back on days and nights of fear. He wrapped an arm around me. His mere presence spoke volumes. Without him uttering a word, I felt myself regaining some of the safety and security that had been lost to us.

In the evening, we reached the marina in Calvi. The port administration had told us by radio that there were hardly any berths, but that they'd find room for our small yacht.

In the town, the world seemed to be turning as it always had, and it was easy to ignore the pandemic. The medieval citadel, shining bright orange in the setting sun, presided over the old town, which was teeming with life.

I walked with Patrick for hours through the alleys of the town, fervently soaking up its fleeting joie de vivre and crumbling longevity. I was overcome with melancholy at the thought that this beauty might be in danger.

We had hardly anything to wear besides what we had on. So, we bought two, three jackets, pants, underwear, and pairs of shoes, driven by the fear that we would never be able to buy anything ever again. We stocked up on provisions at the supermarket and returned to the boat in the early evening. For the first time in weeks, we would finally be able to spend a whole night in safety.

DAY 29 A.I.

The aroma of freshly brewed coffee drifted into the bunk. For a brief moment, I forgot the danger that had been tracking us for weeks. Pure joy. A relaxed breakfast, vacationing on my grandfather's sailboat. At first, I smiled, reclining with my eyes closed and stroking the familiar boat with every movement it made.

But bliss was soon displaced by reality. I took a deep breath and crawled backward to the edge of the bed. Outside, Patrick was setting out silverware and dishes. Through the curtain, I watched him preparing breakfast. Bustling around the tiny kitchenette, he looked like a bear plundering a beehive.

My heart was pounding. Without turning his head, he asked, "Are we having breakfast in here or outside?"

"Outside," I replied with a smile, wrapping the blanket tighter around me and climbing the small staircase. As I passed, I brushed my lips against his back. He followed me, carrying a plastic tray with coffee and fresh rolls. Where had he gotten them so early?

Over breakfast, we discussed how to approach the next few days. Inevitably, this meant I had to face the reason for our flight here. I immediately wished it had all just been a nightmare.

DAY 32 A.I.

Our souls gradually healed in Corsica, though we took pains not to let ourselves be thrown off course by what was happening on the continent. Long strolls on the beach and good food made us feel safer and safer. Nonetheless, we bought foods with long shelf lives every day, stuffing them into every last space on the boat, no matter how small. One morning, we gave the water tank a thorough clean and filled it with drinking water. At night we slept well. Well, not "well" exactly, but better than before. Calvi seemed like a paradise where we could survive the apocalypse unscathed.

But nothing could ever take away the sense of threat. In the background, part of me was always on the lookout for the least sign of danger. I flinched at every loud shout and every quick movement, ready to sprint in the opposite direction. Patrick was on his guard too, although he wasn't as frightened.

Despite our detachment from the situation on the mainland, I feel an increasingly sense of urgency. But I can't quite place it. Are these the alarm bells that supposedly sound when you're in imminent danger? There's nothing I can do, though, but continue to keep a watch on the situation.

DAY 33 A.I.

There is something morbid about people's behavior here. Patrick brought it up at dinner the day before yesterday, confirming my own concerns. As if the good mood wasn't just being artificially maintained, it was being heightened every day. It's not right to ignore the danger like that.

The two of us would soon set off on our great voyage. The boat was fueled, packed full, and ready to go. The sails were intact, and the engine serviced.

The news we were getting every day did not bode well. France had succumbed to the plague, and things didn't look any better in the neighboring countries. My parents had made it to Iceland. Patrick and I were feverishly considering whether we should venture north as well. But Iceland was a hell of a long way away. However, we had to hold out here for a few days. The weather report was predicting a bora over the Mediterranean, and we didn't want to get caught in it. After that we'd see. From now on we'd be staying on the boat and only leaving it if we really had to.

DAY 35 A.I.

Despair had me in its grasp again. Corsica would fall. No, that wasn't right: Corsica had fallen. The infected made it over to the island with a shipment of food.

That morning, Patrick and I were still at the market buying fruit and vegetables when screams of pain and horror broke through the general confusion of the busy marketplace.

Some of the people around us looked for the source of the distress, but others pretended not to hear. The grace period we had enjoyed here was over. Patrick quickly dropped a hundred-euro bill onto the counter, and before the merchant could hand over any change, we were on our way to the boat at full speed.

The next day, we learned from the radio that several people had hidden in the shipping containers and arrived in Corsica as stowaways. Unfortunately, some of them were already infected. During our morning walk to the market, we'd seen the ship, which, as it turned out later, had been given either a cursory inspection or no inspection at all by the crew of the naval cruiser.

The cargo was unloaded until the undead broke out. I don't know exactly what happened because I immediately ran for my life. Out of breath, we reached the dinghy. I started the engine and opened the throttle before Patrick had even loosened the mooring.

The telescopic tiller extension in his hand, he helped me maneuver through the narrow harbor. Other sailors were also trying frantically to leave the marina. In the confusion that quickly arose, many of them blocked each other's way. We were better prepared and left far ahead of them. I even remembered the name of one of the yachts: *Bahama Mama*. Who the hell comes up with something like that?

No more than ten minutes had passed since we heard the first noise. From a safe distance, we watched the chaos erupting in the harbor. A scuffle here, an angry argument there.

My gaze kept wandering to the marina entrance, which was standing open.

And then I saw the inevitable. The infected ran into the harbor area, as fast as I had ever seen them run. Two of them immediately rushed into the gatehouse. Seconds later, I saw silhouettes through the glass panes, perishing in a bloody dance. The rest headed unerringly for people on the jetties and fell on them. The creatures leapt from boat to boat, sowing infection and death among the stunned mariners. A few managed to save themselves temporarily by jumping into the water, but nowhere was safe. I sped up, pushing the ancient motor to its limits. The noise of the elderly internal combustion engine superimposed itself on the screams that followed us far out to sea. We drove in a big arc, east, north then west, past La Revellata. I didn't turn around once. Nor did I notice when the island disappeared over the horizon behind us. Now we were on the west-southwest course we had plotted. We hoisted the sails. The wind, at least, was with us. The sun was setting. I was tempted to shake off the tension, to prevent the emotional stupefaction from taking ahold. But this time, it wouldn't be easy. The fear was firmly embedded, like a thorn sunk deep under the skin. Uncertainty about the days to come fueled the feeling of lostness even more.

It is shortly before midnight. The light of myriad stars is glittering in the sheer endlessness of the sea around us. We have extinguished our position lights. After the incident in Calvi, France declared a ban on sailing in its territorial waters. Fortunately, our craft is so small that it could not easily be detected by radar. But we were not the only ones ignoring the prohibitions. We made out several larger ships on the horizon, heading south. A few minutes before, a single-engine propeller plane flew low over us, despite the ban. I listened to its hum for minutes until it disappeared westward. I am covered with a blanket while I keep watch at the tiller and hold our course, to shield the light from my headlamp. I turn it off every few minutes and look around. I have no way of knowing if someone is following us, but I keep on looking through my mother's binoculars.

Then I sit here and think again about how Patrick has been with me through thick and thin over the last few weeks. How stoic he's been about all the hardships, and how he's fled with me across half of France. His unshakable spirit has so often given me strength. He's not a daredevil; he's not combative like you'd expect. But he always does what needs to be done, no matter how unpleasant it is. Of course, we've argued, too. Our nerves have often been on edge, so it doesn't take much to make one of us explode.

But being exposed to constant danger has focused us on what is important: survival.

It's midnight. Patrick is lying down in the cabin. I can hear him snoring softly. Three hours until he comes to relieve me.

DAY 36 A.I.

The wind has picked up. A breeze is blowing from the north, driving us forward. We've had to make minor course corrections, but that was to be expected. What worries us is the weather report, which has confirmed the bora that is forecast to blow from the northwest tonight. And it's likely to be much stronger than previously expected. But we might be able to reach Mallorca before the storm. At this speed, we should make it, even if it is close. Patrick relieved me early in the morning as agreed. I stayed by his side until sunrise and then went below deck, where I tried to cook something edible in the pronounced swell. We had canned chili.

Am I finally going crazy???

Pirates!

Pirates, for the love of God!

Here, in the twenty-first century, we are being pursued by Mediterranean pirates!

They showed up a good two hours ago and changed course immediately, heading straight for us! I almost had to pinch myself to make sure I wasn't dreaming. After having failed in their attempt to cut across our tub with their three-master, they are now sailing just under a hundred and fifty meters behind us.

Patrick sailed past their barricade at a safe distance. One of them even threw a grappling hook at us! A grappling hook!

In fact, it was only a galvanized anchor, and it flew harmlessly past us—but still! The world is being overrun by the infected undead, but European pirates are experiencing a renaissance. What a time to be alive.

Our pursuers hoisted all the sails they had and drew inexorably closer. I could see their faces clearly and counted twelve of them—women and men alike—standing at the rail ready to disembark. A black Jolly Roger flag like the ones that were sold in toy stores until recently, was flying from the main mast.

All of them appear to be of European descent. A woman about my age gave me a look intended to frighten us. But I saw only insecurity and despair. The face is deeply imprinted on my mind. It spoke volumes about the wrong life choices she had made so far. We looked at each other as the boats slid past each other.

The pirates' sailboat was faster, but we were more maneuverable. Patrick zigzagged masterfully ahead, and it has taken them a long time to adjust at first.

Nevertheless, they are continuing to gain ground. Ahead of us, the sky is getting darker, and the sun is dropping behind the horizon. We are heading straight for the big weather front. My God, what a bora this is going to be! It's going to hit us in about an hour.

The swells are getting bigger. We're literally sliding down into the deep troughs between the waves. We are coping far less well with this sea than the big pirate ship astern. I don't know what they want. Our boat doesn't look like much. They probably want to practice because they think we are easy prey. It's starting to rain, and I have to stow the diary. I don't want to lose this one, too. Besides, it's so dark now that I can hardly see what I'm writing. I have to get our oilskins; tonight isn't going to be any fun. The storm is starting. The pirates are closing in.

DAY 37 A.I.

Despair intensifies my sarcasm, and that's why I haven't been able to find the words to describe last night. The good news is, we're alive. And we have food. And the pirates are gone. Okay, that's three bits of good news. The not-so-good news is we can forget about Iceland and Gran Canaria for now. As soon as we hit the storm, we realized we had underestimated how bad it was going to be. The waves were soon so high that they almost capsized the dinghy a few times. The pirates also quickly had other things to worry about than chasing us. The sails they had hoisted presented a large surface for the wind to attack, and it tossed them around on the crests of the waves like a child's toy. By the time they had hauled in the ropes, we were out of view. What fate befell them, I can only guess. We fought the storm all night.

In the darkness, were fully occupied with trying to stay alive. We could hardly use the compass. Powerful waves, meters high, sloshed over the deck like an animal. We had had the foresight to tie ourselves to the railing and sailed almost blind through the night.

Our course had taken us much farther north than we would have liked. Whenever I could, I tried to locate our position and chart our direction, but I rarely succeeded. When we saw the Formentor light-house flashing on our port side, we turned south. We had driven no more than five minutes, which seemed like an eternity, when our journey came to an almost fatal end. A bolt of lightning crashed into the sea a few hundred meters from us, illuminating a dirty white wall—right in our path.

Pirates again, I feared at first, but I was wrong. A passenger ship, almost invisible in the darkness and concealed by waves and rain, was plowing through the churning sea just a stone's throw away from us. There was nothing we could do except minimize the inevitable damage. Patrick jerked at the rudder, but we continued to sail straight for it and crashed into it.

For a moment, we lost control of the boat. The mast swayed violently, but it held. The sails flapped abruptly this way and that. We had to keep our heads low to avoid being hit by the lurching boom. Patrick crawled over to the sheet and adjusted the mainsail, while I took care of the jib. We idled alongside the passenger ship for a time and finally managed to get away from it. As soon as we were sailing reasonably normally again, I stood up to survey the damage.

I didn't get far. The sheet came loose again. The mainsail flapped uncontrollably to the other side. Patrick saw it coming and ducked, but not low enough. The underside of the boom hit him hard, hurling him to the ground. I dropped everything and rushed over. Without a helmsman, our boat was tossed wildly back and forth. I couldn't tell if my husband was breathing. He lay there, lifeless, soaked through with seawater and rain. I screamed. I roared out all the frustration of the last few weeks, leaving our little yacht unskippered. I didn't care, I just wanted my Patrick back. There was no sense in existing without him. I begged the sea to take me, too, but it had other plans. A high breaker caught us and flushed the boat into a small, secluded bay. The wave pushed us up the sandy beach, jamming the starboard side of the boat against the stone wall until the boat burst apart. And then it stood still, at a slight incline, as if held by an invisible force. It was a huge effort to pull Patrick below deck. In the light of my headlamp, I identified a large bump on the back of his head, felt his pulse, and heard him breathing. Then I took off his wet clothes, put him on his bunk in the recovery position, and let him sleep. A short time later, my eyes closed with exhaustion.

DAY 38 A.I.

In view of the hopelessness of the situation, my general motivation has now dropped to zero. Our supplies will get us through the next few weeks, but then what? Our vessel is damaged beyond repair, but it still makes a good roof for our heads. The storm has moved on. The sky is a bright blue, dotted with a few clouds. By noon even those will have evaporated.

I've thought for a long time about where we might have landed and reached the tentative conclusion that it is Mallorca. The high cliffs to the southeast match the descriptions I've found in the old navigation books. So here we are again on an island that, like the rest of Europe, will soon be overrun by the infected. I have no doubt about that. Not after what happened in Corsica.

Patrick has regained consciousness. Except for a terrible headache, he's fine. He listened to my report on our new situation, drank some tea, and fell asleep again. Since I'm afraid he might have a concussion and could vomit, he's lying in the recovery position again. My mood has hardly changed at all. As soon as something new happens, I'll write more. Even setting down these few lines has cost me effort. I've run out of steam.

DAY 41 A.I.

Patrick is halfway recovered, though a bit wobbly on his feet. We've decided to go for short walks every day.

DAY 43 A.I.

The supplies will only last another week, then we'll have to think of something else. Staying here isn't an option. And our wreck of a boat offers little protection against the infected.

DAY 50 A.I.

Every day, I become more and more withdrawn. Only Patrick's words of encouragement sometimes bring me out of my shell. He always manages to give me emotional support. Without him, I would have gone under long ago. He says that it would have been even worse for him without me. That's how it is in a real relationship, I guess—you're always there for each other. I'll try to recount the key events of the days that followed, even if every word is difficult for me. After that, I'm going to put down my pen for good.

We've been living with Nils since yesterday. After using up our supplies a few days ago, we left the boat with a heavy heart. Moving southwest through a wide green valley, lined both to left and right by high cliffs, we passed some uninhabited houses. At the end of the valley, we chose the southeastern route, walked up the road, and soon reached a pass between two ridges, looking down on most of the island. The plain below was silent. All over it, columns of smoke were twisting into the air. I knew immediately what had happened and made to turn and run back to our boat, thinking I'd be safer on the secluded beach. But my husband pulled me onward. We had nothing left to eat and had to return to civilization. Or to whatever was left of it.

Debilitated and discouraged, I let him lead me. We walked for half an hour until we saw a blue car coming toward us. Patrick pointed to a nearby fig tree where I could hide. I didn't know exactly how he managed it, but the driver offered us to take us in. We accepted with thanks. Nils lives in an opulent villa which has everything: electricity, water, food. He has the house set up so that one person could be self-sufficient here for years. He is welcoming and friendly but behaves more like a loner. Nils has given us our own room, and it's more luxurious than anything we've seen in the last few weeks. He tells us there are other people living here, but they're out collecting supplies. The house stands in the middle of a huge estate surrounded by a high fence. The entrance gate looks sturdy enough to withstand the attacks of the infected. On the surface, everything here seems safe. Oh, how I want to believe that. But I know better.

Eva closed her diary and placed it lovingly on the low coffee table. Patrick slid closer and put his arm around her shoulders. She drew her knees up, snuggling into his embrace.

On the fifth day after the rescue operation at Hotel 23, I had finally regained enough strength to go downstairs and spend the evening with my friends. I had listened spellbound to Eva. Now—as always after a tale had ended—there was a thoughtful silence. We sat for a long time in the dimly lit living room, offering each other wordless consolation.

CHAPTER 8

FAREWELL

As Franca had predicted, it was seven days before I had recovered enough to leave the room during the day. My head hurt with every step. Bright light bothered me, but that subsided after another week.

Immediately following my injury, I had barely moved and had eaten almost nothing but liquid food, so I lost some weight and muscle mass. As soon as I felt halfway fit—though I was nowhere near as healthy as before—I went out onto the lawn with my spear and tried to remember the training sequences. The blows I accidentally gave myself with the rock-hard shaft helped me realize which of my martial arts skills required improvement.

I took frequent breaks because my fitness was appalling. It took a shamefully short time for me to retire, exhausted, into the shade to doze for a while. The community permitted this. I made my usual contribution to the household chores.

Days later, when I could do at least an hour's practice with the spear, I joined the shooting and hand-to-hand combat training. The crew was pleased to have me back and immediately gave me a hard time. The swelling and hematoma disappeared completely after three weeks. Only a thin, blistered scar on the bridge of my now slightly bent nose bore witness to the accident.

As the days passed, the Mallorcan weather changed. The rainy pre-summer season arrived, and it poured continually. Humidity rose to almost a hundred percent and temperatures dropped below ten degrees in some places. Everything was damp and clammy. The rooms cooled down, so we had to turn the heat back on to prevent mold from forming on the walls. During this time, we hardly went outside, and with a household of thirteen, our supplies were now dwindling rapidly. We continued to train diligently in the basement, day in and day out.

Several times a week, despite the rain, I went outside and ran along the inner wall for an hour. I couldn't stand it in the house anymore. The ground was soggy and the red Mallorcan clay stuck heavily to my shoes, but I ran lap after lap and felt my fitness returning. Our days were occupied largely with planning for when the rain stopped. We had to use the lights sparingly, because the solar panels didn't provide enough power to charge the batteries. It went on like this for two weeks until the rainy season suddenly ended. If you looked over Es Plá early in the morning, you could see huge clouds of fog rising, tinged with gold by the first of the sun's rays. The streets remained empty. Plants ran rampant over towns and villages, and the achievements of human civilization crumbled to dust in eerie silence.

After three days without rain, we decided to try out a new route. Though we had plundered most of the western part of the island by now, the east remained—if other survivors had not already cleared it out. Our canary yellow pickup had suffered from reduced power levels during the sunshine-free weeks, but these had improved again over the last two days. Since the enormous size of its batteries gave it a range of over a thousand klicks, we weren't concerned about driving thirty kilometers on half a charge.

My physical condition was as good as it had been at my fittest on Dragon Island. The only thing I hadn't done was endurance work. Back then, I'd been able to train by running up and down the mountains. Still, I could do ten kilometers right off the bat, without needing a break.

As our small convoy rolled along the rain-rinsed highways toward Costitx, I sat in the Mercedes at Nils's side. I was glad to finally be back on a supply run. Besides the Glock at my hip, I had the spear, whose tip was sticking out the window and whose shaft was beneath my right calf. Through my lower leg muscle, I felt the fine vibrations of the wood in the wind. The sky was bright, almost painfully blue. Jens and Franca, with Patrick at the wheel, drove behind us in the pickup. Close to our destination, we slowed down. I leaned forward and watched in the side-view mirror as the elite fighter moved to the loading area.

She had lost much of her gracefulness and was moving awkwardly, as if she were fighting her usual flow. Since we had rescued the young people from the hotel without her help, she had become increasingly taciturn and more and more withdrawn every day, often avoiding our company.

Nils crawled along the winding road north of Costitx. Patrick followed three car lengths behind us. We reached the village. Both drivers braked abruptly. A walking corpse in a terrible state staggered out of the shadows onto the street. It was dragging its foot, which had been broken several times. One eye was missing. Its left arm hung loosely under its torn shirt. The other shoulder seemed to have been dislocated and was stiff. It came toward us with its right arm raised, the fingers extending rigidly.

"Damn Nazombie!" growled Nils, loading the Beretta with a fluid motion.

I put my hand on his arm and, glancing at the spear, said, "Let me do it."

He nodded.

Without opening the door, I got out of the car through the window and told the rear guard to keep an eye on the surroundings, which they were doing already. The infected made greedy sounds and approached, twitching. I lured him away from the middle of the road. After three steps, he was within reach. With a single movement, I stabbed the Nazombie in the brain through the empty eye socket. A heartbeat later, I felt him slump and finally drop dead. A jerk was all it took to get the weapon free. His right arm remained rigid.

It was not essential to get back into the car. The first supermarket was about a hundred meters ahead. I preceded the column on foot, hearing it crawling along behind me.

My vigilance increased with every breath. We passed the empty village church and the terraces of two lonely cafes. Before we reached the store, I saw the entrance to a pharmacy behind a green gate on the right. I waited for the vehicles to approach and then pointed to the store. Franca jumped from the pickup and joined me.

"First the pharmacy, right?" She nodded and strode toward it. As she walked, she fished out a small black case from the pocket of her pants. Before kneeling to pick the lock of the gate, she looked quickly over her shoulder to make sure I had her back. I nodded affirmatively and she began her work.

After less than a minute, it popped open. Franca pushed the grille aside, folding it up like an accordion. She got through the front door just as quickly. Jens had gotten out in the meantime and was keeping watch on the entrance. We entered the pharmacy.

The little sales room was silent. Light was streaming through the big windows. Franca pulled a cotton bag out of her pocket, jumped over the counter, and began stuffing random medicines into it from the shelves.

I followed her. On the other side of the counter, I found a bundle of folded paper bags under the cash register. I tucked a good dozen of them into my waistband, unfolded one, and started throwing in boxes of pills, ointments, and liquids. We didn't know what each medicine was for, but we sure didn't have time to read through the instructions.

Two of the shelves formed a passage to the back room where we found more cabinets full of medicine. I filled five bags to the brim before we agreed that the pharmacy wasn't going to yield anything else of value. I lined up my haul, ran the shaft of the spear through the bag handles, and slung the weapon over my shoulder. At the pickup, I set the paper bags on the truck bed and pulled out the shaft. Franca came out with her hands full and set her loot down next to it.

We looked at each other, grinning with satisfaction. She seemed to have relaxed a bit now that we had successfully cleaned out the pharmacy. It could hardly have gone better.

Suddenly, I noticed that something had changed. My smile faded. I looked down the street past the Mercedes, puzzled. There was a short, sharp sound somewhere and a whirring that approached horrifyingly fast. At the same moment, the windshield of the coupé ahead of us cracked, a spider's web spreading immediately around a hole the size of a thumb. I saw Nils's head jerk back and hit the headrest. Then the rear window exploded in a jumble of dark red blood and black splinters of bone.

I heard another bang. Before I could react, a linear buzz raced past me, missing me by about ten centimeters and knocking Jens off his feet.

"DOWN!" roared Franca, throwing herself against me. We hit the floor as more bullets whistled close over our heads. "Snipers!" she shouted as she pinned my body with her weight.

The next moment, she crawled over to Jens, grabbed his ankle, and dragged him toward the pickup. I clasped the shaft, which had almost slipped from my grasp, and crawled behind her. She examined the wound on Jens's torso, where his chest met his shoulder. The shock of the injury and the force of the hit had knocked him unconscious.

"Patrick!" I yelled. "Are you okay?" More bullets whizzed through the air, hitting the facades and crumbling the fine sandstone onto the asphalt.

"Yes, but Nils is gone!" His voice cracked in anger. "Those mother-fuckers killed Nils." I heard a Velcro strap ripping open inside the truck as he grabbed one of the pump action guns from the back seat.

"Did you see where the shots came from?" I asked.

"No, pulled my head back in right away."

"Jens is badly wounded. If we don't get him treated, he might bleed to death!" Franca shouted over the crack of the precision rifle. She was trying to staunch the bleeding.

The car swayed slightly as Patrick moved inside it and opened the rear door, almost tossing the first aid kit into our laps. Franca reached for the plastic box and frantically broke it open. She took out some bandages and gauze, tore them open and pressed them as hard as she could to the wound.

Then she noticed that Jens was bleeding from the back and drew my attention to it. "Shit," she cursed, though immediately realizing that this might even be a good thing: "Straight through. I just hope none of his vital organs are injured. Backup, give me a hand, damn it!" She lifted Jens's hip and gestured for me to hold it in place. I obeyed. She wrapped the remainder of the bandage around his torso.

A bullet ricocheted off the cobblestones a meter from our feet. Franca yelled over the whir of bullets, "Patrick! Jens is unconscious, but we need to get him in the car. Now! Backup and I will jump into the back of the truck."

"All right. Get him to the door!" His hands came into view, signaling that he was ready. Without lifting our heads, we carried and pushed the injured man to him. Patrick grabbed Jens by the forearms and pulled him into the cabin.

When her hands were free again, Franca brought the HK forward. Cautiously, she peered over the edge of the vehicle toward the suspected location of the shooter or shooters. Two bullets immediately whizzed by. She stood up and fired several short bursts. What—if anything—she was aiming at, I couldn't tell. But the sniper fire stopped.

"Go on, get in!" she hissed, slamming the door. I jumped onto the truck bed, more carefully this time than last time. Again, she raised the gun and fired.

"Yeah, one down!" she cheered as she joined me in a mighty leap and pounded her fist against the back window. It took Patrick a second to move off. He turned around in the church square and accelerated back the way we had come.

"How did you even see anyone there?" I yelled over the wind.

"You don't unlearn something like that; it's like riding a bike." She surveilled our surroundings through the rear sight of her fully automatic weapon. "You have to learn to watch for movement and react to it fast! And to have already fired the shot in your head. So as soon as something comes into your line of fire, you pull the trigger."

"Hold tight!" thundered Patrick, turning into a serpentine bend almost without braking. We obeyed. I risked a look through the windshield at the back seat where Jens was lying, held in place with several seat belts. His skin was ashen. The bandages around his upper body dripped dark red with blood.

"What the hell . . . ?" Franca burst out in surprise and fired a short volley in the direction of Costitx. I looked back and saw three vehicles turning onto the straight behind us.

I immediately recognized the first of the cars as our blue Mercedes, the top of which had been removed. I thought sadly of Nils, who was now growing cold in a godforsaken Mallorcan village. Franca fired again and changed her empty magazine. I reached through the sliding window for a shotgun.

Patrick drove as fast as he dared on the narrow road, which was lined with stone walls. If he strayed from the path, it would mean certain death for Franca and me—and even more certain death for Jens. The Mercedes came inexorably closer. The passenger stood upright, taking aim at us over the windshield. We heard him shooting, but this time none of the projectiles came even remotely close. "Why are those assholes shooting at us?" I yelled. Franca hardly seemed to hear, took a single deep breath, exhaled deeply, and with total concentration, raised the HK to her shoulder. Kneeling, she became one with the movements of the truck.

In the heat of the moment, she found her flow again. I saw her switch into her fighting mode. She exhaled again, pursing her lips and fired a single shot. A quarter of a second later, the enemy gunner's head jerked back. A fine red mist sprayed up briefly, then he fell over. His driver made the mistake of jerking the steering wheel sharply in shock. Stones the size of heads flew fifteen meters into the air. The centrifugal force pulled the battered car farther in the direction of travel, flipping it over and over and flinging its occupants into the air. They came down hard on the side of the road. The demolished coupé traveled a good seventy meters before coming to a halt sideways across the road.

The vehicles behind it had stopped as soon as Franca took out the gunman. Even if they had had the courage to follow us, they would not have made it past the barrier with any ease. We saw them turn. Then we turned left, and the pursuers disappeared.

Patrick raced onward, the empty streets allowing him to drive at almost maximum speed. Franca and I squeezed into the back seat next to Jens and pressed our balled-up T-shirts against his wounds. Either our efforts were having some success or he had already lost so much blood that he had less and less to lose.

At the exit, Patrick warned, "Look out, it's going to get bumpy now." The vehicle rumbled over the gravel road. A gigantic cloud of dust rose behind us. Franca and I swayed to the rhythm as the truck dodged the potholes. Jens's blood was flowing in fine rivulets onto the back seat. After a while, the truck stopped, and our driver hurried to open the gate.

He pressed the button on the remote control. Nothing happened.

He pressed again, harder this time. Again, nothing happened.

"Goddamn it! Open up already, you piece of shit!" Patrick was now pounding the key fob with his fist.

At some point, the gate jerked and slid to the side. "Okay then!" he growled. We drove through hastily. He pressed the button again to close the gate and accelerated away.

Eva and Waltraud had heard the pickup approaching and met us at the front door. We headed toward them faster than usual. By the fountain, Franca and I jumped out almost at the same time.

She thundered, "Bandages, now!" while we pulled Jens carefully out of the car. On the small balcony over the door, I saw the young people watching in horror. In the meantime, Patrick had run into the house—before Waltraud or Eva had taken in what had happened—and returned with a blanket.

Waltraud opened her mouth in shock at the sight of Jens but had the presence of mind to fetch some sheets.

"What happened?" she burst out in a shaky voice.

"We were ambushed," I replied. "Nils was hit in the head by a sniper. Whether they were waiting for us there or we were just unlucky, I don't know."

In the meantime, Eva had brought an orange first aid kit with the word *Policía* emblazoned on it. It was as big as a suitcase and even contained a defibrillator. Franca examined Jens's wounds more closely. "Damn, I hope he didn't lose too much blood." With one hand, she rummaged in the box and fished out a sterile wound stapler. "Backup, clean it!" she snapped at me as I stood idly by, nodding toward a bottle of iodine and a stack of gauze sheets. I wiped away the partially clotted blood all around the injury using the disinfectant. As she stapled the wound, Franca said again, "Bullet went clean through. At first glance, it doesn't look like life-threatening. I just wonder why he's bleeding so much."

"He's a hemophiliac. Not the bad kind, but it takes longer than usual for his blood to clot," explained Waltraud, her voice thick.

Franca made liberal use of the staples. "Why wasn't I told this before?" she cried. Then we turned Jens's body over to treat the exit wound. Franca charged into the house. Out of curiosity, I followed her and found her in the kitchen, where she had turned on the kettle. She retrieved an empty bottle from the cupboard, rinsed it frantically with half of the hot water as soon as it boiled. Into the rest of the water, she tipped some salt and sampled the mixture, diluting it with the tap water. She added more salt until she seemed satisfied with the taste.

Then she screwed the cap back on the bottle, took a corkscrew from the top drawer, and ran back outside.

The first aid kit contained several meters of thin transparent tubing. Franca cut one short and one longer piece with her combat knife. Using the corkscrew, she drilled two holes in the cap of the bottle until they were about the same diameter as the tubing. Then she pushed them in, the short one as far as she could, the long one about an inch. She squeezed a cannula into the other end and stuck it into the crook of Jens's left arm. His blood loss had made the vein clearly visible, and she couldn't miss it. As Franca held the bottle aloft and bent the short tube upward, the saline immediately flowed down to the cannula. Patrick approached and took the vessel from her hand.

"This should compensate for some of the blood loss," Franca explained. "Do we know what blood type he is?"

We looked at her, perplexed. Waltraud knelt by him. She stroked his waxy, bloodless face gently and shook her head. "We never talked about that." Tears ran down her cheeks.

We stood silently around our injured friend. I watched the contents of the bottle diminish. It seemed to me that some color was returning to Jens's dark skin.

The staples held.

The bleeding seemed to have stopped. Suddenly, Patrick turned his head, looking toward the driveway. "What the . . ." he spat out.

We heard the sound of an engine.

Calls rang out from the balcony.

"Someone's coming!"

"There, from the gate!"

Seconds later, two vehicles came hurtling toward us. They had approached slowly, and once it was too late for us to react, they sped toward the house. They came to a halt, tires squealing, a few meters away from us.

Around four or five scrawny, dirty figures jumped out of each car, pointing their guns at us. They were the ones who had set the trap for us in Costitx an hour ago. There was no doubt about it. One of them, dressed in a sturdy but dirty military uniform, was even aiming a bazooka at us.

We were unarmed. The pistols were lying on the blood-soaked back seat, the shotguns and Franca's HK were somewhere in the footwell. My spear was in the loading bay, barely a meter away and yet out of reach.

Patrick's eyes widened at the sight of the unexpected visitors. Eva whispered in bewilderment, "This can't be happening . . . ! The goddamn pirates!" She murmured, her lips rigid. "Those are the pirates who pursued us at sea!" I noticed some women among the crowd of marauders.

One of them looked suspiciously in her direction. A young man got out of the rear car, casual and overconfident. The one we had rescued from Hotel 23, and whom Franca had cold-bloodedly cast out in Sa Pobla. He smiled broadly and without any warmth as he came toward us. He strolled past me. As he approached Franca, I saw in his waistband a matte black pistol that I immediately identified as Nils's Beretta. Ignoring me, he waved up to the balcony with feigned friendliness and stood before the ex-elite policewoman, smirking.

"Good afternoon, everyone. Nice to see you again." He spoke loudly. His voice had no kindness in it, despite his gracious words. "Do you know how long it took us to find you again? This fucking island has more dead-end side streets than Amsterdam has canals! But finally we meet again! And I brought some friends for lunch." He gestured with his thumb to the ravenous pack behind him. "My new buddies have had you in their sights for weeks but never had the courage to introduce themselves in person. You were far too"—with imitated revolvers with both hands—"well-equipped for them."

I remembered our first trip to Inca, when Patrick thought he had seen a reflection in the rearview mirror. Had it been them?

"I have assured them that you are not as dangerous as they suspect. The quality of my arguments is unsurpassed," he bragged, laughing loudly, as if he had told a joke that only he understood. His eyes lit up fanatically. "And you guys? What's been going on with you?" His voice took on a sarcastic, questioning edge.

"Oh, no!" He put his hand over his mouth in mock horror as he spotted the unconscious Jens behind the pickup. "What's that? Has someone been injured? And where's fatty?"

Grief over the loss of Nils, the person who had saved us all and brought us together, gripped me. My breath caught and my eyes filled with tears.

"He's fucking your mother right now!" Whatever had driven me to say this, it couldn't have been healthy. He turned slowly and stiffly toward me. As he did so, he pulled the Beretta from his waistband.

He approached, pointing the gun at my head. I looked past him and noticed Waltraud and Franca exchanging a glance. The Norwegian turned her buttocks a few degrees in Franca's direction. A bulge was visible under her shirt. She saw it, too, and gave an imperceptible nod.

"My mother, I see!" he hissed in my face. His breath was horrible. What had he been feeding on, zombie meat? The cold iron of the pistol's muzzle touched my left temple, but my disgust drowned out my fear.

"Do you know my mother? No? Yes? No? I don't think she's alive any more than fatty is. You know how I know fatty is dead? Huh?" he said, gesturing from one of us to the next with the gun. "Because my best shooter here took him out!" He pointed at the man who was aiming at us through a scope. Then he pointed at Jens with a snide gesture. "And he got that one, too. But the fat one is dead now! So, it's not possible that he and my mother are fucking each other right now. Unless they get together as some kind of ghosts . . . Wait a minute; now I get it." He laughed theatrically, and his eyes bulged so much that I was worried they would burst and stain me with his madness. "That's what you meant, isn't it, that they're both ghosts . . . ?" Again, he laughed like the lunatic he clearly was. "Funny, very funny."

Unexpectedly, he punched me in the stomach, bringing me to my knees. "Anyone else want to be funny? Is there another comedian among you?"

His shadow told me that he was waving the Beretta around, threatening the others, while I struggled to catch my breath.

Suddenly, an ice-cold female voice rang out, "Is that you, John Wayne? Is this me?"

Enraged, he jerked the pistol around to where Waltraud was standing and marched toward her, engaging the trigger with his thumb. At the same time, the smell of decay and feces washed over us, stronger even than his mouth odor. We heard inhuman moans and the stamping of dozens of feet moving closer.

The teenagers on the balcony cried out in panic and fled into the house. Ignoring my stomachache, I stood up, supporting myself on the pickup truck.

As I reached over the side of the loading bed for my spear, Franca took advantage of the momentary distraction, disarming the madman and striking him a brutal blow behind the ear. He went down without a word, like a rubber doll filled with water.

Waltraud hurled a throwing knife in the direction of the sniper. The blade entered his throat almost without resistance, blocking his air supply before he could fire a shot. Startled, he dropped his weapon. His eyes grew huge. With superhuman effort, he pulled the knife out of his throat and inhaled in panic. Instead of air, a gush of blood flowed into his windpipe. He fell lengthwise, twitching, his eyes glazing over.

The would-be soldier next to him lost his nerve and fired the bazooka. The projectile came loose with a hiss and sped toward us. It snaked past us with astonishing speed, disappearing through the front door into the house. The massive explosion shattered the windows, sending shards and debris flying. Everything quaked, even the earth beneath my feet. The shock wave hurled me against the pickup truck. A high-pitched sound registered in my ears over the noise. I struggled to my feet for the second time in ten seconds. Smoke was billowing from the ground-floor windows.

At that moment, the wandering corpses came into view. They charged down the slope toward us, stumbling, limping, and enraged. When they smelled fresh blood, they went into a full-blown frenzy. The marauders, deprived of their leader and shocked by the brutal death of a comrade, took a moment too long to turn their weapons on the undead. The few shots they fired missed their targets. Two or three sought salvation in flight and headed for the entrance to the house. The rest were buried by the first wave of zombies that descended on them like oversize killer ants.

Within a heartbeat, Patrick had climbed into the pickup, and he emerged just as quickly with two pump-action shotguns. As he got out, he loaded one of the shotguns with one hand and tossed it to Eva. He didn't have time to fire. A zombie was only an arm's length away from him. He took a step to the side and let the infected smash into the pickup truck. Then he struck, slamming the handle against the zombie's ear with all his might. There was a cracking of bones, and the undead sagged. Patrick fired and quickly mowed down half a dozen walking corpses.

Eva caught the shotgun he threw her in midair. She put her index finger to the trigger while the gun was still falling, and simultaneously raised it. A bang like a thunderclap made me start. Barely a meter in front of me, a zombie face was cut in half. With a *crunch-crunch*, she loaded a new cartridge into the barrel. Another shot and it was farewell to another of the undead.

Franca emptied Nils's recaptured Beretta. She fired at close range, and the bullets were sure to find their targets, but there were too many attackers for us. "Retreat! Into the house!" she ordered between shots. "Waltraud, Backup, take Jens inside! Now!" She took a step backward and stumbled. In the process, she lost her balance and slammed backward onto the cobblestones. The leader of the land pirates she had knocked unconscious had now come to, and he had grabbed her ankle and pulled hard just as she began to run. The Beretta slipped from her grasp. Before she could react, he threw himself on the gun, raised it, and pointed the muzzle at Franca's face. I followed his finger as it moved toward the trigger, reached out with my arm, and hurled the spear.

Once again, I saw everything in slow motion: the blade nearing its target, the index finger pulling the trigger. A few milliseconds before the bolt detonated the cartridge's black powder, the tip of the spear embedded itself in the biceps of the arm holding the gun, prompting the injured nerve endings to send pain signals to the brain. That—and of course the force of the impact—made the shooter yank the gun, and the bullet grazed harmlessly past Franca's shoulder.

The spear bayonet pierced the muscle of the upper arm. As the centrifugal force caused the shaft to describe a circular motion around the bone, the blade cut clean through the tissue. The spear fell clattering to the ground. Blood gushed from the large wound. More gruesome than the cries of pain emitted by the injured man was the sight of the edges of the wound, which were rapidly turning black. Even his lifeblood was turning a dirty gray. A milky substance formed over the entire wound. As we watched, the bleeding stopped. The whole thing took two seconds.

He stopped screaming, saw dark veins assimilating his tissues, rolled his eyes, and slumped back, lifeless.

My mouth dropped open. Had the parasite learned that wounds represented a danger to its host—and that it had to treat them? What else was it capable of? Thought transmission? Fascinated, I dragged myself away.

Our head start was gone. Waltraud and I grabbed the corners of the blanket on which Jens was lying and ran for the house. Franca followed hot on our heels. Patrick and Eva ran backward, firing all their guns. They jumped through the front door at the last moment as the ex-elite fighter threw herself against it, slamming it shut. She almost landed on her back as the zombies crashed into the door from outside. But its solid wood and sturdy hinges held firm. Unspeakable noise reached us in the form of hungry, frenzied screams and the sounds of kicks and jolts of those trying to get through.

The lower floor was on fire. Shell fragments had pierced the walls all over the room. I ran to the cellar door, forcing Waltraud to follow me, since we were both still carrying Jens, and pushed the doorknob with my elbow. Behind us, I heard Franca screaming at the top of her lungs, "Children, where the hell are you?"

Three of them came out of the kitchen, two girls and a boy. They were crying. The youngest girl had blood flowing from her ears.

"Where are the rest?" I asked.

The older one pointed upward, as if in a trance. Franca didn't waste a second, but ran to the upper floor, or at least tried to, because the stairs had partially collapsed. She scrambled along the banister and stretched forward, peering down the second-floor hallway. Turning around immediately, she came back to us. "What are you standing around here for?" she chided us. "Down to the damn basement with you!"

No one resented her tone of voice. And no one asked what she had seen upstairs.

When we arrived in the training room, we set Jens down. Before Franca could lock the door, Waltraud rushed past her into the blazing living room. Barely ten seconds later she was back with us, holding the glowing remains of the router in her hands. Franca turned the key in the lock and followed her downstairs. The Norwegian pulled out the SIM card from the partially melted device, which she immediately threw away.

We heard footsteps from the room above us. The undead had entered the burning house through the patio doors and were searching for us. They wouldn't find us down here, but if the building collapsed while we were waiting in the basement, it wouldn't look good for us. I realized that I had lured us into a trap!

Jens was breathing deeply and evenly, and his skin had regained some of its natural color despite the ruckus. His stapled wounds were no longer bleeding.

"What weapons do we have?" asked Franca. We put everything on the floor and added the rest of the weapons from our basement stash.

There were two shotguns and about sixty shells, four 9-millimeter pistols of various makes, and over two hundred 9-millimeter bullets. We also had some cold weapons.

"Damn, what happened up there?" She spoke softly while she and Patrick inspected the shotguns. I could hear anger and reproach in her voice.

Shaking his head and continuing to reload, he replied, "It's my fault. The key fob isn't working properly. I didn't make sure the gate was closed."

"Shit, man! Now we've got a badly injured guy on our hands and a burning house full of zombies." She pushed a cartridge into the barrel. He did the same.

"At least he's still alive. And we have enough supplies here for a few days, if not weeks," he replied.

"Yes, but no plumbing!"

"Never mind, we'll poop in a bucket."

She sounded cranky. "Do you see a bucket here?"

"Calm down, Franca! I know I messed up, and I deserve a hard time. But bellyaching won't get us anywhere right now. We've survived worse, and we'll survive this, too."

Patrick turned away from her, went to the blanket, and knelt beside Waltraud and Jens. She was wiping off the dried blood with a piece of cloth. He squeezed Jens's motionless hand before getting up and going over to Eva.

Eva had gotten the young people somewhat calm, and they were sipping water from bottles and staring blankly ahead. Patrick and Eva exchanged a few quiet words and hugged each other close.

My chest tightened. More than ever, I wished I had someone by my side with whom I could form a unit. Someone I didn't have to wear a mask for or have any secrets from.

A crash from upstairs snapped me out of my melancholy and back into the present. The zombies were screaming more loudly. We noticed the load-bearing structures of the house slowly starting to give way.

Two hours later, we were still sitting in the basement and listening to the undead roaming around. We still hardly dared move.

Apparently, despite the smoke, the house was so full of our scent that the infected couldn't help but think we were up there. The scratching and shuffling sounds did not diminish. At some point, I dozed off briefly. When I became conscious of my surroundings again, I spotted Patrick and Franca sitting on the floor not far from me. They were holding their heads close together and talking quietly. Waltraud had snuggled up to Jens and was asleep. Eva sat amid the youngsters, leaning against the wall and holding two of them who were slumbering restlessly. As soon as they realized I was awake, Patrick and Franca beckoned me over. I crawled to them on all fours.

He spoke first. "We've just been assessing our chances. Long story short, we need to get out of here as soon as possible." I nodded, and he continued, "If we make it out of here alive, what are we going to do? Staying in this area doesn't make much sense, given the number of zombies picnicking in the backyard."

Yes, what do we do, I wondered.

Then an idea came to me that could be our salvation for the next few weeks if we succeeded in breaking out. "Let me worry about that," I said. "We have to get out of here first! What were you thinking?"

Patrick looked at me, waiting, as if he wanted to know more about the idea right away. Then he thought better of it and replied, "First we have to lure them away from the house." He pointed to one of the walls, which had windows. "We won't get him through there too easily. The windowpanes all shattered in the explosion. Their frames were bent in the process, but I think those ones there"—he pointed to the smaller ones on the shorter side of the basement—"will still open. Someone needs to climb out and distract the infected so we can get to the truck."

"Someone?" I asked, raising an eyebrow. They looked at me mutely.

As soon as the way was clear, two people would have to bring Jens up. The strongest of us were Franca and Patrick. I could run the fastest, and my stamina was above average; that's why I was chosen as the bait.

The two of them gave me a few minutes to think the process over—and to get my head around the fact that I could quite possibly die. Then we let the rest of our companions in on the plan. Eva folded her arms over her body as if she were cold. Waltraud hugged me. Franca gently put a hand on my shoulder, nodded, and said nothing.

Outside, dusk was falling. I was equipped with two 9-millimeter pistols and fifty unused rounds. If I could not fight myself free for at least a full minute to refill the magazines, the bullets would be useless. Left loose, however, they would fall out of my pockets. We briefly tested a headlamp before I put it on.

In the meantime, Patrick had cleared the entrance to one of the windows and was peering out through a crack into the gathering darkness. Then he nodded at me and raised his right thumb in the air. I looked at everyone as if to say good-bye.

Patrick whispered in my ear, "You can hear them trotting, but there are none right in front of the window. Good luck. And thanks!"

"Thank me later!" I replied more confidently than I felt and climbed into the zombie-infested yard at the back of the house. The lack of wind increased my almost nonexistent chances by a few percent, as it meant my scent would not be carried to them. Between the bushes, I saw the silhouettes of many figures swaying back and forth on the lawn. Behind me, the window closed quietly again.

Then I halfway straightened up and walked toward the main entrance, a pistol in each hand. When I peeked around the corner, the sight of the swarm of zombies left me breathless. At least a hundred were moving haphazardly around the square in front of the house. They seemed to have lost interest in the front door.

The sun had just set, and if I didn't want to be running from them in complete darkness, I had to act now.

Time to make some noise.

I straightened up, turned on the headlamp, and strolled resolutely out, breaking cover. The first zombie to notice me didn't get far. I liberated him with a bullet from five meters away. The bang seemed to wake the others. They turned their heads in my direction and started howling in unison. I shot three more wandering corpses before opening the front door and blindly firing three or four shots through it. I didn't think I would have inflicted any significant damage, but my primary goal was to draw out the stray ones inside. Then I sprinted off as fast as I could. Looking over my shoulder, I saw with mixed feelings that the plan seemed to be working. Some of the zombies ran out of the house, following hard on my heels. I was faster, but it took some effort not to panic. Every one of the undead that got too close, either head-on or from the flank, got a bullet. It was damn close, but I escaped by the skin of my teeth and could consider round one a success.

The biggest blind spot in my plan was the gate. I couldn't know whether—or how many—were behind it. They could well be blocking my way. If that happened, our maneuver would have become short-lived.

But there was no one there. I slowed my pace, looking back. They were right on my heels! One of the pistols was almost empty. I put it in the back of my waistband. With the other, I aimed with a shaky hand and shot the magazine, too quickly for my taste. My accuracy left much to be desired, but I took out three of the nimblest. Now I had fifty cartridges that I wouldn't be able to use anytime soon and a pistol containing only three or four rounds. My pockets rattled mockingly with every step I took.

I ran onto the dusty gravel road, turning the headlamp backward. The undead wouldn't be able to miss a point of light moving in the darkness. It was bizarre to be going for a jog on such a beautiful summer evening, pursued by murderous zombies. It was several kilometers to the main road. I had to adjust my speed to the infected so there was no chance I'd run out of steam. They had to keep on seeing me as a potential victim so that they didn't lose their desire to pursue me—in particular when shots rang out from the nearby courtyard.

As I ran, I pulled out a pack of the 9-millimeter bullets. It took a few seconds for me to hold about half of them loosely in my hand. Judging from the shouting, those chasing me had stopped. I glanced in their direction. They were obviously distracted by the new sounds of battle.

This bought me time to load the pistols and safely stow the remaining cartridges in a pocket. I aimed at the zombies, who had turned back about thirty meters behind me.

"Hey! Over here!" I yelled at the top of my lungs, firing twice. It was enough to change their minds again. Daylight was fading. I had to let them get within twenty meters to land any lethal hits, and again I limited myself to taking out only the fastest five or six.

Then I turned around—and almost ran right into a wandering corpse. She had probably been part of the pack that had overrun our safe house and had been left behind hours ago—and no wonder, given her condition. The headlamp had guided her to me while I was concentrating on controlling the pack behind me. She was dragging one leg. There were large bite marks in the skin around her neck. Her bloodless lips revealed rotting teeth. Barely two meters separated me from her hungry embrace.

Startled, I dodged out of the way. As the creature stumbled past, I kicked it with full force behind its knees. It fell headlong and I put a bullet in the back of its head. My training had paid off.

The wailing of the horde then grew louder. I ran. With the loose cartridges in my pocket, it was relatively easy to load the magazine in the barrel, even if I lost a few rounds in the process. The last few meters of the gravel road were clear. Once I reached the asphalt access road, I could run at full tilt all the way to the highway. But there was still quite a way to go.

The thin line of the Ma-13 appeared just as the light of day was fading. I had to turn the headlamp forward so that I could see. I had fulfilled my part of the mission, so I increased my speed to give myself a bigger lead. I passed the last of the side roads leading to other homesteads. After less than a minute, I stepped onto the warm asphalt of the highway. I could no longer see the zombies behind me, but that meant nothing in the darkness of the night. Since I couldn't hear them either, I must have lost them. Before taking a breather, I emptied the remaining cartridges into my pants pockets. Then I turned off the light and tried to steady my breathing. Normally I would have been able to run this distance effortlessly, but due to the fear and excitement, my pulse was much faster than usual.

The stars were flickering clearly in the firmament. More and more of them came out. With the darkness, the evening breeze came down from the mountains. I was sweating and longed for something to drink, but the cool wind would have to suffice for the time being.

Taking a deep breath, I enjoyed the clear air and focused all my attention on my powers of hearing.

Five minutes passed. Without any change in the direction of the wind, the smell of decay suddenly mingled with the breeze. The stench increased rapidly. I turned around, looked around in panic, but I couldn't see or hear them. In the darkness, I should have at least been able to see their outlines. Shining my headlamp the way I had come, I caught sight of the group that had been following me before. But they were far away, about where I had thought they were. They could do me no harm. They groaned hungrily as soon as the beam of light hit them. Behind me, on the other side of the highway, was a tall fence with barbed wire at the top. Even if I had been assured of safety behind it, it would not have been an easy barrier to overcome.

I shone the light to the left, then to the right. Then to the left again, and to the right. Silently, like stalking cheetahs, they were coming at me from both sides. Some were limping, some staggering, but all were silent as they approached their prey step by step. Both lanes of the highway were clogged with the walking, silent undead. I almost dropped my pistols in horror. The light of the headlamp illuminated the front rows, but I sensed countless others behind them. They were barely fifty meters away from me. I looked at the weapons in my hand and calculated how many seconds I had left to live.

Once Backup had left the basement, Franca and Patrick placed Jens's body carefully on the blanket.

"He's lucky he's so anorexic, or I'd leave him here," Patrick whispered, panting. He tilted all the windows so that at least some fresh air could get in. More and more smoke was coming into the cellar through the gaps in the doorframe, making it difficult to breathe. When the first shots rang out outside, they took up position with the injured man on the makeshift stretcher. Eva and Waltraud, heavily armed, led the way, stopping at the top of the basement stairs. Patrick and Franca followed close behind, holding a corner of the blanket in each hand. Jens's wounds didn't look too bad. The teenagers, carrying essential food in improvised bags, waited at the bottom of the stairs.

The sounds died away. The smoke became unbearable. Eva carefully opened the door and let Waltraud out. Waltraud checked the dark room with a glance over the rear sight of her shotgun and stepped into the hallway. Here and there, the fire was blazing. The load-bearing beams had been so badly damaged that there was no hope for the house. It was only a matter of minutes before the upper floor collapsed. Without stopping, Waltraud strode out the door and straight to the pickup truck. Looking around continuously, she saw many zombies roaming the lot in the fading light. But they were far away and not an immediate danger. The Norwegian opened the rear vehicle door and beckoned her companions to join her. Franca and Patrick crossed quickly to her. Franca climbed in, pulling the injured man with her. She laid him on the back seat and stepped out the other side. The three teenagers climbed in after her and tried to find themselves some space on the floor. They secured Jens with the seat belts and locked the doors. Eva sat down in the passenger seat. Waltraud jumped in the back. Franca ran a few steps, bent down, and picked up the spear with which Backup had saved her life.

Patrick pulled away. In the mirror, he saw her carefully throwing the weapon onto the truck bed before leaping lithely up over the shoulder-height side of the rolling vehicle to join Waltraud.

At the top of the hill, the vehicle stopped. They looked back wistfully at the ruined building that had been their home for the past several months. At that moment, one of the beams gave way and the left half of the villa collapsed. Smoke and sparks rose into the sky.

Patrick stepped on the gas. The pickup rolled onto the gravel road. Some of the slow creatures heard the crunch and turned around. Waltraud pulled out her pistol, and before Franca could react, she shot. Three of the wandering corpses fell. Franca put a hand on her arm and said reprovingly, "No, leave it! Patrick should just drive through!" The Norwegian, who was in shock, said nothing in reply. The daylight was fading by the second. Soon all they could see was the outlines of the Tramuntana Mountains ten kilometers to the northwest.

Patrick drove over one undead after another. The women on the loading platform had to hold onto the roll bar, on which the imposing LED spotlights were mounted. He deliberately left the lights turned off, driving in darkness for several kilometers, slightly faster than walking speed. Franca tapped the roof twice after they had left the gravel road. Patrick stuck his head out the window.

"How much farther?" she asked.

"We should be nearly there. It shouldn't be more than a hundred yards to the highway."

No sooner had he said it than there were two flashes followed by loud bangs. That was enough to see Backup firing to left and right on the multilane highway in front of them.

"Hang on," Patrick roared and hit the gas. When he had counted eight shots, he switched on all the lights and rolled up his window. Suddenly, the scene was so brightly illuminated that it hurt his eyes for a moment. Twenty meters ahead of them was Backup, surrounded by hundreds of greedy wandering corpses. When the lights came on, it seemed as if they were too late to rescue their friend.

Patrick raced onward.

Backup ran toward the pickup truck.

The car shot across the asphalt, and the first of the undead smashed against it.

At the last moment, Backup dropped to the ground and the pickup rolled over the body, braking. The teenagers in the back seat screamed at the top of their lungs.

"Fuck, it's about time! What the hell took you guys so long?" I bellowed, getting the fright off my chest. I had barely crawled under the truck and jumped onto the loading bed from behind when we began to reverse. Franca and Waltraud almost shot me at first, thinking I was one of the undead. Then they pulled me up, holding me by the arms until I found my footing. Patrick drove back down the road at breakneck speed, yelling at us to get out of line of sight. He turned into the first alley, stopped, then opened the throttle and tore off to the southwest.

We also encountered small groups of zombies here. The massive truck swept them effortlessly off the gravel road. A few kilometers and several turnoffs later, no new ones appeared.

Patrick switched off the lights one by one, leaving only the parking lights on to enable him to see the road ahead. We gave settlements as wide a berth as possible. We didn't want any more confrontations today. Near the Cementiri Santa Maria, we risked getting back onto a sealed road. We followed this to El Caulls, where we switched to the Ma-13 toward Palma. Eva told us she wanted to consult the road map; meanwhile, we drove farther and farther south. It would do her good to concentrate on one task at a time.

In between, she consulted me to see if we were on the right course. I opened the sliding window and gave her instructions. Speeding through the night on the empty highway with a minimum of lighting was both scary and breathtaking. Where the Ma-13 came to an end, we had to maneuver past broken-down vehicles to turn onto the Ma-20 toward Andratx. This arm of the multilane highway described a large arc around the north of Palma, which we followed for another twenty kilometers. So close to the city, we drove carefully and kept a lookout.

We reached Andratx without incident, but here the highway ended. The final part of the route would take us into towns, and we didn't know what awaited us there. I gave Eva all the necessary information. She navigated us safely to Saint Elm. Sadness overcame me as we rolled the last few kilometers to the small fishing village. It was on this road that I had been rescued by Nils weeks ago. I thought about what it had meant to me when he had shown up that day.

My companions seemed to be in a similar mood because no one made any effort to talk. I spoke to Patrick through the window while we were driving through Saint Elm, but only because he needed more detailed instructions on the route. Then I asked him to stop. We had arrived.

In the pickup's indirect parking lights, the street and its buildings looked as familiar to me as if I had never been away.

I instructed the troops to wait in the vehicle. Then I jumped off the loading bed and disappeared into the passageway below the balcony. Climbing up was child's play. The balcony door was still open. I had almost completely closed the shutters, but a small horizontal gap gave me enough space to reach in and push up the blind. I crawled into the living room. The familiar surroundings—even in almost total darkness— calmed my nerves. With my headlamp on, I inspected all the rooms, relishing the sight of the pantry. I walked down the stairs and felt myself slowly relaxing. My friends were waiting impatiently in the truck. Grinning, I stepped out onto the street.

"Here we are," I whispered. "This used to be my sanctuary. It's safe here, though not quite as comfortable as the villa."

Pain showed in their eyes. No doubt they were thinking of the losses we had suffered today. I didn't want them to torture themselves. To distract them, I asked, "How's the invalid?"

As if on cue, Jens stirred in the back seat. Waltraud immediately switched on the interior light and put her hand to his cheek. The Dutchman slowly opened his eyes and looked around. He groaned as he tried to stretch.

"Slowly, slowly!" she admonished him.

Barely audible, he muttered, "What happened? What did I miss?"

For a moment, no one dared to breathe. His partner's eyes moistened, and she whispered in his ear in a shaky voice, "Get yourself well first. You've been shot"—she stroked the skin around the bullet hole—"and we've lost Nils. It was a shitty day. But now I'm glad you're with me."

"Oh, shit!" he wailed. "I remember now."

"Let it go, please. You lost a lot of blood. We had to give you improvised saline. When you're better, we'll tell you everything. But right now, you need to rest."

He nodded.

Patrick and Eva secured both sides of the alley while the teens got out and waited outside the front door.

I turned to Jens. "We're going to carry you up a flight of stairs. It's not long, but it's narrow and steep. It may hurt a little."

He raised his right thumb in reply. I grabbed the blanket at his feet and pulled him toward me. Waltraud helped from inside the truck until he was halfway out. Then Franca took over, waiting impatiently for her turn next to the truck. Together, we carried him up the narrow staircase. We had to maneuver carefully around the corners of the small apartment. The whole time, he didn't make a sound, but in the light of the headlamp, I saw how much he was sweating from pain and exertion. I wanted Jens and Waltraud to have the bedroom.

We laid him down on the big double bed. The Norwegian joined him, and we left them alone.

The others had followed us into the apartment and made themselves comfortable in the living room. Eva had lowered the balcony blinds with the help of her flashlight, ensuring that no light could escape.

Franca and I had barricaded the front door of the house with a sideboard.

I showed them the supplies, most of which were still edible. Only two apples in the refrigerator were shriveled.

My water reserves would serve us well in the coming weeks. Of the medicines we raided from Costitx, most had survived the bumpy ride and were in the hallway.

Tonight, we would be able to sleep undisturbed. We spread out in the living room. Someone fetched some blankets from the bedroom and reported that Jens had drunk some water and was sleeping soundly. None of us thought to celebrate our safe arrival in the apartment. We were all mourning the loss of a friend who had been brutally taken from us—and without whom maybe none of us would have been alive.

The tension of the day had faded, leaving us with a sense of loss. I lay awake for a long time, with a blanket between me and the floorboards, listening to the sounds of the others sleeping. It was well past midnight when exhaustion carried me into the realm of dreams.

In the days that followed, we were able to appropriate the apartment across the street and settled in there. We spent hours racking our brains over what to do next and working out a detailed new survival plan. Even though we had different opinions on many points, we all agreed on one thing: we could not stay on the island. Almost every day, the wind carried the stench of the wandering corpses to us. Large groups of them showed up in the village several times a week. They were undoubtedly on our trail, which made it an enormous risk to venture outside. Nevertheless, we tried our hand at looting. But the yield was pitiful, not least because I, myself, had plundered the village and its immediate surroundings months ago.

On one raid, Waltraud found a functioning tablet. She managed to hack it on the same day. Of the dozens of routers she had also stolen, there was one that could connect to the internet via the mobile network. Equipped with this, she tried to contact Berlin again. But the system's poor performance meant that video chats were no longer possible, only cumbersome email communication. Waltraud and Dr. Koller exchanged information on a regular basis until the internet connection became less and less reliable and broke down completely after a couple days.

During one of our meetings, the Norwegian, with a sideways glance at the young people, said, "We need to get the kids out of here."

Patrick nodded. "We all need to get out of here."

Franca looked up from the table. "And how do you propose we do that?"

"First we need a sailboat big enough to take us all. The supplies we have should last for five or six weeks. Theoretically, that would get us as far as Hamburg. The harbors on this island are full of boats. I know it's dangerous out there, but I'd like to go out and look for a sailboat. It shouldn't be a problem to find at least one we can use."

We did not object. Patrick and Eva set off the very next day. In the meantime, we prepared for our departure. Jens's wound had not healed as well as we would have liked, but his condition also hadn't worsened. Waltraud had recovered from her shock over his injury, but she still hardly ever let him out of her sight.

The three young people were now fully integrated into our community. But I couldn't find that we had anything in common personally. It was rescuing them that had brought about Nils's death, albeit indirectly. I knew it was unfair to blame them for it, but I didn't make any active attempt to escape from the maelstrom of my thoughts.

Like me, Franca seemed to have become more introverted. We avoided each other as best we could in the cramped living conditions. Sometimes I had the feeling she was about to say something, but she never did.

Three days later, early in the morning, Eva and Patrick sailed into the small harbor of Saint Elm. We saw them from the balcony and waved to them. They were steering a large yacht with white sails and a blue hull.

I couldn't believe that our desire to get off the island was going to become a reality. We had planned what we would do when they returned down to the last detail.

Waltraud and Jens took the rifles and ammunition and marched the few hundred meters to the jetty. The depth of the water meant the boat could dock directly in the harbor. The rest of us carried water and food supplies tied up in blankets and sheets. We made several trips back and forth while Eva and Waltraud covered us. As if to say good-bye and wish us a good journey, hundreds of zombies appeared. We took the rest of our belongings and headed for the yacht at a safe distance. Patrick started the engine and steered between the half-sunken sailboats and llaüts. The wind caught in our sails and carried us southward as if it was personally concerned with getting us out of there quickly.

The wandering corpses stumbled to the end of the jetty, the foremost ones disappearing like lemmings under the water. The rest stood hungrily on the pier and waved at us desperately.

"What do you think," I asked Franca, "happens to the zombies when they have nothing left to eat? When there are no people around? Do you think they'll eventually die?"

"Hmm, good question," she replied. "I suppose so. Apparently, despite everything, the organism needs nourishment. Not the human body, maybe, but the parasite that infested them. And as Nadine told us, they may even turn to cannibalism. What the consequences of that will be in the long run, I couldn't tell you." She sighed. "I still don't quite understand it all. Hopefully, we'll have time to talk to her about everything sometime when we're in Berlin.

I just hope they'll find a cure or a vaccine soon, something that will put an end to all this shit before we're completely wiped out."

I wondered if that would even be relevant to our planet. "Sometimes I think we humans have it coming. As if nature is taking revenge on us after being treated so badly for so long," I replied.

I looked out to sea, feeling nothing but hopelessness. Franca stood just an arm's length away from me, yet I felt alone in this contaminated world. Trapped in the gloom, I didn't dare take the first step and bridge the gap.

The sun was high in the sky. We looked north over the stern with mixed feelings. No one said anything as our sailboat shot along over the swell. It took hours for the final summit of the Tramuntana to disappear over the horizon. Only then, as if freed from a burden, did I go below deck and begin to put the galley to rights.

ACKNOWLEDGMENTS

No one creates anything by himself—especially not a book. I would like to thank everyone who motivated, inspired, and encouraged me to write this novel.

If my parents had made different decisions in their lives—who knows where I would be today? To them, my undying gratitude for what I have achieved in life so far.

Children are great. I don't understand why some people don't want children. They're making the incomprehensible decision to miss out on encouragement ranging from, "Dad, I don't think anyone would ever want to read this," to "It would be mega if Netflix made it into a series." My dear daughters, thank you for letting me be your father—you're a better adventure than I could ever imagine.

Regarding my characters, I have used a few people from my own environment. Any similarities to persons still living are entirely intentional.

To the one person who has—with a couple of breaks—been with me on the journey for over twenty years, I dedicate all the love I am capable of. Thank you for helping me to become a better person every day.

A thousand thanks also go to the following: my editor Björn Schultz, who transformed incoherent gobbledygook into something readable and rigorously eliminated anything too long-winded; Punkrock Miri for her fabulous input, which really helped the characters and story come alive; Marcus Dorau for the ingenious logo and cover design, you are the world's best pixel pusher; Uve Teschner for kicking my ass to get the first version thoroughly revised, and for agreeing to lend your voice to the audiobook.

Without you, this book would not have been anywhere near what it is today.

I love you all.

Dinko Skopljak
Würzburg
February 1, 2020

ABOUT THE AUTHOR

Dinko Skopljak is the Yugoslavia-born author of the Anno Initium trilogy, which launched with his debut novel, *The Stranded*. Prior to becoming a writer, Skopljak worked variously as a dental technician, a photographer, and a web designer. A lover of science fiction and fantasy, cinema, and nature, he lives in Würzburg, Germany, with his two daughters.